BLACK EARTH
EXODUS

David N. Alderman

I0637964

ISBN: 978-1-945712-44-9

Visit **DavidNAlderman.com**

This book is dedicated to my grandfather, Earl Bailey, who taught me the importance of preserving the past.

Dear Reader,

Nathan Pierce's story begins in *End of the Innocence*—the first book in the Black Earth series—and continues in *The Broken Daisy* and *Dark Masquerade*. If you haven't read any of these books yet, it would be to your benefit to do so before venturing into *Exodus*. There are many plot twists and character developments that take place in the first three books to prepare you for what's to come in this final installment in the Black Earth series.

David N. Alderman
Author

"Greater love has no one than this, that one lay down his life for his friends."

– John 15:13 (NASB) –

"The sun hides behind the dark veil
As all the while evil prevails
A sixpence caught in the storm of war
Snagged by winds of hate, shattered, forlorn
Legion rises on a stage of oppression
Violence and blood the world's latest transgression
A hero will rise, with *Shadowbanish* in tow
For who else to oppose the indestructible foe?"

– Violet Dawn –

EULOGY OF LETTERS

y dear sister, Daisy. Even as you lay six feet in the ground on a hill in the Broken Lands, I find I have to write to you, to communicate in some way that doesn't leave me thinking I'm crazy. I have to write this out, because the speech I gave at your makeshift funeral did no justice to the relationship you and I had all these years. You were more than a sister to me. You were my best friend. You were the mother who was there for me. You were the friend who didn't treat me like crap. The sister who would give her life—and did give her life—for me. But not just for me, for all of the world. To set an example. To prove that evil cannot win. To prove that even though the president of the United States murdered you, she cannot take away the spirit of what you stand for...freedom.

Now, simply by living, I am showing the world that your death was not in vain.

Daisy, I miss you so much. It's only been a couple of days since our group—Daisy's Defiance—left your burial spot, and I can hardly stop the urge to run back to it and set up a home there so I can be close to you. You were the last piece of familiarity—and of family—I have. Macayle died to give me a chance to save you. I don't know where Heather went. Serenity, Katt, and the other residents of the Westgate Plaza Mall may or may not have survived the mass murder that Henry performed, or the attack from the monstrous creature that crawled out of one of Legion's portals. Pearl has been taken from me—by God, I believe. Who is left? Ginger is a great friend, and she's probably the closest thing I'll ever have to familiarity. But it's not enough. Your death has left a gaping hole in my chest. I fear it will never be filled.

If I can't build a home near your grave, I just want to get off this planet.

1

I want to run away to Anaisha and not look back. The things we've all seen, heard, and experienced are more than a person should in a lifetime. I want to forget most of them. I want to start over. I don't know what to do really. A woman—an angel possibly—told me to head toward a city we spotted in the distance. She said the city is Providence. We watched a plane descend into that city, pouring smoke from its engines as it went down. Who is on that plane? What will we find in Providence? What does any of this have to do with you or God's plan for things? Will we run into more members of Daisy's Defiance? Or will the president's supporters be waiting there to avenge the president's assassination?

I'm going to end this letter now. We're about to leave for another town on our way to Providence. This abandoned playground I'm sitting in, this sunset I'm staring at—a pleasant change from the blackness threatening to swallow the sunlight out here in the Broken Lands— brings me peace. I don't really want to leave here, but I was instructed to go to Providence. Ginger thinks that would be our best bet right now. It's the closest major city that hasn't been named a sanctuary zone.

I love you, Daisy. I hope God is taking good care of you now. I don't know whether or not you're looking down on me, but you're definitely in my heart.

CHAPTER 1

Tuesday, June 10, 2008

athan Pierce took a few minutes after writing his note to enjoy the sunset from his perch on the stationary merry-go-round. Washing the cloudy sky in brilliant shades of crimson and orange, the setting sun squeezed out the remnant of the day's warmth to make way for the chilling night. It was a serene scene, one Nathan had come to enjoy the last few evenings he spent in the untainted section of the Broken Lands.

A cool breeze moved in from the distant mountain ranges, blowing across Nathan's bare arms, carrying the scent of rain with it. *I should grab my jacket from the pickup truck, he thought, but I don't want to miss any part of the sunset.* He knew the sunsets wouldn't last forever—in fact, he was surprised this portion of the Broken Lands hadn't been smothered in complete darkness like most of the world had.

The rest area the small playground resided in had been bombed. The restrooms and snack machines were nothing more than rubble, but miraculously, the playground had survived. It served as a sanctuary.

Nathan picked up his backpack and shoved his notes and pen inside, next to his pistol and a mask made of black stone. The backpack and its contents were the only things he owned besides the clothes on his back, his ichthys necklace, and a profusion of memories of his harrowing journey that began on the stage of his high school graduation and continued across Arizona and California.

"Hey." Ginger sat down on a patch of yellow grass next to the merry-go-round. He looked down at her and smiled. Her hair was still up in pigtails, and she still wore her khaki shorts and green long-sleeve shirt, with the sleeves rolled up and a yellow and white daisy patch she had crudely sewn onto the left arm. She had added a long black sweater coat to compensate for the lack of pants, and her pistol hung snugly from the holster on her right hip.

As much as he wanted to be alone, to enjoy the sunset by himself, Nathan didn't really mind Ginger's presence by his side. Over the last few days, since his sister's burial, he had gotten to know Ginger a little better each day. She had many qualities that reminded him of his sister, like her swiftness to take action, her sense of humor—something that took a while to come out, and her positive outlook regardless of her circumstances.

"The sunset is beautiful tonight," Ginger whispered.

Nathan nodded, agreeing with her more than words could express. At one point in time, not too long ago, he had taken each sunset, each sunrise, and everything in between for granted. The splash of colors on the horizon was a second chance for him to appreciate God's handiwork, even if these beautiful paint strokes were sure to fade soon. Each day, Nathan kept a close eye on the darkening storm clouds surrounding the Broken Lands, and each day he noticed they were growing larger. By his estimate, the clouds would overtake the clear sky within a matter of days.

This made each sunset special.

"The next town is about four miles ahead of us," Ginger said.

"Good." As they traveled across the Broken Lands, they

continued to find abandoned neighborhoods, towns and houses, some utterly destroyed by the bombs President Stone had ordered to be dropped on the landscape—giving the Broken Lands their name. But some homes and buildings still stood, as if in vehement opposition to the president's will to annihilate them. Most of these had been abandoned, left behind to rot away in the darkness. These were the ones that Nathan, Ginger, Ericka Shane, and the rest of Daisy's Defiance used as shelters to sleep in and recuperate. Very few locations held any useful supplies, but some areas had vehicles from which the group siphoned gasoline and pulled parts to keep their trucks running, while others had food, which kept Daisy's Defiance fed.

"We can stay there for the night," Ginger said. "I think we'll be able to reach Providence—and the plane wreckage—tomorrow."

Nathan closed his eyes and took a deep breath. The scent of rain relaxed him almost to the point of slumber. If it rained, he would dance in it until it stopped. He knew if his sister were still alive, she would do the same.

Her death had not been in vain. Through snippets of radio broadcasts, Nathan and his friends had learned that Daisy's death had upset everything the president had strived so hard to establish. Instead of bringing the world together by demonstrating the consequences for disobeying the Falling Star Directives, the execution of his sister had only opened everyone's eyes to the depths this country had fallen to—the public murder of a young, innocent woman to prove a point. The president's sanctuary zones were being overthrown by those within, opening the cities to those who wandered the Broken Lands. The American Government had all but dissolved, especially with the president's death—courtesy of Ginger's sniping skills—and it seemed as if small colonies of people were already beginning to separate themselves from anything to do with the president or the Falling Star Directives. All of this was conveyed to Nathan and his friends via rogue radio broadcasts.

Nathan understood now, for the most part, why his sister had to die. He missed Daisy, but at least her death hadn't been a waste. Nathan opened his eyes and caught sight of the sunset again. He smiled at its beauty. *Please, God, give us safety.* He prayed the same prayer each time Daisy's Defiance approached one of these abandoned or mostly destroyed settlements, and each time the group found safety. He felt a sense of peace, which he attributed to the absence of Legion's malevolent forces.

"The smoke from the plane wreckage stopped yesterday," Ginger said.

The plane they had witnessed shortly after Daisy's burial resembled a stealth bomber and had gone down across the horizon with a plume of smoke pouring out its engines. It looked to be heading into Providence, near the foothills. Ericka Shane—at one time a reporter for the Global News Network—had told Nathan she did a special on the leader of Providence a while back. She said she remembered him being an ultra-billionaire who was criticized for creating the city—with the help of SilverTech Industries—with castle-like walls and a special energy field to appease his paranoia about invading countries and World War III.

Coincidentally, before leaving Nathan, the woman with the blue eyes—the same one Nathan had seen on his graduation day and whom had recently told him it was time to fight—instructed him that the Almighty—God—wanted him to head south toward Providence.

Aside from that, and the crashed plane, he had received no other directions. And when he decided to make it his goal to reach Providence to see what God would have him do next, Daisy's Defiance—every remaining member of his section of Daisy's Defiance—agreed to go with him. It was a grim but sobering realization that nobody really had any other direction.

Nathan wasn't sure if it was his imagination or not, but he could have sworn the plane that crashed looked like one of Vector's transport ships—like the one Heather had boarded when she left him back in Los Angeles weeks earlier. He tried to ignore the possibility that it could be one of Vector's aircraft. If it was, though, he knew there was a chance Heather could have been on it. And if she had been, she may not have survived the crash, meaning she could be just another corpse in the wake of Nathan's journey across a darkening world. For the moment, he was content not knowing Heather's whereabouts, not knowing if she was dead or alive. Content with the unknown. He could spend the rest of his life not knowing where Heather was or if she was even alive, but keeping hope that she was. If he found out otherwise, that she was dead…if he discovered that another of his friends had died…

"We should leave soon," Ginger whispered.

Nathan knew she was being kind with her request. It was more a hint of what Daisy's Defiance was going to do than a request for Nathan's permission to move on. They all knew it wasn't safe to stay in one spot for too long. Although they had enjoyed safety the last three days, there was no telling how long it would last.

Nathan stared at the sunset a minute longer, attempting to burn the image into his mind, give himself something to refer to when the darkness ate the rest of the world. Then he zipped up his backpack and stood with it in hand and stretched. A strong breeze moved the nearby swings back and forth. The creaking sound from the metal chains reminded Nathan of when he was younger and would swing so high that he swore he would flip over the bar.

Ginger stood up, brushing dead grass blades from her rear. "Sorry to rush you. I know you like to wait until the sun has completely disappeared behind the mountains to move forward."

"It's okay," he said with sincerity. "I'm getting hungry. And tired. We need to reach the next town and find cover before it gets too dark."

They walked back to one of the pickup trucks parked along the rest area curb. Ginger gathered everyone from their loitering spots along the way. The rest of Daisy's Defiance had been watching the sunset, chatting with one another, or reading from the few books they had taken out of the city with them. When Nathan passed by, the people looked on him with awe and respect flooding their eyes—the same looks they had been giving him since his sister's burial. He didn't want to be looked at in such a way. He wanted to blend in, to disappear. He didn't feel he had done anything special—at least nothing anyone else wouldn't have done if their sibling had been on the president's chopping block.

Nathan tried to put his thoughts behind him and focus on the task at hand. The group was headed toward Providence, together, with no way of knowing what lay in store for them along the way or once they reached their destination.

Heather could be there, Nathan told himself. He quickly

shook the thought away. *She's not there. She's safe and sound with Vector. Could Pearl be there?*

Hope rose in him. He missed Pearl more than anything but tried his best not to think about her. He feared he would never see her again and didn't want to have his heart broken and beaten more than it already was. The last time he saw Pearl, she was unconscious, being taken away by one of Heaven's elite, who saved him from Evanescence's Soul Eater.

At least now she can't be used as a key to unlock Earth's most demonic creatures.

"Hey, Nathan."

He turned and watched as Ericka Shane, dressed in a pair of jeans, and a hoodie, climbed into the back of one of the pickups. She sat against the back of the cab and crossed her legs, setting her hands in her lap as if she was ready to receive a gift from the sky.

"Hey," he replied, climbing into the pickup with her. He grabbed his jacket off the top of the wheel well and slid it on as Ericka moved over to give him room to sit next to her. The old Ford Ranger's glossy green paint was chipping away—probably a result of untold adventures—to reveal gray primer underneath.

Ericka smiled at Nathan as he sat down. Other members of Daisy's Defiance climbed into the back of the pickup until the bed was full. Others climbed into the cab, and the engine started with a rumble. The other pickup came to life, and the caravan took off toward the highway and the next town, guided by bright headlights and the soft glow of the moon overhead.

I don't remember when I saw the moon last, Nathan realized. Looking up, he could make out a few stars here and there between the broken cloud cover. He remembered the gift Hwami had given him the night of his graduation—the star named after him. *Which one is mine?*

The trucks exited the highway just past a sign that read STERLING CITY LIMITS.

"Sterling?" a young man sitting next to Nathan asked. "Why have I never heard of these towns we're finding? I've lived in California my whole life, and I never even knew Echo existed."

"Me neither," a dark-skinned woman sitting across from them replied. "It's almost as if these towns and cities are just appearing out of nowhere."

Nathan remembered the strange school—Mercy Springs Elementary—which had appeared from 1983, the one in which he and Heather found Olivia. He recounted the disappearing apartment complex in Los Angeles—again tied to Olivia. *Did she—or Ryn, the bizarre man she said haunted her dreams—cause more buildings and cities and towns to appear around the world? Or is it just everyone's imaginations that these names don't sound all that familiar? California is a pretty big state.*

The pickups slowed through the main street of the town, allowing everyone to view the destruction.

"Well, the president's bombs have certainly been here," Ericka mumbled. Everyone murmured agreement. The buildings along the main street had been reduced to rubble. Brick and mortar, wood and glass. Heaps of destruction greeted the group at every block. An old bowling alley looked promising to Nathan, until he saw that the roof had caved in.

The pickups moved farther down the main street, into the center of the seemingly abandoned town. In the center of a parking lot to their left, a missile stuck out of the asphalt. *It doesn't look like it went off,* Nathan noticed. He was just grateful the president hadn't decided to drop nuclear warheads. That would have definitely brought an end to everything.

A mile farther down the road, they came upon what looked to have once been a small neighborhood—now piles of rubble, except for one lonely house that still stood, despite the destruction around it. A small iron fence surrounded the yard, which was full of overgrown grass and weeds. No lights emanated from the windows, but the moonlight brightened the white shingles on the roof.

The trucks stopped along the curb.

Ericka stood up and stared at the building before remarking, "*Looks* abandoned."

Everyone started to exit the truck bed. Nathan took his time, not all that eager to find out if the house was indeed abandoned or not. They hadn't run into any trouble yet—no demonic hordes, no visits from good ol' Evanescence, no friendly conversations with Legion. *Maybe everyone and everything thinks I'm dead, or maybe, because my sister actually passed—and the president was assassinated—it's the end of things.*

Ginger approached as Nathan hopped out of the truck. He tightened his backpack over his shoulders. *Maybe I'll get a chance to examine the mask I obtained from one of Legion's prisoners without anyone noticing.* He didn't want to draw attention to it, especially if what he heard was true and there was an actual soul trapped inside. *Maybe I can rescue or free the soul somehow.* At the very least, he had to keep the mask out of the hands of the enemy—all of his enemies.

"Cover me?" Ginger asked, tightening the straps of her own backpack. "Someone has to check the house before we decide to make it our temporary home."

Nathan nodded as he took his backpack off, pulling his pistol from it.

He caught a glimmer in Ginger's eyes—happiness, possibly—but only for a moment. It was quickly replaced with seriousness as she pulled her own gun from its holster and opened the iron gate. A long cement path led from the gate to the porch. Three steps up, and Ginger and Nathan were at the front door. The others stood around the low iron fence, watching with anticipation. Some had their weapons drawn, ready to run inside if the situation warranted. Ginger carefully pulled on the handle of the screen door and swung it open on creaky hinges.

Nathan stood with his finger on the trigger of his gun, waiting for something to lunge out at the group. It had been too long, he realized, since he had held his somewhat civilized conversation with Legion back in Echo—before his sister's death and the assassination of President Stone. It had been too long since Evanescence or the man in the red suit had paid Nathan a visit. It had been too long since he had seen any sign of demons or monsters or anything else out of the ordinary. Even the crashed vessels they passed on their journey through the Broken Lands, transports Legion had arrived on Earth in, seemed barren and stagnant, void of any signs of life.

With her gun in one hand, Ginger slowly turned the door knob with the other and pushed the door in. It swung open silently to a dark living room. Ginger reached around the corner to the wall and fumbled around, finally finding a switch that surprisingly illuminated the room.

There shouldn't be electricity here, Nathan thought. *The bombs would have taken everything out.*

Ginger and Nathan stepped across the threshold, letting only the screen door shut between them and the outside world. Their footsteps cast clouds of dust into the light pouring out of the bowl-shaped lamp in the ceiling. A stained couch covered in a revolting flower pattern sat in one corner, abandoned by its owners like one of the many derelict vehicles Nathan had seen in recent weeks. A tall armoire with glass doors showcasing various glassware and plates took up half of the wall. A kitchen waited in the distance, while a short hallway extended off the living room and gave passage to darkness and other rooms. Rooms Nathan was not looking forward to investigating.

Ginger led the way into the kitchen. Once illuminated, it too revealed it had been abandoned, with cabinets and counters caked in dust, a bone-dry sink, and a refrigerator full of rotten food. Ginger and Nathan managed to find a cabinet full of canned food—various soups, vegetables, and Spam. It was enough to last them another day. Another day to reach Providence.

Quietly, Ginger motioned for Nathan to follow her into the dark hallway. The light switch didn't work, but Ginger had her flashlight out and used it to reach the first room on their right. The door was closed, but Ginger didn't tarry long before she opened it, tried another broken light switch, and filled the dark space with the glow from her flashlight. An empty toddler's bed and a bookshelf full of children's storybooks greeted them. Nathan briefly remembered the children's classroom in Mercy Springs Elementary School—the room he had found Olivia in.

Ginger moved on to the next room. She found the door wide open, and when she turned the switch on and filled the room with artificial light, Nathan lifted his gun at the woman sitting on the edge of the four-poster bed. Her hair was a startling white, and she wore a white dress with black polka dots across its surface.

"You?" Nathan whispered.

Ginger raised her weapon. "Who is she, Nathan?"

"Legion."

The woman nodded. "It is true. I am a single part of the whole entity. I do not wish you two harm, though. Nor do I wish to meddle with your friends outside. I simply wish to speak to Nathan Pierce of Earth. Alone."

"I don't think so," Ginger snarled. "You better give me a reason not to shoot you right now before you have a chance to stand."

The woman simply smiled. "Please," she said softly, looking at Nathan. "I wish to speak, as we did back in your city of Echo."

Nathan lowered his weapon. "Talk about what? My sister is dead. The president is dead. What do you want?"

She gave a suspicious glance Ginger's way. "Alone. That is my requirement. It is not much to ask, is it?"

Ginger turned to Nathan for an answer. He nodded. She lowered her weapon and headed into the hallway. "I'll be close by."

Nathan put his gun away. He knew if she wanted to, this woman could easily obliterate him, regardless if he was armed or not. She scooted over and patted her hand on the bed, signaling that she wanted him to sit next to her. He hesitated just long enough to reveal that he was uncomfortable with her proposition.

"Please. If my intention was to harm you, I would have done so already."

"I'm sorry, but I don't really feel comfortable around you."

"You mistake me for the rest of my kind. Psychotic. Murderous. Hungry."

"Hungry?"

She nodded. "For power. For ash." She stood up from the bed and took a few steps toward him. She swayed her hips from side to side, clumsily at that, as if trying too hard to walk like a true woman might. "I told you before that I have been observing you. You fascinate me. I can't say the rest of my kind share my fascination."

"Why are you so fascinated with me? This whole time, all I've been trying to do is save my sister. And she died. Part of the reason she died was because Legion invaded Earth, so I guess I have you to thank for that. Now I have nothing left."

"You have everything left."

"I don't follow."

"The plane that crashed in your Providence city. Aboard is what you will need to win your war. For now."

"My war?"

"Light against dark. Good against evil. Whatever you want to call it. Your real enemy isn't necessarily Legion, is it? It is the one you call Satan. The Devil. The Dark One."

"As far as I can tell, Legion is working with…him."

"Legion *has* been working with him. But some of us…some of us want something more. More than this hunger for destruction, for chaos and madness. Some of us want what you would call peace."

Nathan found himself stifling a laugh. He couldn't bring himself to believe this rogue representative of Legion would want peace.

"You doubt me. I understand that completely. But I truly want to help you destroy the Dark One's servants. Chaos and Evanescence."

"Chaos?"

"The one who wears the red suit."

"Why would you help me? And how?"

"More questions. You are always questioning. I find it…remarkable. Instead of shouting answers, instead of assuming to know all, you ask and you search and you blatantly let others know that you don't know. You aren't necessarily humble, but you take pride in your search for understanding. Understanding which has served you well."

"I don't have time for this. I'm not going to help you."

The woman put a hand to her chest. "It is not I who I am trying to help. It is you." She turned away, as if embarrassed by the confession about to leave her lips. "I am more than just fascinated with you. I feel…sympathy and respect for you. Your sister has been killed—fellow flesh and blood— and yet you continue moving forward."

"I don't know what I'm doing," he confessed. "I take each day as a gift. But I'm not sure where this road will ultimately lead me."

She attempted to grin, again clumsily, her lips instead forming something between a frown and a grimace. "You have only further proven my point. You don't know the end result of your actions of today. Yet you continue to move forward. You continue to…strive. There is a strange strength within you that I do not fully understand. This causes me— the individual me—to feel something between respect and adoration for you.

"I have not felt these things for any other human, any other species, in the universe. I have taken part in the obliteration of worlds. I have participated in what you would call genocide, of entire species. I am filled to the core with darkness. It is all I know. I see in you a light, one that I do not comprehend. One that I do not have the ability to comprehend.

"My time is coming soon when I will be consumed by my siblings, by myself."

"What do you mean consumed?"

"Legion is one. We are many. But some of us are individual. We…we are what you would call rogues. I have developed my own…self-awareness. It hurts, it stings and burns, but it feels good. It feels…alive? My kind will not tolerate this. My kind will consume my essence soon, and I will be no more." She looked at him with urgency flaring in her eyes. "I want very much to help you, Nathan Pierce of Earth. To help you destroy those who I know have plans to destroy us. The Dark One seeks to destroy Legion—sooner or later—and then my kind will be no more anyway. If I can somehow…turn the tables…I can bring advantage to my kind. To Legion."

"Why would I possibly want to help you get an advantage? You'll just turn around and destroy us if he doesn't."

"Yes, Legion will destroy the human species, as it has other species. But I…I, Viranda DelaCourte, desire to help you destroy the Dark One's servants, Chaos and Evanescence, before I am destroyed myself."

"Viranda?"

"I gave myself that name. I read it…in one of your species' marvelous books. Stories…stories are the breadth of your imagination, I have learned. Beautiful stories. Wonderful stories. Stories of hope, of betrayal, like the betrayal I am currently taking part in. Treason against my kind. Treason against myself."

Nathan heard Ginger shuffle her feet in the hallway near the edge of the doorway. He knew she was listening to everything, and he didn't expect her to understand any of it—he didn't even understand half of it—but he figured it was a good sign that she hadn't lost her cool and interrupted their conversation yet.

"I desire to give you time to think this over. But there is no time. My kind—Legion—is already moving forward to destroy you. You, Nathan Pierce of Earth, and you, the human species. We have already captured enough of your kind and have them imprisoned in the Hopeless Bastille. Now the rest of your species will be decimated. That is the way of things."

Nathan's hand instinctively drew his pistol from his backpack. He refrained from pointing it directly at Viranda, but his finger jittered against the trigger as he pointed the gun toward the floor. "That is the way of things? You talk like it's nothing to destroy an entire planet, to wipe out an entire species!"

She shrugged, adding to Nathan's anger. "In all truthfulness, it doesn't mean anything to me. It is who we/I am. It is what I/we do. Legion destroys. Legion consumes."

Nathan took a deep breath. He knew the others outside were going to head in any minute to look for him and Ginger.

Viranda stepped toward him. When he didn't flinch, she slowly reached out and took his hand, staring into his eyes. Her grip felt cold, like his hand was pressed against the back of a freezer. "The plane that crashed, it holds the key to your victory over the Dark One's servants. It has been…a pleasure…speaking with you, Nathan Pierce of Earth. I desire to continue watching you, learning from your tactics and unconventional strategies, but I sense my kind are already on their way to destroy me for my treason."

She let go of his hand and sat on the edge of the bed again. "I will wait here," she said softly. "For nothing, no one, can escape Legion's grasp. Not even Legion itself. Not even me."

I wish I could take her with me, Nathan thought, though not sure why. She's the enemy, clearly. Legion is the enemy. But has this lone female—or whatever she is—indeed gone rogue? And is she truly struggling with her independence from this cohesive unit known as Legion?

She waved him away. "I must apologize. I lingered too long, and now my kind know you are here. The Sphere has brought the Age of Restraint to an end. Now the Age of Destruction has come, and I am…curious…if you will be able to avoid its effects."

Nathan backed into the hallway, keeping a close eye on Viranda.

Ginger flanked him, her weapon still drawn. "We should kill her now," she whispered.

Nathan felt conflicted. *Legion can't be trusted. But Viranda confirmed that we're on the right path headed to the crash site. It can't be a trap, can it? I sure hope not.*

Screams erupted outside. Nathan and Ginger rushed to the front door. When Ginger opened the screen door, Nathan caught a glimpse of a naked female outside with bright orange hair. He grabbed Ginger's wrist, pulling her to the side of the doorway, out of view. He turned toward the window to his left and peered through the blinds. He saw two nude females—the one with orange hair and another with a shaved head. Swirls of black ink covered their most intimate parts. They moved through the crowd like phantoms, barely touching each member of Daisy's Defiance before turning them into pillars of black and red ash that lingered in the air like frozen snowfall.

Nathan pressed his back against the wall and tried to catch his breath. It took him a minute to realize he was squeezing Ginger's hand. He let go, and she peeked around the wall to see what was going on through the screen door.

When she gasped, Nathan pulled away from the wall and grabbed her wrist again, this time yanking her toward the kitchen.

"We have to get out of here," he whispered.

"They...they're gone?"

"Yes." He turned off the kitchen light and made his way toward the back door. When he saw the back door boarded up, he quickly hid himself and Ginger in the bottom cabinets nearest the refrigerator.

"What the hell was that?" Ginger asked. "What the—"

Nathan put his hand over Ginger's mouth. "Shh. They'll kill us if they find us. Just keep quiet," he whispered.

They crouched silently, crammed into the small, dark space together. Nathan could smell his own sweat. Bare footsteps pattered across the kitchen tile.

"Where is she?" one of the Legion females asked.

"She is here. I can...I can sense her. She is attempting to cut off her Chord of Conduct and break away from the control of the Sphere completely."

"Yes. She must be stopped before...wait, I hear her breathing. I sense her human form in the next room."

Footsteps trailed out of the kitchen. Nathan closed his eyes and waited. He heard voices through the wall behind him.

"You cannot run anymore."

"I don't wish to run anymore. I have done what I desired to do."

"You contacted the human, Nathan Pierce of Earth."

"Yes, I did. I could do nothing to help myself. I am... enthralled...consumed...by him."

Silence.

Nathan shifted his knees, pulling them closer to his chest. Ginger sighed. Her breath smelled like rotten onions.

"Your rebellion must be purged."

"I understand. Please…make it quick."

"No."

A scream traveled through the surface of the wall. Nathan couldn't hear anything beyond that.

He and Ginger waited for what felt like hours. Trembling, Ginger crawled out of the cabinet and stood in the kitchen.

Nathan crept out behind her. *We should flee the house, but I have to see what occurred in that room.* And then, to his surprise, he wondered, *is Viranda okay?*

Nathan cautiously entered the hallway, weapon drawn. He reached the bedroom and looked inside. To his disgust and surprise, Viranda's body hung naked, her arms and legs spread and fastened between the posts of the bed, stretching her in an X position. A frightened look remained on her face, her eyes large but empty, her lips turned downward. A contraption the size of a soup can—a silver metal cylinder etched with glowing blue neon— had been shoved into the center of her chest, just far enough to tear the skin. A large circle at the end of the contraption hummed with a yellow glowing pulse. Blood pooled underneath her hanging corpse. The device appeared to be doing something to her.

Ginger entered the room and gasped. "What…We have to leave."

Nathan reached out and took hold of the end of the machine and tugged. It slid out of Viranda's chest. When it exited the wound completely, blood spilled out, splashing his shoes. He felt the pulsing in the machine slow to a stop and fall dead in his hands. Dropping his backpack to the floor, Nathan unzipped the main pocket and shoved the bloody device inside. After resealing the bag and strapping it back on, he followed Ginger into the kitchen. They pried off the boards blocking their exit and opened the door to the backyard.

CHAPTER 2

ricka Shane spotted the two Legion women from a distance before they reached the loitering crowd of Daisy's Defiance. Besides the fact that they were two nude women with black swirls marring their intimate parts, roaming a deserted town, Ericka sensed something—darkness or emptiness—that made her turn and run in the opposite direction. Taking refuge behind an old station wagon parked along the curb, she watched as the members of Daisy's Defiance were turned to ash. The scene filled Ericka with panic and fear, but she quickly brought herself under control and waited until they entered the house, where Nathan and Ginger were, before emerging from behind the vehicle and making her way toward the house.

A buzzing sound stopped her in her tracks. She hunkered down behind another vehicle and scanned the area, only then realizing the sound was coming from her. From her hoodie, to be more exact.

She looked over her sweatshirt and noticed a very small disc sticking to its side. The disc was smaller than her thumbnail, and was the same tan color as the fabric, making it almost impossible to see.

"Ericka?" a voice spoke from the disc. *"I have you on my satellite. If you head a mile east, I can get a transport to pick you up."*

"What?" She pulled off the disc and squinted at it, examining the intricate copper circuitry embedded in the surface of its back.

"This is Absolute. I planted the chip on you when I asked you to shoot the video of President Stone's atrocities."

"You've been tracking me?"

"And listening to you. You and Nathan and your pathetic little group. I'm not sure what happened over there, but you're on your own now, aren't you?"

Ericka glanced toward the house. "I'm not on my own."

"What happened?"

Ericka crushed the disc between her fingers and blew the tiny pieces to the ground. She pulled the gun from the back waistband of her jeans and analyzed her situation, resolving to help Nathan and Ginger. If they were smart and quick, they would more than likely head out the back door leading to the open field. Or possibly, if they were able to, they would head out the front door. But that seemed unlikely, especially if Nathan or Ginger had seen the destruction the two females had caused moments earlier.

Ericka took a deep breath and decided to head toward the side of the house to cover the back door. She stood up and then jogged toward the house. When she reached the side of it, she took a moment to catch her breath, still unable to completely shake the images of her allies turning into pillars of ash.

Something dark and stocky moved in her peripheral vision. She lifted the gun and felt a stabbing in her left thigh. She grabbed her leg with one hand while the gun was knocked out of the other. Something struck her in the throat, and she hit the soil hard.

A foot pressed against her spine, pinning her to the ground. "Don't move," a deep voice thundered.

Pain spread through her lower half. Then numbness settled in.

"You're paralyzed from the waist down." Another stab, this one to her neck. "This will make sure you cooperate."

The last thing Ericka saw was Nathan and Ginger running out the back door of the house before her world drowned in black.

CHAPTER 3

Cynthia Scarlet Ruin's body lay on the floor of Petrina Rilar's living area, her throat cut open with glass, her blood staining the once immaculate white carpet. Petrina cried herself to sleep after the event. She had done what she could to save Cynthia. Petrina blamed the statue. It had always been the statue. The little carving of a black cathedral that her husband had picked up at a swap meet before the stars fell.

Petrina hadn't really wanted the statue in her home. She told her husband that, said she had a bad feeling about it. But he didn't listen. He didn't care. He cherished it just as he did the other antiques and knickknacks he kept in his armoire. The very armoire that was at least partially responsible for Cynthia Ruin's death.

As Petrina slept, her mind spinning nightmares, Cynthia's body lay still and lifeless. But her soul and spirit resided elsewhere...

Cynthia sat upon the stone throne, staring out at the long chamber before her. Dark pillars lined the corridor that stretched for almost a half mile and ended at a set of double doors, which opened into the main hallway of the Black Cathedral. A long black rug, edged with bright silver threads and dotted with variegated gems, stretched from the bottom of the throne to the double doors. This was, as Cynthia had been told, her ruling chamber. As princess of the Black Cathedral.

She closed her eyes as a servant's hands, soft and talented, massaged her bare shoulders. The black corset gave some of her flesh room to breathe, while the dark gown covering her bottom half felt like a soft, velvet blanket across her legs. She wore knee-high stiletto boots that were a little too tight, and she made a mental note to trade them out for something different, like regular stilettos or some Lolitas, when she returned to her sleeping quarters.

The last thing she remembered before leaving her world to join this dark fantasy was her body bleeding out across Petrina's carpet. She remembered agreeing to join Ryn, to be spirited away from her world, her reality, into his. And now here she was, in the Black Cathedral, as royalty.

Her memories of the last few days were somewhat blurred. After dying in Petrina's living room, she remembered waking here, in this very throne room, on the black rug before her. She had been naked, shivering, and coated in a black gooey substance, which took three washings to rid herself of. An older gentleman who seemed to have no name had greeted her. He explained that she was the new princess of the Cathedral, destined to rule by Ryn's side for the rest of the war. When she asked what war, he simply grinned and left her to wash the gooey substance from her bare flesh and pick out an outfit to rule in.

Every ensemble in the wardrobe was black or red. The colors appealed to her, but she found herself wanting something a tad more vibrant. In the few days she had been here, she found practically everything within the Cathedral—which really resembled more of a castle on the inside than an actual cathedral—to be crafted out of dark substance. Dark stone, dark tile, dark marble. The clothes the servants wore were made of black cloth. The meals they served her consisted mainly of dark meats and dark fruits, like pomegranates and cherries. Even the bedding and decorations of her sleeping quarters were dark in theme.

Cynthia found it depressing. She had grown up loving Gothic themes—to a degree—but this place seemed a bit over the top. And to her dismay, she hadn't yet met Ryn in person, which she found disconcerting.

From what Cynthia understood, the Black Cathedral was a way station of sorts between her reality and the afterlife. If one believed in such a thing. Ryn offered humans the chance to give up their souls to reside in the Black Cathedral, instead of passing through to darkness, Hell, Heaven, or wherever people believed they would go after they died. Ryn essentially caught a person's soul as it passed through the Cathedral, giving it a home here.

Cynthia ruled over these souls as their princess. Well, that's what Ryn said, and that's what she told herself. But each day she spent here, she found herself doing more of the same dull tasks, almost none of which involved interacting with the souls within this realm. She ran into many souls as she walked the halls of the Cathedral, but the souls didn't bow to her or even acknowledge her half the time. She figured they would simply need to get used to her presence here.

She spent most of each day on her stone throne—sitting and thinking, mostly about what might be happening in the realm she had left behind. *Did Nathan Pierce save his sister? Had someone gotten the guts to kill President Stone? Whatever became of Alpha 1?*

She ruminated on these things, but was happy to be here, to be thought of as royalty. She wasn't sure if Hell existed beyond this realm, or even Heaven—which she would most absolutely be denied entrance to—and she didn't really care. She felt safe here, within the walls of the Black Cathedral, under the protection of Ryn.

The servant giving her the massage, a man by the name of Gerolic, finished his work on her shoulders and then packed up his oils and lotions and left the throne room, saying nothing as he went. Nobody around this place seemed to say much. Some of the souls wandering the Cathedral looked as if they had died in this realm instead of the previous one, depressed expressions stamped on their faces. A few of the souls conversed with Cynthia, but she found the talk brief, usually only containing minor details of the previous world, of the horrible things Legion and the president were doing, of the darkness that had engulfed the planet.

These talks made Cynthia all the more happy to be within the Cathedral—as princess, no less.

She sat staring at the double doors Gerolic had just passed through. Crossing her legs, she felt the thin, soft fabric of her gown brush the skin of her thighs, and she sighed. When she had agreed to come here, she didn't know what to expect. After her sensual dream that Ryn had somehow invaded, she thought there would be ways for her to indulge her sexual desires. Sitting on this lonely throne, however, she found herself yearning for something more. *Is it sex? Excitement? Maybe companionship?*

Regret continually snuck in. *Where is poor Petrina now?* Cynthia had saved the woman's life. *But to what end? So I could steal her trinket, the last monument to her late husband's memory, and then die a gruesome and painful death in the end? Only to wind up here, in another realm, possibly another reality, waiting for what?* She didn't know. She didn't know why she was here, other than to be royalty. She felt empty, like a doll with no heart.

The double doors at the end of the long corridor swung open, and the hourly Mirror Man started his long trek down the black rug toward her throne. Each time he arrived, Cynthia would stare into his mirror and revel in her beauty. It was one of the few things that brought her a sense of fulfillment, even though she wasn't doing anything but basking in her vanity. Before she died in her other world, she had noticed a very positive change in her physical structure. Magical, maybe. She had lost weight, and she looked enticing instead of just appealing.

Since her arrival here, though, she had transformed from enticing to downright enrapturing. Her arms and legs had become ivory columns, her breasts plump fruit ripe for a firm squeeze, and her hair seemed to flow from her head like a dark river of silk. Everything sexual about her seemed to be enhanced—even her libido. It was as if she had stepped into a realm of her own creation.

Yet it lacked the most basic of necessities to be a realm of her own: sex. If she had devised this Black Cathedral, she would have given herself more attractive partners to exert her urges upon. The servants seemed to be nothing more than dolls who wandered mindlessly, doing the miniscule bidding of the Princess of the Black Cathedral, bringing her meals, grooming her, or giving her the occasional massage—which she always hoped would turn into something more. But every servant, both male and female, seemed to be void of any sexual nature.

And the residents who transferred here from her *old world*—a term she found she liked—didn't even give her a desirous glance. Male or female. She found the situation disappointing and frustrating.

The sight of the old man trudging his way toward her throne, large vertical mirror bouncing haphazardly in his hands, didn't appeal to Cynthia's tastes, as varied as they were. Even now, as he drew closer to the steps leading up to her throne, she could see bags of wrinkled flesh drooping from his chin. His ears looked two sizes too big, and his eyes appeared large and frightening, like those of a nocturnal animal. His very presence made her want to gag, but she kept her decency about her, realizing he had probably dwelt within this realm longer than anyone else she had encountered here.

"Your highness," he wheezed as he set the mirror before her.

She took a look at her reflection and marveled at how magnificent she looked in the black corset. The bright pink rabbit tattoo peering out from over her left breast brought a splash of color to the otherwise dreary atmosphere.

"Is there anything you require?" the old man asked, staring at her.

"Yes," she said after some thought. "I want to meet with Ryn."

The old man stepped back, shifting the mirror to Cynthia's other side. "Ryn?"

"Yes. I want to meet with him. Today. Now."

"He is busy."

Cynthia stood to her feet and looked down on the decrepit man hunched over the steps leading to her throne. "I want to meet with him today, and that isn't a request."

The man began trembling. He set the mirror down and folded his skeletal hands together. "Y-your highness. He…Ryn cannot be d-disturbed. He has m-m-much work to do. P-please, save your desire to s-s-see him until a later time, when he d-deems it prudent."

Cynthia felt rage building within her. "He is the one who transported me here. He is the one who called to me in the old world, who summoned me to this place. And he doesn't have time to meet with me?"

The soft fluttering of wings resonated through the cavernous chamber. Cynthia looked up to see a murder of crows circling near the ceiling. One of them carried something large in its talons. The crow dropped the object, which landed on the steps with a thump. A rotten pomegranate. A closer look revealed that a symbol had been meticulously carved into the fruit: a key.

The crows flew away. The old man stumbled backward a few feet, speechless.

Cynthia reached down and picked up the fruit, examining the key symbol, black with mold and filth.

"R-R…my master, the King of the Black Cathedral, has summoned you to his chamber."

Cynthia dropped the fruit when she found a maggot crawling out of the key. Wiping her hands on her gown, she realized she had no idea where Ryn's chamber was located. She had only been given access to certain areas of the Cathedral: living quarters, dining hall, bathing area. Other areas were off limits to her, guarded by beings in black robes, sentinels with no faces—just darkness under their hoods.

"Take me to Ryn's chamber," she demanded.

The old man wrung his hands together and attempted to speak but couldn't manage anything beyond simple stuttering and spitting. Finally, he took a deep breath, one that looked painful for his frail frame to accomplish, and nodded. "As you desire."

He led Cynthia out of the massive throne room and into the main hallway. They passed through a set of double doors guarded by the faceless sentinels and entered another hallway, this one made of walls crafted from beautiful stained glass illuminated from behind. Cynthia stopped and stared at the jagged chunks of colored glass that had been meticulously set within the surface of the wall, all in no particular pattern or image, at least none that Cynthia could discern.

"C-come. The king waits for you. You m-m-must not keep him waiting."

I am the princess, she wanted to say. *I agreed to come here, to be by his side, but he hasn't had the balls to show his face to me yet. How dare you hurry me along!*

They continued through the corridor until it emptied into a very large courtyard. Tall pillars rose from the center, capped by a massive stone canopy. Various stars and planets studded the night sky, and a light breeze moved through the concourse, skittering across Cynthia's bare shoulders.

"Th-this way."

She followed the man to a separate section of the Cathedral. This part, from the outside, looked like a lone tower that had been built as an afterthought. It rose high into the night sky, yet when they stepped through its large doorway, the room they entered was only one story, an antechamber. Red carpet blanketed the floor, and display cases along the walls held various indiscernible objects beneath panels of thick, lightly frosted glass.

The old man gave her no time to tarry, instead prompting her toward a set of large double doors guarded by more faceless beings. "His majesty...he is behind this door. You m-must bow when you s-s-..." he stopped, frustrated, and took a deep breath before speaking more. "You must bow when you see h-him."

"We'll see," she whispered.

The old man opened the doors and signaled for Cynthia to head inside.

A long black rug led from where she stood to his throne atop a tall flight of stone steps. That much resembled her own throne room. Along the edges of this rug, however, stood tall statues—ivory on one side of the rug, black marble on the other. The ivory statues had been sculpted into naked women, some of which didn't look human. One had what appeared to be flesh ribbons pouring out of her sides. Another had a long snout, like a fox's, and still another had no eyes. They were all in different poses depicting various actions, like a woman mending a wounded dog's appendage, another tending to a garden.

This is nothing like I expected. Although, she had to admit, *I didn't know what to expect from Ryn*. She had never formally met the man, but his hands had touched her...intimately...sensually. The act had created a bewildering bond between them.

The marble statues depicted naked men—again, some of them not exactly human: one with a horn protruding from his shoulder, another with a large, square, block torso. Each of the men had been shaped in a position of action: one with a raised fist, yelling, and another with a sword through the back of a man lying against the floor.

She walked slowly, carefully, between the two rows of

statues. Many things about them disturbed her. Aside from the nakedness, she noticed that the women were all in positions of peace, while the men were in positions of anger and dominance. Each statue seemed to be staring at her with eyes that weren't really there, but that she felt were tracking her movement toward the throne. *Are these actually guards in the clever disguise of statues? Are they demons? Or are they real people turned to stone?*

As she drew closer to the throne, she saw that behind it, behind the figure sitting in it dressed in engulfing black attire, towered a massive tree, the twin trunks of which snaked and spiraled around each other—one black, one white—until they both met at the top and ended in a cluster of brilliant blue leaves, which seemed to glow with power, with life. Cynthia watched as a single leaf broke free from its branch and sailed down into the grass surrounding the tree's trunk, joining other leaves that had already fallen there.

She stopped at the base of the tall flight of stairs and looked up toward the throne at the pinnacle. The figure sitting there was clothed in what she could only assume was a black blanket or wrap since it appeared to swallow the being in darkness. The air surrounding him shifted the silver throne and the tree in the background in fragments of blurry jitters and swirls.

"My, my, my. You certainly do fill that outfit well."

Cynthia said nothing to the borderline lewd comment. She realized the old man had left her alone in the throne room and that the double doors she had entered through had been sealed shut. She was alone with Ryn, with the man she had handed her life to. She smelled something sweet, like honey, moving through the air, and the scent almost clogged her nostrils with the simple act of breathing.

"Did he not tell you to bow in my presence?"

"I am the princess," she stated matter-of-factly.

"Yes. I am the one who made you *my* princess. And you will bow to your king. To me."

Cynthia hesitated, but then decided she didn't want to start her relationship with this man on a bad foot. So she knelt and bowed her head toward the floor, waiting five long seconds before standing up again.

"Very good. Whether you understand or not, you certainly do acknowledge that I am the one who is above you."

Cynthia literally bit down on her tongue to save herself from saying something foolish.

"I would certainly like to examine you up close. Come up here."

She started up the steps, her stiletto boots clacking against the stone, echoing in the chamber like the pendulum of an old grandfather clock. As she climbed higher up the stairs, the air seemed to get easier to breathe, and the musky scent of cedar replaced the sweet scent of honey.

When she reached the final few steps, the man put a hand up to stop her from getting closer. "That is close enough. For now."

Through the blurry distortion around him, Cynthia could make out a face, void of any distinguishing elements like eyes, nose, or mouth. She simply saw pale skin pulled taut over an oval skull.

"I," he started while motioning to himself, "am King of the Black Cathedral. I am Ryn."

"You know who I am," she said, realizing only too late how rude her tone had come out.

She felt his nonexistent eyes staring at her. "Yes," he finally said. "Yes, I am the one who handpicked you to be my princess. To be my servant."

"I am nobody's servant. And I'm not sure what I'm supposed to be doing here. I've been here for three days, and I've done nothing but sit around in a chair and stare at myself in a mirror."

Crows filled the space above her head and descended on her at once. She swung her arms madly, fighting to keep her balance on the steps as she felt the sharp points of beaks strike her exposed flesh, rip at her hair, and tug at the threads of her clothes. She screamed and hollered and stumbled down a step, catching herself before she took a nasty tumble. The crows disappeared seconds later.

Cynthia stood, panting, her corset frayed, her gown torn. She was bleeding from small wounds in her shoulders and neck, and she wanted nothing more than to strangle the man sitting before her.

"You," he said softly, "will learn your place here. You, human girl, are in my domain. This is the Black Cathedral. You are no longer on Earth. You are no longer in the reality you left behind. You died back there, bled out until there was nothing left but an empty framework of flesh missing its most vital component—a soul. Your soul now resides here. And here, I am the King. You will bow before me. You will serve me. Nobody but me!"

Cynthia closed her eyes and pushed past the pain from the bites across her flesh. They hurt, but her anger toward this callous man overrode whatever irritation she felt from his bird attack.

She opened her eyes and saw him standing before her. The air around him remained distorted, but she felt his presence enter her personal space—even though it didn't look as if he was physically touching her. His soft caress—the same she had felt on the boardwalk and in her erotic yet disturbing dream where he first offered to bring her to the Cathedral—soothed her wounds, healing them immediately. She felt flesh close up with a very soft vibration in the areas where the crows had bitten her. Her muscles relaxed, her tension melted away, and she suddenly felt calm and at peace.

"I need you, Scarlet."

"My first name is Cynthia."

"Scarlet is your middle name. That is your name here."

"Fine," she conceded. "That is my name here."

"An appropriate name for such an exotic woman."

She felt his hands—though they didn't appear to move from his side—grab at the ribbon holding the front of her corset together. Untying it, he pulled a section of the ribbon out through the holes. He pulled a second. After a third and fourth, the cloth separated to expose the top half of her breasts.

Before the sixth and seventh sections could be undone, exposing her chest completely, she backed away, shaking her head. "No. No, this isn't what I came here for." She heard her heart pounding in her ears, and her hands trembled. She attempted to retie the corset, fumbling for a few seconds before finally restoring the garment to its fastened state.

"Oh dear, it seems you mistake my intentions. I can understand why you would do so, seeing your extraordinary nature. I assure you, I am not interested in your flesh for lustful purposes. I am merely an acute observer of the human body. An observer actually of many different species. But I find the human body to be the most fantastic, the most interesting."

Cynthia turned away from Ryn and looked down the stairs, her mind racing. Part of her wanted her old life back. The other part wanted to dive so deep into this realm that she completely forgot her whole past and assumed a new identity—the identity of Scarlet.

"My persona lashed out at you once. The crows...they can be relentless when I neglect to control their bloodlust. But in all honesty, I really just want you to understand me. To understand your purpose here."

Scarlet turned back toward him, her eyes full of sadness, her heart dragged down with sorrow. "Why am I here? If you don't want me for my body, why did you summon me here? Why did I have to die, back in Petrina's house? Why did that little statuette call out to me, urging me to steal it? Why?"

Ryn sat on his throne and sighed. "Interesting questions. The most important questions, actually. All species seek purpose. They seek to know why they are in existence, regardless of what galaxy, what plane, what realm they reside in. But not everyone receives the answers they seek. To soothe your worried heart, I will tell you now that I am androgynous. I care for both male and female species, and I can take the form of either. But I do not give in to sexual temptation toward one or the other. My attempts to undress you are simply so I can observe your naked flesh in all of its beauty. I want to see what it is that the others—the men and women of your world—find so intoxicating about you. Right now I simply see a young girl, barely of age, but ripe as any woman fifty years older. Your flesh is tender, soft, without blemish. But your spirit...your spirit is so powerful." He turned his face to the side in a blur of motion.

"What is it?" She yearned to have her question answered. *Why am I here?*

"To be honest, I am trapped here. Banished by those closest to me. It is a sad tale I will not bore you with. It seems you are already bored with the rest of this place. I will not bore you in my own chamber. I am trapped here in this Black Cathedral. This has become my home, but not necessarily out of desire. More out of force."

"Why were you banished here?"

"That is the linchpin question, isn't it? However, I will not answer it. Private matters are private, and the reasons for my being caged here like a carrier dove are neither my business to tell, nor yours to discover. Regardless of my circumstances, I strive to make this kingdom an oasis along one's journey to the other side."

"Am I only here temporarily? I was told you wanted me here until after the war. What war?"

"The war does not affect this realm. And you may stay here permanently, if you'd like. However, if you decide you want to leave, to journey onward toward the Great Unknown, that is your choice. You may go at any time. However, I would like it if you stayed, with me, by my side as princess. I think I have the ability to make your stay here more enjoyable than it has been thus far."

Scarlet glanced up at the tree, unsure of the glowing blue leaves and the twisting trunks of black and white. "I don't know the first thing about ruling a kingdom."

"You aren't just here to rule, you know? I believe everyone's purpose is what they make it to be. Most of your adolescence has been steeped in sexual immorality. Yet you enjoy it. Every moment of it. The way you torture the men, the way you tease the girls. The things you can do with your hands are equivalent to the things a painter can do with a brush. And with each stroke of the brush, you paint more of your own self-portrait. You are Scarlet, and you are now mine—as long as you are here. I wish to see you at the peak of your potential."

"I don't know," she said, crossing her arms over her chest. She wasn't eager to have him untie her corset again. Although…

"I felt that," he said. "I felt the tug of your spirit, how it relented, giving way to the core of your being. You don't want to be violated like you were in that nightclub in Scottsdale. That was rape. Yet there is something within you, a voice, that screams to be allowed to lose control. Just once. Completely."

"I don't know what you're talking about. I was raped. I never wanted to be raped."

"I believe that. To some degree. But you asked to be raped, did you not? The way you dressed, the way you enticed others, the way you rejected those you deemed unworthy. And it was one of those rejections, one of those unworthies, who lashed back, who took control away from you for one night. One night changed everything. But in actuality, my dear princess, it changed nothing.

"Most would have assumed you would finally realize a grand mistake in your scheme of things. That you would finally see the 'error' of your ways and turn from your life of sexual promiscuity. Some, as misled as they were, even believed you would turn your face to the Heavens to call upon the deity who is rumored to reside there. You did none of those things. Not completely. Instead, you decided to carve your own path through whatever life you had left and control the world you walked through. Much like I control this world.

"You see, you and I are the same. We are two creatures, two

sentient beings, who simply want to control the world we inhabit. We don't want that control to be taken, and we will fight with everything we have to keep that control. And if by some nefarious means, that control is stripped from us, we will self-destruct, destroying those who hijacked our precious control."

His words rang so incredibly true, they almost brought tears to Scarlet's eyes.

"I would like you to take control here, Scarlet. Take control of your gifts. Take control of your talents. I will give you the pawns you desire to control. I will give you the warmth you want in your bosom. I will give you the home you deserve…for you and your child."

Scarlet rubbed her stomach with her palms, remembering the child growing inside her. When she first transferred here—however that had happened—she thought she had left the baby behind, in her corpse. But then she sensed—knew—it was within her, even here in the Black Cathedral.

"I need time."

"To think?"

She nodded.

"I presumed as much. Humans like to think. Thinking is good, it is healthy. While you think, I will have you escorted back to your sleeping quarters. You may rest, relax, indulge."

The way the word indulge left his mouth gave Scarlet's gut a jolt of electricity. *Could he mean—*

"I will have another of my servants take you back." The double doors at the other end of the chamber opened. Ryn stood and entered her space with light caresses on the back of her neck. She shuddered. "You are so easily controlled, yet so fluent at controlling others," he said. "It is a conundrum that I wish to understand at some point. For now, it was a pleasure speaking with you, my lovely princess."

Scarlet turned and headed down the stairs, her mind overwhelmed by the heavy discussion. When she reached the bottom, another of Ryn's servants met her. Scarlet looked up at the young girl and almost shrieked with surprise.

Standing before her, staring her straight in the face, was Olivia.

CHAPTER 4

r. Silver took a deep, painful breath and exhaled slowly, letting his body process the taxing movement. It was the price of science. The price of immortality.

After experimenting with his immortality serum on Shaonna Ryshay—now known as Mira Tracer after he wiped her memory—he was sure the serum would work on him as well. He was wrong. Instead of giving him rapid healing abilities, like the serum had given Mira, it had gone in the reverse direction and was methodically destroying his body.

"What is the status of our defenses?" he asked.

Stanton, the head of Mr. Silver's security, sighed. "They're holding. For now. We have the outer shields up over the complex, and security measures are being implemented in the ventilation system as needed."

"Will Legion be able to stop us from taking off?" Secretly, Mr. Silver had no plans to fly in one of the shuttles being housed in SilverTech. He had his own private shuttle, stashed away below Providence.

"I don't believe so. The shuttles depart so far below ground..."

Mr. Silver took another deep breath. *I'm going to end up on a breathing machine. And possibly in a wheelchair.* The thought frightened him to no end.

"Mr. Silver, I suggest we get you out of here if your plans are to travel to Anaisha. Dr. Reeves tells me if you don't leave now, your body may fall into worse shape, and then you won't be cleared to go anywhere."

Mr. Silver shot up from his chair and threw his chief guard up against the wall. "Nobody gives or takes away my clearance, you understand? I'm the one who makes the rules around here. I'm the one…" He stepped back, realizing his bladder released into his pants. He picked up the chair he had been sitting in and threw it at the wall, watching with satisfaction as it bounced off and tumbled to the floor.

"Mr. Silver, you need to calm down."

He leaned against the desk and took a deep breath. "Yes, I know."

"We should go."

"I'm not going yet. I have more to do around here before I leave."

"As your chief of security, I highly advise that we get you as far away from SilverTech Industries and as far away from this planet as possible."

Mr. Silver looked over his shoulder at the man. "Are you pressing this issue for your own sake or for mine?"

"Both of ours, sir. Who are we kidding? Legion can't be stopped once it enters the building."

"Legion won't bother with me. Not yet."

"How do you—"

"If you actually came into my office to tell me something important, please do. Otherwise, leave. I have many things to prepare before I'm ready to travel. There are several more shuttles out there that haven't taken off yet. Countless high-ranking people have not had their chance to escape this darkness. I need to make sure those things—and my laboratories—are in order before I go anywhere."

"I understand that, sir. And I understand that you don't think Legion is anywhere near us. But the darkness outside…it's gotten thicker. It's starting to climb over the walls of SilverTech."

"Let it. Bring our men inside. Seal everything off. If that doesn't work, I will hold you personally responsible."

"Sir, do you really think—"

Mr. Silver put a hand up to stop him. "Do you have something important to say?"

Stanton kept silent for a moment, then sighed. "Dr. Reeves wanted me to pass along a message to you. About Metal Man. They've retrieved the storage core of Metal Man's brain, but to do so, they had to preserve it within special cutting-edge technology to keep it from being damaged by Earth's atmosphere."

"Wonderful!"

"Sir, Dr. Reeves has been working on something for you. An outfit of sorts."

"No. Now, where is the data bank? We need to get it implanted in my head before we get things rolling to wrap this place up and head out of dodge."

Stanton huffed. "Sir, can't you just talk to Dr. Reeves about all of this directly? I have other duties I need to perform if you want this building sealed up."

"No. Tell me what Reeves said."

"He said the data bank can't be surgically implanted in your body—especially with it reacting the way it has to the immortality serum. Metal Man's body—his flesh and muscle and bone—are all designed to hold the data bank and preserve it within him. It was…symbiotic in nature. It won't be so with you. You're human, not Wedge."

"I am fully aware of what I am, damnit!"

"The data bank has been incorporated in the outfit that Dr. Reeves has created for you."

Mr. Silver lunged at the man, slamming him against the wall again. "I swear to the gods that don't exist that I will kill you if you piss me off any more than you already have. SilverTech is mine! I will not allow anyone to change that."

Stanton carefully moved Mr. Silver's hands away from his neck. "Mr. Silver, you better get a hold of yourself. I work for you, but my life is not yours to take. We aren't against you; we're trying to help you. You can't travel to Anaisha in the condition you're in without assistance. Dr. Reeves has developed cutting-edge technology that I'm sure you'll appreciate." Stanton picked Mr. Silver's chair up off the floor and set it upright. "Now, if you'll have a seat, I'll have Dr. Reeves come in and show you the outfit. I do have other things to do, things you yourself ordered me to do."

Mr. Silver paced the room in an effort to calm himself. His body was giving out—starting with his lungs and his bladder, and he hated the feeling more than anything. He felt so weak all of a sudden, so vulnerable. First, Shaonna had turned on him, attempting to murder him multiple times. Now his chief of security had no fear of him…his power was starting to fall away. He couldn't let that happen.

He sat back down in his leather office chair, quietly and without persuasion. Stanton left the room. Minutes later, Dr. Reeves entered, holding a thick, black suitcase. He set it on Mr. Silver's glass desktop, his hands trembling.

"Mr. Silver, sir, I took a lot of time—"

"Cut the shit, Reeves. Show me what you've created, and let's get on with this."

Dr. Reeves entered a pass code into the top of the suitcase, and the lid opened. He pulled out a folded black garment and held it out in front of Mr. Silver. It looked like a wet suit, with gray lines running along it.

Mr. Silver stood up and took the suit from Dr. Reeves. "What the hell is this?"

"It's made of very flexible, highly resistant Terustin. Fifteen times more bulletproof than Kevlar. Stronger than titanium, flexible and lightweight."

"This is the material you extracted from Metal Man?"

"Yes, sir."

"What are these lines running along the suit?"

Dr. Reeves smiled. "Those are conduits to deliver synthetic nutrients and minerals to your body. They run from this small canister you plug into the suit." He pulled a canister from the suitcase. Through the clear casing, Mr. Silver could see a blue glowing liquid. "Each canister will last you six months."

"Six months? This includes all the nutrients I would normally get from food?"

"Yes. They go directly to your muscles, bones, and flesh. Even your organs. The suit knows where each nutrient should go and directs it to that location through the skin with the right intensity to get to the organ, bone, or muscle it needs to reach. I created the design under the assumption that the immortality serum would eventually destroy your body's ability to process foods normally. In essence, this suit was designed as a worst-case scenario."

Looking closer at the canister, Mr. Silver saw "SilverTech

Industries" etched in a metal ring surrounding the cylinder. "How many of these have you made?"

"Well, I sent the design to our labs within the building, and they have already started manufacturing them for you. By the end of the next hour, we should have enough made to last you a few hundred years."

Mr. Silver's eyes widened at the news.

"You must understand, we take the immortality serum seriously. Even though your body seems to be falling apart right now, we have foreseen this and created countermeasures to sustain you. My team is already working on a way to possibly reverse the negative effects, giving you the same abilities Mira has—if we can get it to work."

"Yes." Mr. Silver rubbed the texture of the suit between his fingers. He noticed reduced feeling in his hands. He didn't mention this, simply assumed the suit would give him back that sense. "And what of the data bank?"

Dr. Reeves smiled. Although Mr. Silver wouldn't say so, he was proud of Reeves. The man had, for lack of a better explanation, saved Mr. Silver's life.

"Sir, I embedded the data bank into the suit. Metal Man's core wasn't necessarily a container of information, but information itself. A mass core of knowledge and data. So I embedded it into the texture of the outfit, and it relays the information to your brain in segments."

"Segments?"

"Yes, sir. Segments. Your human brain—since you are not a Wedge—could not possibly contain the data core all at once. It would fry your brain, regardless of your immortality, and render you a vegetable."

"How does it give it to me in segments?"

47

"Well, another aspect of the outfit is the face console. In the suit, you will have a computer screen in front of your face. It will react to your thoughts. In the computer bank are different categories—say, planets or species, for example. You think about which category you want, and the suit will pull up a detailed table of contents regarding those items from the data core."

"You've outdone yourself."

Silence fell over the room. Mr. Silver figured it would. He rarely complimented anyone—aside from his late daughter—and to receive a compliment from Mr. Silver was the equivalent of a god reaching down to touch a person on the nose.

Dr. Reeves, unsure of what to do in such a situation, half bowed toward Mr. Silver. "Thank you, sir. It's an honor."

"Does this suit have any…offensive capabilities?"

"Yes. Yes, I designed it with an electric pulse, in case someone tries to tamper with the suit. Like I said before, the suit is made of Terustin, which can repel almost every type of ammunition made by man—and even some made by alien life, which I researched from part of the data bank using SilverTech's servers."

Mr. Silver looked at the man suspiciously. Dr. Reeves had suddenly lost favor in Mr. Silver's eyes, just for analyzing some of the information from the data bank. Mr. Silver wanted to be the only one graced with the wisdom and data on the core, and he would not share that with anyone. "Anything else I need to know about?"

"Yes, I designed the suit with a hacking mechanism. The gloves in the suit can emulate fingerprints and data codes they pick up. So if you come across a data pad you can't unlock, the suit will scan the fingerprints that were used last and put them back into the pad, unlocking it for you. If there was a code put in, the suit can quickly analyze the millions of combinations according to the fingerprints left on the buttons and spit the right combination back out in a matter of minutes—sometimes even seconds."

Mr. Silver stared at the suit in his hands. It felt lighter than an everyday shirt. "What is powering this suit?"

"Your brain waves, body heat, body movement, sunlight. It has over a half dozen ways of generating power. Just in case you became an invalid, though, it has a backup supply of power made from nitro carbon batteries, which will last a hundred years. All based on SilverTech's own technology."

"Very good. Is there anything else I need to know? Anything else about the suit, like flaws or security measures that should be taken?"

"You will have to wear it all the time. The suit will recycle your waste into energy for the suit itself."

Mr. Silver remembered he had wet his pants earlier. He squirmed in his seat as he realized they hadn't completely dried yet. "Very good."

"Also, the suit has a temperature control system. If it's too cold, you can set the suit up to warm you, and vice versa. All from the face display. There are dozens of applications, all of which I could go into in detail if you'd give me the time."

"No," he said. "I know the most important aspects of it and would like to try it on."

"The sooner you can get your body into it, the sooner the suit can preserve your failing structure."

Mr. Silver waved Dr. Reeves away. "I will contact you if I need any assistance with it."

Reeves nodded and started to walk backward toward the door. "Yes, sir. Also, in case you're interested, the suit does have a name."

Not really caring what stupid scientific name Dr. Reeves and his team had come up with for the suit, Mr. Silver said nothing.

Before leaving the room, Dr. Reeves stopped and put a finger in the air. "Her name is L after your late daughter, sir. I thought you might appreciate that." With that, he left.

Mr. Silver sat in his chair, staring at the suit in his hands. *This will change everything. I have immortality on top of all the research—both alien and human—that we've obtained over the years, all at my disposal. And now this data core, which could contain limitless amounts of knowledge from across the universe.* Anxious to put the suit on, he left the office and returned to his living quarters.

I don't know if I should kill Dr. Reeves or commend him. It was rare for Mr. Silver to feel this way about someone, but he decided not to put too much thought into it and to allow Reeves to live…for now.

Mr. Silver set the suit on the edge of his bed and undressed himself, slowly, painfully, and most of all, clumsily. His limbs weren't reacting the way he wanted them to. His skin had suddenly developed bizarre, multicolored sores, their swelling making it difficult to fit into the tight suit. Somehow he managed to get it on, and instead of zipping in the front, the suit halves simply sealed together by themselves. When they did, he was relieved to find that the suit felt like a second skin.

"Marvelous," he said. And just as Dr. Reeves had told him, a display materialized before his face. Through it, he could see the room perfectly. The display showed names and descriptions of objects for him, like the bed—what type of bed it was, the materials it was made of, where it had been manufactured. After a few minutes of analyzing everything in the room, Mr. Silver decided it was a nuisance. *I wonder how to turn it off.* It suddenly went off, as if the suit had read his mind.

It has.

Mr. Silver smiled. With the suit, he could be invincible as well as immortal. And all-knowing. Mr. Silver began to think of categories to pull from the data bank. They came up as easily as if he had just typed them into a computer system. And with that, he settled down on his bed and stared into the face panel of the suit, analyzing everything he possibly could of other planets and other species, striving to know everything there was to know about the universe.

CHAPTER 5

ricka awoke in an empty cement canal feeling nauseous, a massive headache in her temples. She spotted a highway bridge in the distance, lit by the glow of amber street lights. The rest of the terrain around her, as best as she could tell, appeared to be empty fields surrounded by darkness. Three men, all dressed in black, stood at attention around her, their rifles pointing straight at her. A bright, portable flood lamp stood in the middle of the group, casting light on their forms.

Another man stepped through the group, motioning for the others to lower their weapons. He looked down on Ericka. "I'll give you a few minutes to come to. Then we're heading out."

"Who are you?"

The man whom she assumed to be the leader of the group grinned like an idiot, holding his shoulders high. His face was clean-shaven, and he had short black hair, meticulously cut. He pointed his finger at her. "You don't ask questions. You have two minutes, and then we're taking you back to Absolute."

"Absolute? I'm not going back to him."

"On the contrary."

"What does he want with me?"

"I don't know. I don't care."

Ericka closed her eyes wishing her pain away. "Can you give me something for this headache?"

"It's a side effect. It should wear off soon."

"I can't even stand up. It hurts so bad."

"Stop talking and maybe it will go away."

Ericka took a deep breath and attempted to stand. With a bit of wobbling, she managed.

"Good," the arrogant man said. "You're ready to go."

"I said I'm not going to Absolute. He's a traitor of everything I believe in. I want nothing to do with him. And why on earth would he send you to bring me back to him? He has no use for me."

"Those are the things I don't care about."

The man on her right, a lanky fellow, approached her from behind, pulled her wrists behind her, and fastened a zip tie around them.

"That's so you don't try to escape," the arrogant one said. "It would now be to your benefit to stay close to us, what with all that's hiding out there in the dark." He reached down and turned off the floodlight, picking it up by its handle before they started to move through the canal toward the highway bridge.

Ericka's body refused to execute every command she gave it. She tripped and stumbled, doing her best to catch her balance but failing miserably, bumping into the men escorting her. "How long is this stuff supposed to last?"

The leader shrugged. "You'll find out, I guess."

Ericka finally straightened her walk and moved amid the group of men, feeling more protected than she would if she were on her own. Each man carried a large rifle and various other weapons. Each wore a flak vest, black cargo pants, and a black backpack. They appeared ready for an all-out war. Ericka thought it overkill to send such a huge squad of mercenaries to capture her. *And what does Absolute want with me?*

As they came within a hundred feet of the bridge, the head of the man to her left exploded in a burst of blood and brain matter, splashing Ericka's face and knocking her to the ground. The other four men immediately positioned themselves in a semicircle in front of her.

The leader of the group tossed a disc to the ground, and it opened up into a brilliant blue energy barrier in front of them. "What was that, Alpha 9?"

"Sniper. On top of the bridge."

A bullet hit the shield but zinged off.

The leader of the group set up and turned on the flood lamp so the light illuminated the bridge and their attacker in a wash of white. "Take them out, Alpha 16."

The man to Ericka's right took off his backpack and unloaded various pieces of a weapon, setting them on the ground in a specific order. When he finished, he began clicking and sliding the pieces together. Within seconds, a full-size sniper rifle materialized. The man took position behind the shield.

"I'll keep them distracted," the leader said. "You make sure you get them in three shots."

Alpha 16 nodded. The leader rose up from behind the shield and fired his rifle toward the assailant on the bridge, while Alpha 16 peered out and aimed steadily before firing the first shot from the sniper gun. "Missed," he mumbled to himself.

Ericka squinted through the shield but couldn't make out who was on the bridge.

A second shot from the sniper gun missed.

The leader stopped firing and crouched down behind the shield. "This time, you hit them or you're dead."

Alpha 16 didn't blink. He took a deep breath, aimed the rifle, and fired. The bullet missed its mark.

The leader pulled a combat knife from a sheath tied to his ankle and, without warning or dialogue, plunged it into the man's neck. Blood spurted across the others, some freckling Ericka's face. Alpha 16 looked straight into his leader's eyes and then fell to the ground in a puddle of his own blood.

The leader picked up the sniper rifle and aimed it over the shield. His first shot looked like it hit the bridge assailant in the arm, the second in the leg. The assailant disappeared from sight behind the small bridge wall.

"Takes care of that," the leader said. "Alpha 20, Alpha 13, finish the job."

The men to Ericka's right and left rushed out from behind the shield and headed toward the bridge, each heading up a different side of the canal to flank their attacker. This left Ericka with one other man and the leader.

The leader pushed a button on the disc, and the energy shield collapsed into the mechanism. He picked up the disc and stuffed it into his backpack. "SilverTech's stuff is simply the best," he muttered. Turning to Ericka, he smiled. "Once they come back and confirm that our way is clear, we'll keep moving. We have a few miles to traverse tonight, and I'm in no mood to be late. So you'll need to pick up the pace once this is finished."

Ericka said nothing, simply lay on the ground, hands tied behind her back, perpetually wondering what Absolute wanted with her.

The leader put his finger to his ear. "Is that so?" he said. "Bring her down here. I would love to show her what we do to those who mess with Alpha Team."

Alpha 20 and 13 both returned to the canal, one carrying a sniper rifle, the other carrying a female over his shoulder. The men set both the weapon and the woman down on the ground in front of the leader and Ericka.

Marigold!

The woman with blue hair had been the one firing from the bridge. Her arm was bleeding out profusely across her white trench coat, but she didn't appear to have any wounds in either leg. She ground her teeth, refusing to scream or cry, but Ericka could tell the woman was in pain.

The leader of the Alpha Team moved the floodlight to the middle of the group and then grabbed Marigold's wound and squeezed. She couldn't stifle her scream. "Who sent you?"

"Fuck you, dick face!"

The leader chuckled. "You have spirit. I like that. All women should have spirit like you do." He squeezed her arm harder, and blood bubbled out of her sleeve. "Tell me who sent you and how many others there are, and I'll make this quick. If you don't, I'm going to screw you every way I can and then leave you for dead."

Marigold's skin paled. She began breathing loudly, almost wheezing. "You'll g-get nothing out of me."

"Oh, I doubt that." The leader picked her up off the ground and carried her toward another spot in the canal, away from the group.

"Wait!" Ericka shouted.

He stopped and turned. "Yes?"

"Don't do anything to her. I'll...I'll give you what you want."

He laughed, shaking Marigold around as blood splattered across the concrete. "You think I'm going to rape her because I have a sexual need that has to be fulfilled?"

Ericka stared at him.

"You're mistaken. I'm going to teach her what happens when she messes with someone who is stronger and more cunning than her."

Despite her condition, Marigold managed to swing her good arm around and strike the man in the larynx. Then she slipped out of his grip—grunting as her wounded arm moved through his fingers—and lunged to the ground. She rolled, got up behind one of the other men, and put him in a headlock with her good arm. She slid the hand of her wounded arm down and pulled the pistol from the holster at his side. Shoving the barrel into his neck, she fired a bullet that exited the other side of his neck in a spray of blood.

The leader pulled his pistol out, but Marigold shot his hand, forcing him to drop the gun. She sent another bullet into the head of the man who had brought back her sniper rifle. Then she pointed her gun straight at the leader of the group. He wore a smug look on his face, but he raised his hands just the same. "Very nice."

"Shut up," Marigold snapped.

"I'm not sure why you're interfering with our capture of the reporter."

"I didn't ask about your sureties. Get on your knees."

He shook his head. "I see a killer in your eyes, but you won't kill me because you want to know if there will be more of us. And if there are, you're going to be in trouble if you kill me. I ask again: Why are you interfering with the job I was paid to carry out?"

Marigold fired a shot into the man's shoulder, the same side as his wounded hand. He took the bullet, hardly flinching. She shot another one lower in the same arm. Blood poured out his entire limb.

"Why don't you just kill me?"

Marigold smirked. "This is more fun."

Another bullet to his leg dropped him to his knees. Ericka wanted to stop Marigold's rampage, but she feared the woman would turn the gun on her and finish her off as well.

"I think I'll leave you out here to die with your little douche-bag friends," she growled as she came up behind Ericka and, using a combat knife from one of the corpses, cut the zip ties off. Ericka stretched her arms, happy to be free again. Marigold clutched her bleeding arm. "Let me see your wrists."

Ericka held them out in front of her.

Marigold smiled when she spotted the four-leaf clover bracelet on Ericka's arm. "You do have it."

Ericka pulled her wrist back, feeling suddenly protective of her father's gift. "Of course I do."

Marigold pointed toward the bridge. "We need to go. You and me. Now."

The leader of the mercenary group lay on the ground, groaning. He pulled his flak vest off and ripped cloth from his T-shirt to create tourniquets.

"Where?"

Marigold didn't answer. Instead, she looted the dead bodies, taking two rifles, a handgun, knives, and even stripping two of the men of their flak jackets. She gave a rifle, gun, knife, and jacket to Ericka.

Trying to find somewhere to store the weapons Marigold had given her, Ericka didn't see Marigold collapse to the ground, clutching her wound.

"We have to get you medical attention," Ericka said, ripping one of the corpse's shirts to create a tourniquet.

Marigold shook her head. Ericka wrapped the cloth around the top of her arm, just above the bullet wound, and tightened it as much as she humanely could. Marigold squirmed in pain. "We don't have time."

"Time? What do you mean? We're out in the middle of nowhere. I'm in no hurry to get anywhere but to safety."

Marigold examined the tourniquet, apparently satisfied, and then fired a bullet with her good arm at the portable flood lamp, shrouding the area in darkness. "Let's go." She stood to her feet.

Ericka gave her eyes a moment to adjust to the lack of light. "My plan was to head back and see if I could catch up with Nathan."

Marigold shook her head, sliding the combat knife into her shoe, the pistol into her back pants pocket, and the rifle strap over her shoulder. Ericka mimicked Marigold's actions, not wanting to carry all the weight but realizing the foolishness in leaving the weapons behind.

"Nathan…Don't worry about him. We need to get to this…" Marigold pulled a cell phone from her pocket, showing the screen to Ericka. It displayed a GPS map of their current location. A red dot blinked up near the top left corner of the screen, miles from where they stood.

"How is your phone on GPS? The last I heard, most of the satellites orbiting Earth were destroyed during Legion's invasion."

"Absolute…it's his satellite."

"He really does have his own satellite?"

"Look!" Marigold shouted. "Just listen to me. The map will tell you where we need to go. It's our only chance to stop everything. Legion…the demons…please…hel…" Marigold leaned to the left, then to the right, and then regained her balance. "Help me get there. And your bracelet…" She took hold of Ericka's wrist. "Guard this with your life. It's our last hope."

"I don't understand. What does my bracelet—"

Marigold put her hand up. "No more talk. Let's go before more of the Alpha Team—or worse—shows up."

She started in the direction of the bridge, swaying left and right, gripping her arm.

*****

As much as it pained him to let the women go, this wasn't the first time Alpha 1 had tasted defeat. He slowly lifted his finger to his ear. "Alpha Team Core?"

Seconds passed. Then he heard static, then a female's voice. "Alpha 1? Core copies."

"I need extraction."

"Copy that, Alpha 1. Passage to Anaisha is secured. We will have a transport pick you up. Do you require medical attention?"

He almost laughed. "Affirmative."

"Copy that. ETA one hour."

Alpha 1 glanced up at the dark sky, imagining what this area might have looked like when the stars still shone. A warm breeze crossed the back of his neck. *This place is already long gone*, he thought. *Even Mr. Silver and all of his technology is no match for what I've seen.*

Alpha 1 wanted badly to close his eyes, but he knew if he did, it would be the end of him. He had lost a lot of blood, and he wasn't certain he would be able to last an hour for his transport to arrive. He wasn't one to have regrets or to worry about the past, but sitting under the starless sky, bleeding out, alone and uncomfortably warm, he wondered what Shaonna was doing these days.

CHAPTER 6

r. Silver opened his eyes, realizing he had fallen asleep examining the tomes of information his suit had given him. His body felt refreshed from the power nap.

He pulled off the hood and mask of his suit, taking a breath of fresh air. When he tried to think about any one thing, millions of things came to mind. The names of planets—Rhodenine, Earth, Anaisha, Absooo, Crena, Semar; the names of species—Wedges, humans, Croillians, the Rosh. Mr. Silver's brain flashed images of secret weaponry from every planet in the data core's banks.

"Stop!" he screamed, sitting up on the bed. Panting, he glanced around the room, pushing all thoughts out of his mind as best he could. He realized there was one thing that could always take his mind off matters at hand: women. But one specific woman came to mind: Mira. The woman previously known as Shaonna Ryshay.

Mr. Silver got up and opened the top drawer of his nightstand, pulling out a small remote. With the press of a button, a large rectangular panel on his bedroom wall slid down, revealing a plate of lit glass. Behind it stood Mira, in a small chamber made to preserve her memory wipe and monitor her vitals in the wake of the immortality serum that had been placed inside her earlier. The longer she stayed within the memory wipe state, the more of her deep memories faded completely—eventually remaking her into whatever Mr. Silver wanted, which was an assistant. A slave.

He sat on the edge of his bed, staring at her behind the glass.

Her eyes were closed, her arms at her sides, and she wore a black blouse, black skirt, and black business jacket with matching heels. Chills ran across Mr. Silver's skin when he thought of everything he'd be able to do to her. She wasn't like the robotic assistants he had created in the early stages of his work. This was a true human, her brain wiped and reprogrammed to do all of Mr. Silver's bidding without resistance.

Another button on the remote slid the glass panel down. Mira's eyes fluttered open. "Mr. Silver?"

"Yes," he said, standing. "Come out of there."

She stepped out of the chamber and into his room, a bewildered look on her face. "Where am I?"

He walked back to his nightstand, sticking the remote in the top drawer. Then he slowly circled her, examining the curves her skirt and blouse enhanced. Her long black hair—which had been multicolored before he dyed it the shade of a raven—splashed across her shoulders. He was eager to run his hands through that hair, but first he wanted to check on his experiment.

"What is your name?" he asked.

He watched her face scrunch a little as she processed the question. "My name? My name is Mira Tracer. Why are you asking me that?"

"Why are you here?"

"I am your assistant."

"What does that entail?"

She grinned. "Attending to your every need. Professional, intellectual, spiritual."

"Spiritual?"

She nodded. "Yes, spiritual."

"I have no spiritual needs."

"Have we had this conversation before?"

"Never mind that." He had had this same conversation with her yesterday, hours after she had first been put in the chamber. "What other needs of mine can you attend to, besides the three you listed?"

"Other needs? There are no other needs I can assist you with."

"What about my physical needs?" he asked calmly.

"Mr. Silver, are you referring to your sexual needs?"

His eyes lit up. "Yes! Yes, sexual."

She grinned slyly. "I am your assistant, Mr. Silver. I am here to give you whatever you require, in whatever capacity you require it."

Mr. Silver paused for a moment, staring at her. Mira had tricked him on a number of occasions. First, pretending to be his assistant, using the position to get close to him so she could assassinate him. The second time, pretending to be affected by volatile poison he had introduced into her system. And now she stood before him again, ready to attend to his most basic, primal need. *Is she tricking me again?* he wondered.

His team of scientists had assured him the memory wipe was successful, that the immortality serum was no longer healing the memories he had attempted to wipe. In essence, she was completely dead inside, a blank slate for Mr. Silver to write a new future on. A future all about him.

He took hold of her suit jacket, sliding it off her shoulders. She let it drop to the floor without protest.

"What would you like me to do, Mr. Silver?"

He began unbuttoning the top of her blouse, a feat he found more frustrating than pleasing using the clumsy gloves of the powerful suit he wore. He stopped halfway down and took a seat on the edge of the bed, motioning for her to finish the job.

He watched her unbutton the blouse and found himself salivating when he saw the delicate curves of her breasts in her plain-colored bra. He admired the scar running across her abdomen, something he kept meaning to ask her about.

He remembered a time when Hush—Sasha—was the only female he wanted to commit himself to. She was the pinnacle of human evolution and was to eventually become his bride, before she had been abducted and lost somewhere in the world.

Now that he had Mira, this mindless zombie of a woman who would do any and all of his bidding, he found it a little easier to move on from Sasha. Besides, he had Anaisha to look forward to. Anaisha to build and sculpt into the world he wanted. Forget Sasha. Forget those who had tried to betray him. He had the upper hand in everything, was always two steps ahead, and now would be his moment.

Especially with Mira.

"Attend to my sexual needs," he said.

She removed her blouse, started to unzip her skirt, and his heart somersaulted.

***

Mira slid the zipper of her skirt down and let the clothing drop to her feet. Standing in her underwear before Mr. Silver, she felt disgusting, degraded. Satisfied. The way he stared at her hips, the way he drooled over her breasts, she had him right where she wanted him. And this time, she wouldn't fail.

64

She slipped her heels off and walked slowly toward him. The man's eyes were scouring every inch of her flesh. She had tried to entice him in this manner at an earlier time, in the locker room when she returned from watching Sasha fall through a portal to wherever. But Mr. Silver had been so obsessed over Sasha that he would have nothing to do with Mira, then Shaonna.

Now Mira had him right where she wanted him, thinking she was dead in the head. Little did he know she had new friends on the inside. Friends who wouldn't let her mind go to vapor. Friends who wouldn't allow Mr. Silver to live another day.

Giving Mr. Silver the illusion of control had been the key to his end.

Mira pushed the old man back on the bed. He offered a little resistance, probably unsure of her intentions. She had to make this convincing, so she straddled him. As much as she wanted to gain pleasure from the act, she had to stop herself from gagging.

When he closed his eyes to take in the emotions of pleasure, she slid a blade out from the back of her panties and hovered over his face for a moment, dotting his cheeks and forehead with soft kisses. When he moaned, she felt bile rise up her throat. He would get no final act from her, or from any other female ever again.

"End of the road," she whispered, nibbling on his ear.

She buried the knife deep in the side of his throat, letting his warm blood spray her face. She had waited so long for this moment, for this fresh taste of vengeance, and she savored it like she would a last meal. Pulling the blade out of his neck, she shoved it into a new spot, below his neck, near his collarbone. He struggled weakly, but she slapped his fumbling hands away and pulled the knife out again, driving it into his manhood, just for kicks. The exasperated and pained look on his face gave her a new sense of pleasure. She relished it for a moment, watching his blood-spotted face contort into shifting masks of agony. Then she made one final puncture, into the side of his head, twisting the dagger as it went in, scraping metal against bone.

As she pulled the knife out, she watched his body twitch and spasm, the last remnants of his sordid life floating away into the atmosphere of the hell he had created.

Using the blade, she tried to cut Mr. Silver's suit off, but a powerful electric shock deterred her from putting any more effort into it. She could handle electric shock, but she knew the intensity that came at her from the suit would be enough to kill her if she attempted it again. As much as she wanted to destroy all of his technology, she would have to settle for his death and move on. Move out.

She scooted off the bed and stood, pressing her finger to a small, nearly invisible piece in her ear. "It's done."

"We're on the move," she heard in her earpiece.

"I'm going for the safe. I'll meet you in ten."

"Got it."

Mira went to the wall behind Mr. Silver's bed and pounded on its surface three times. A large, square panel sunk into the wall and slid to the side, revealing a touch-screen computer display. Mira input the password she had been given, and the safe beeped and unlocked, swinging open like a safe-deposit box.

Rifling through the safe, she found a number of *Playboy* magazines, all stacked in order of publication month, newest to oldest. She pulled them out and tossed them into the room. She pulled out a 9mm pistol and two boxes of ammo, glad her assumption that he kept a weapon in the safe had been proven correct. She set the items on the nightstand to her left, away from Mr. Silver's bleeding corpse to her right, and then grabbed small stacks of American hundred-dollar bills, putting them with the gun. *I don't know if this currency is worth anything anymore, but it doesn't hurt to have the money just in case*, she reasoned.

"The suit triggered some kind of alarm," her earpiece squawked. *"Security is on its way there."*

"Got it," she said, checking the 9mm to make sure it was loaded. "I wasn't able to destroy it."

"Just get out of there."

She placed the gun on the nightstand, reached back into the safe, and pulled out a small black box. Opening it revealed a black, brittle-looking blade half the length of her arm that appeared to be made of copper. Intricate symbols—she had no idea what they meant—had been etched in the metal. She shut the box and put it with the ammo and money.

The door to the room opened, and within a couple seconds, Mira lifted the gun from the nightstand, turned around, and fired twice, hitting two security guards in their helmets, which caught the bullets but knocked the men back out the door.

Mira leaped off the bed and fired shots into their legs, crippling them. She raced to the door, shut it, and destroyed the room's locking control panel by smashing it with the butt of her gun, sealing herself in the room. She returned to the safe and pulled out small black satchels, which she assumed contained gems and Mr. Silver's horde of drugs.

Mira reached under Mr. Silver's bed and pulled out a black knapsack that had been hidden there for her, filling it with her treasures. She slid her skirt and blouse back on, opting to leave the heels behind to make her escape easier.

A grinding sound vibrated through the door, and she realized Mr. Silver's security team were trying to cut their way into the room. She glanced up at the vent cover in the top corner of the wall, estimating whether or not she could fit through it. She would have to.

The door burst open, and shots were fired. A bullet punctured her left arm, but she managed to drop and slide under Mr. Silver's bed. She aimed her gun down toward her legs and struck the feet of the guards in the doorway. She slid out the side of the bed and leaped to her feet, firing more shots into the guards' arms, crippling them. She shoved her way through the guards and exited into the hallway with her bag of goodies and every intention of getting out of SilverTech Industries alive.

CHAPTER 7

The sun had completely set, and darkness engulfed the small town of Sterling by the time Nathan and Ginger reached the parking lot a safe distance from the house in which Nathan had confronted Legion. With flashlights drawn, they confirmed the parking lot—which looked to belong to a grocery store—void of any trouble.

Nathan sat on one of the concrete parking blocks, set his backpack on the ground in front of him, and buried his head in his arms. Tired as he was, he told himself he couldn't afford to fall asleep. Not here. Not now. He still wasn't sure what had happened back at the house. Legion—a rogue sect of Legion—had told him how to win one battle of this war, how to kill Chaos and Evanescence. *But will that be enough to give us the edge we need to take back our planet?* Nathan wasn't sure. But he was willing to die trying.

"I've heard the stories of Legion," Ginger whispered. "But what just happened back there…I haven't heard anything remotely close to that. It looked like they executed one of their own."

Nathan lifted his head. "They did." He took a deep breath, catching warm, thick air in his lungs. He found it strange that the air was no longer cold.

"Our team is gone. It's just you and me now."

He nodded.

"I don't know of another faction of Daisy's Defiance between here and Providence. That means it may just be me and you the rest of the way."

"That's fine," Nathan replied. And he meant it. *The more people we travel with, the more attention we draw to ourselves,* he thought. *I don't mind it just being me and Ginger until we reach our destination, but I long for Pearl and Heather to be with us as well.*

Nathan glanced up at the grocery store in front of them. The building was intact but looked to be in sad shape. The outside had been bombed, the walls were chipped, the windows shattered. A sign hung, tilted, from the front of the building: "The Grocery Basket."

"That's weird," Nathan mumbled. "I've never heard of that store before."

"Me neither," Ginger agreed. "Maybe it's new to California."

"We might be able to find shelter in there for the night," Nathan suggested as he picked up his bag and stood to his feet. He feared if he sat any longer, he would fall asleep. And to do so here in the open, in the darkness, would be suicide.

Ginger followed him to the entrance of the store. The double sliding doors opened with some effort from Ginger and Nathan. Once the two crossed the threshold, Nathan pulled the doors shut, wishing he had the key to lock them.

Ginger shined her flashlight into the store. Registers with their LCD screens sat dormant, lifeless, soon-to-be relics of a time forgotten or forever remembered, depending on how many survived Earth's greatest catastrophe. Aisles stretched into the distance, their shelves mostly bare.

Nathan found the silence in the store unnerving. As much as he wanted to scour the entire store for enemies, he felt his body and mind shutting down from pure exhaustion, and all he wanted to do was sleep. He and Ginger moved carefully, slowly, through the building. They found a small hallway and bathrooms in the back of the store. They also found a small office and decided to take refuge in it for the rest of the night. Nathan locked the door behind them, fearful that something—or someone—might try to make its way into the store while they slumbered…if someone or something wasn't already hiding somewhere in the building.

"Should we take turns sleeping?" Ginger asked as she stretched out on the couch like a cat.

"No," Nathan answered, setting his flashlight upright, pointed toward the ceiling to illuminate the room. The room felt cool, a significant contrast to the uncomfortable weather outside. "We have the lock on the door, and I'm sure either one of us will wake at the slightest sound. We just need to make sure we get some shut-eye before moving out again. Our next stop will be Providence."

"That's still a ways from here, but I agree with you. We should try to get there as soon as we possibly can."

Nathan settled into a large chair, finding it quite comfy. It almost felt as if the chair was trying to swallow him whole.

"You can have the couch if you'd like."

"I'm fine."

"You sure?"

"I'm okay," Nathan reiterated. "You can have the couch. I'll be fine here."

Ginger gave up and unbuttoned and took off her long-sleeve shirt, revealing a black T-shirt underneath. She placed the shirt, her backpack, and her flashlight on the floor near the couch. Sweat coated her T-shirt and made the room rank. Nathan refused to allow himself to succumb to disgust because of it. They hadn't had time to stop and pick out new wardrobes since leaving Echo, and Nathan knew he didn't smell like a prize himself.

Turning her back to him, Ginger fell asleep. Nathan struggled out of the chair, shut the flashlight off, and then sunk back into the chair and fell asleep almost immediately.

He dreamed.

No longer plagued by images of his sister's head rolling off into the darkness, he instead envisioned Pearl being sucked into a twisting vortex in the sky, her angelic form gobbled up by blood-stained teeth. Macayle entered his dreams at some point, filling the portrait of his hyperactive mind with cigarette smoke. Toward the end of Nathan's dream sequence, Ginger arrived with her bouncing pigtails and gun holster drooping low at her waist. Her long legs stretched out in his mind, and he suddenly found her in his arms, her flesh warm against his. He felt her fingers scour his body for something, anything—he didn't care. Her caress felt good.

He awoke to Ginger shifting on the couch. He wished he had a blanket to give her. The room had grown cooler than it had been when they first settled in. He felt a sudden compulsion to examine the peculiar machine he had taken from the house. Nathan turned on his flashlight, dumped the contents of his backpack on the nearby desk, and took a seat in the high-back office chair, using his flashlight to illuminate his collected treasures.

After staring intently at the machine—Legion's Machine, he decided to call it, assuming Legion had crafted the contraption—he realized he had no clear way of understanding its technology. From what he could tell, the machine was powered by something internally, but he had no way of opening the machine with what was readily available in the small, dark office.

He stuck Legion's Machine—still glowing with blue neon light illuminating its outer shell—in his backpack, relieved that the backpack's material was thick enough to smother the light within.

The mask he had picked up from an eaten prisoner of Legion right after Pearl disappeared sat on the desk, staring at him with hollow eyes. The sapphires in the cheek absorbed the light of the flashlight and returned it in a soft blue hue. The pink feathers pointing up near the side of one of the eyes seemed to glow. Curious, Nathan turned the mask over so he was looking into the back side of it. *Is there really a soul within?* he wondered. His head drew closer, until the mask leaped to his face and filled his vision in flashes of bright light...

Nathan opened his eyes and found himself at a kitchen table. Surrounded only by white expanse, he wondered if he had fallen asleep and was dreaming again. Within seconds, a home built itself around him, and other people fell from thin air into the kitchen. Kids. A man. Even a dog. None of them seemed to notice him...except the woman sitting directly across the table. She wore a white T-shirt, her frizzy black hair up in a ponytail.

Her eyes filled with surprise. "What are you doing in here?"

"Where am I?" Nathan asked, taken aback at the scene before him.

"Are you...are you with them? With the Tormentors?"

"Tormentors?"

She glanced toward the people mingling with one another near the stove. They seemed not to notice either Nathan or the woman at the table. "Tormentors."

"I found a mask. I guess I put it on and came here."

"You found...you found the container of my soul? Where

did you find it?"

"A portal opened. The body your mask was on was...eaten."

"A Soul Eater?"

He nodded.

Her gaze wandered to the surface of the table. "I...I was taken from my prison cell. My body...it was mutilated by some kind of machine. Before that, someone or something pulled me...oh, this sounds so ridiculous...pulled me out of my body and trapped me within this hideous mask."

"I'm inside the mask?"

She nodded. "Yes. But I don't think you're trapped here like me. I was told by others who were imprisoned with me that the masks only have enough room for one live soul. The rest..." She motioned to the people near the stove. "The rest are known as Tormentors. They are...well, I guess I don't know what they are. They are put in the mask by Legion."

Tears ran down her face. "The Tormentors replicate...I don't know how...but they replicate those we love and then are put here to torture us. The teenage girl? My daughter, Elise. The young boy, he was my son, Ren. And that handsome man there was my husband. I...I can't seem to remember his name, though."

"I'm sorry."

She shrugged. "It's all over and done. They're dead. I'm not. Although I wish I was."

"If there's only room in here for one live soul, how is it we're both sitting here?"

"You'll disappear soon. Right out of the mask. I've seen it happen before. Others have worn my mask and have come here like you. They don't stay long."

"Is there any way I can free you from here?"

More tears fell from her eyes. Her body trembled.

"I'm sorry. I just want to help."

She sniffled. "I, uh, I heard you can destroy the mask—well, if you can find a way to destroy it. Then it will destroy me, and I'll be able to rest."

"With God?"

She scoffed through the tears. "God? Really, kid? After everything going on out there, you think I believe in God? Jeez, give me a break. No, once the mask is destroyed, I'll be able to rest. I'm sure everything will go dark, and I can be freed from this horrible nightmare."

Nathan realized he had so many questions to ask. But only one rose to the surface of his mind and raced through his lips: "Where is Legion keeping its prisoners? I heard of a place called the Hopeless Bastille."

She nodded, her cheeks covered in tears. "Where I was taken from. There is…I remember seeing a factory of…oh, it was so awful. I saw a factory of people or puppets. I don't know which. Legion put the masks on those puppets. Use them as soldiers. Whatever happens to the puppets—the pain, the experience—is transferred into the mask. When the Soul Eater consumed my puppet—my host—I fell apart in here. It felt as if someone was stabbing me with a hundred knives. My 'family' did nothing to help me. Half the time they ignore me. When they do interact with me, it's to ask me questions, to conjure painful memories of my life before."

"What happened? How did Legion capture you?"

It only took seconds for Nathan to return to the desk, the

mask sitting in front of him, its inside facing him, a world within its structure. He had returned to his own reality without even getting the name of the woman trapped within the supernatural prison.

A quick scan with his flashlight revealed Ginger still sleeping, the office door still closed and locked. Nathan wanted to enter the mask again, but when he drew his face close to it, nothing happened. *Does a certain amount of time have to pass before I can return to the soul space?*

As exhausted as he felt the last few days, he found he wasn't that tired now. In fact, since he had time, he wanted to resume recording his experiences during these last days of Earth. But he had used the last of his paper to craft his sister's note, and left his recorder back at the Westgate Plaza Mall. *Surely the recorder is destroyed or lost by now. Maybe*, he hoped, *someone found it and is spreading the word about the things I described—the lighthouses that emit dark light, the president's alliance with Legion, even my sister's execution order.*

Nathan turned his flashlight toward the desk drawers and quietly opened each one, looking for paper and something to write with. He found a stack of old *Time* magazines, file folders, some empty cash register drawers—and a notebook and pen.

He set the notebook on the desk, propped the flashlight up on a cube of Post-it Notes, and flipped to the first page. Someone had jotted down a slew of numbers and simple mathematical equations. *Probably to figure out their next paycheck or the price of items in the store*, Nathan decided. The initials JG and DC had been scribbled in blue ink in the margin, with a crude heart drawn between them.

Nathan turned the notebook to the next page, which was

blank, and began writing about his experiences so far. He started his chronicle at the beginning, with his collapse on the stage of his high school graduation. He recounted Hwami and her gift of a star in his name, his quarrel with Shannon, his text messages to Heather. He tried to include every detail, every fine point, so that whoever found this account of Earth's last days through Nathan's eyes wouldn't miss anything. *Besides*, he told himself, *it feels good to get this down on paper*. The simple act of writing out his life over the last month brought healing to his broken spirit.

CHAPTER 8

As Olivia escorted Scarlet to her sleeping quarters, Scarlet did her best to converse with the girl, but she wasn't all that talkative. She seemed to have something wrong with her motor skills because her right hand continuously twitched whenever Scarlet used Olivia's name. It was as if the girl's identity had become a trigger of some sort. *Maybe something's not connecting right in her mind*, Scarlet thought. To her surprise, Scarlet realized the young girl was still dressed in blood-soaked capris and a blue T-shirt—the same outfit the girl had been wearing when Scarlet was last with her and Nathan.

The two reached the door to Scarlet's sleeping quarters. Olivia motioned toward the room and then started to walk down the hallway the way they came.

"Wait."

The girl turned toward Scarlet. "Yes?"

"Olivia, do you remember me?"

Olivia stared for a moment and then shook her head. "No. Should I?"

"From Earth."

"Where?"

Scarlet sighed, convinced of the possibility the girl could be an Olivia lookalike. "Never mind."

Once Olivia disappeared around a corner, Scarlet stepped into her room and shut the door behind her. Everything in her room—her four-poster bed with violet mesh draped over it, the dresser, the nightstand with the book on top—was exactly as she had left it when she went to take her daily seat on her throne earlier. She felt a presence in the room with her. She didn't sense that it was necessarily malevolent—just that it was a presence unseen. *Could it be the room itself, the very walls of the Black Cathedral?*

She suspected that the Cathedral was a live entity. Certain details about the place could not be ignored or pushed aside as anything other than proof to back up her suspicion: the vague outlines of faces in the walls of certain hallways, the groans she swore she heard when walking alone through certain rooms, and the gentle caress she felt at night, sweeping across her cheek like a feather. *It's just my imagination*, she kept telling herself.

Her skin shuddered and bumps rose from its surface. *Don't be ridiculous*, she scolded herself. *The building is not alive. It's a building. Nothing more. A beautiful but dark building.*

Scarlet shook her head and decided to get some rest. She double-checked the lock on her door, then approached the dresser mirror and stopped to stare at herself. The color, she noticed, was slowly leaving her eyes. Her irises, which had once been a beautiful brown color, were fading to gray. *Fading like my soul in this place.* She remembered her mother reading stories of princesses to her when she was younger. Knowing even then that happy endings were meant only for fairytales, Scarlet despised every female in any story that portrayed women needing to be rescued by men. She didn't like women being depicted as helpless and in distress.

But you are in distress.

She silenced her reflection. *I'm not in distress. I chose to come here, chose to take the title of royalty…But nothing feels royal about it. It all feels empty and dark.*

Scarlet turned and glanced at the luxurious bed. She couldn't wait to crawl under those covers and slumber for hours, but she felt eyes peering at her. She wanted to get out of her clothes. Her corset was getting incredibly uncomfortable—it was clearly a size too small for her—and the boots were chafing her poor feet. She turned back to her reflection and saw bags under her eyes.

She sighed, resolving to undress under the covers. Scarlet unfastened her boots and slid them off her aching feet. Then she turned the light off and made her way to the bed, crawling in between the sheets and thick comforter. The Black Cathedral grew extremely cold at night. She cursed for forgetting to ask Ryn for another comforter to keep extra warm.

Although she wanted to read more of the book on her nightstand, she decided she was too tired. The book chronicled her sordid life—a book she thought would have stayed in the other realm but had somehow traveled with her and appeared in the top drawer of the nightstand when she was first brought to this room.

Scarlet drew the covers over every inch of her body, both to keep warm during her sleep cycle and to keep eyes from looking at her, eyes she was sure were in the walls somewhere. *Or maybe in the mirror.* The mere possibility frightened her. And since she had died and transferred over to another realm, she believed anything was possible. Anything.

Slowly and methodically, Scarlet undressed under the covers, pushing her shed clothing to the floor. When she was stripped, she felt confident she could finally sleep.

She woke in a panic upon feeling the trails of fingertips caressing her cheek. She scrambled up against the headboard, pulling the covers tight against her. Through the purple mesh surrounding her bed, she saw nobody else in the room with her. *But what I felt was real. Almost like a father's touch caressing my cheek while I slept.* She remembered her father doing that to her when she was much younger.

She breathed deeply, loudly, panting with fright. She wanted to burst out in a cacophony of shouts and screams, but she kept silent for fear of angering whatever might be in the room with her. She drew back the violet mesh and looked at the dresser, noticing the candle's dying flame. Glowing in white light were the words *I long for you* written on the mirror. Releasing the mesh, she pulled the covers back over her head and shivered for what seemed like an hour before finally drifting off to sleep again.

When she woke, it was morning, although the sun never shone where the Black Cathedral existed, so she had no clear indication it was morning aside from the loud bells that rang out across the premises.

I have to leave this place, she told herself, convinced she could no longer live in ignorance about the touch she felt in the middle of the night.

A knock on the door startled Scarlet from her thoughts. She watched as the lock turned and the door swung open. Olivia entered the room carrying a tray of food. The girl shut the door behind her, engaged the lock, and set the tray on the dresser. She read the words scrawled across the mirror. "Interesting," she whispered. "So his reach does extend to this realm." She turned to Scarlet, recognition in her gray eyes. "What are you doing here?"

"What do you mean?"

"How did you get into this realm? You had the chance to escape, back in Los Angeles."

"So it is you?"

"Of course it's me," Olivia snapped.

"Well, how am I supposed to know? You looked like a brain-dead retard when you brought me here yesterday."

"I'm not. Ryn teleported me here for his own selfish means."

"What could you possibly have that he wants? Unless…" She flashed the girl an embarrassed look.

Olivia shook her head. "No, he doesn't act in a sexual nature that I know of. But he does have a strange fascination with anatomy."

"So I've noticed."

"How did you get here?"

Scarlet recounted her death in the other realm, how she had tried to steal from a harmless woman who had just lost her husband. Telling the tale made Scarlet feel low and filthy. When she finished, she pulled her covers up closer to her flesh, feeling vulnerable and disgusted with herself.

"Interesting," Olivia said. "So you chose to come here?"

Scarlet nodded. "Why did Ryn want you here?"

"My powers. To see the future. But I don't intend on giving them to him. He thinks I'm disabled, mentally incapable of helping him. He believes it's due to his violent attempts to bring me here."

"Is there a way out, back to our world?" Asking the question, Scarlet felt like she was betraying Ryn.

"Your world is not *our* world. I don't come from *your* world. And I've been looking for a way out of here for some time now. I can't find one."

Scarlet frowned. *So I'll be stuck here for all eternity, to carry out the royal tasks of an androgynous madman?* Asking to go on from this realm was out of the question—Cynthia wasn't certain what was beyond this realm, so she would be forced to stick with what she did know.

"He is not a madman," Olivia said in response to Scarlet's thoughts. "He is a powerful entity bent on destroying your world, my world, and all worlds in between."

"You can read my mind?"

"Sometimes."

"I want out of this nightmare."

Olivia shrugged. "I didn't bring you here. You allowed yourself to be pulled into this realm."

"Maybe we can find a way out together?"

Olivia shook her head. "You will succumb to Ryn's traps. You'll allow your nature to take control, and you will become chained and bound by your own filth. The Cathedral has picked up on your nature and has been playing it back to you."

Scarlet grew angry. "What the hell do you know? I'm not going to fall for Ryn's tricks. I *know* he's trying to trick me. That alone prevents me from falling for his deception. I may not know what he's up to exactly, but I do know not to trust him."

"I've seen many things, but never have I seen such an ignorant human being. You think you have power over your nature? That you alone can conquer your sexual vices, by your own powers? You're wrong. And you'll soon see that you're wrong." Olivia turned toward the door.

"Where are you going?"

"I have to leave now. He's expecting me to serve others within the Cathedral. And I have other tasks to attend to—mostly my own. I will find a way out of here—after I find a way to stop the evil that sits on that throne."

Scarlet sat up. "You're going to kill Ryn?"

"I don't know what my purpose is here yet."

With that, Olivia left.

Scarlet lay in her bed, confused. *If that's really Olivia, surely she would want to pair up with me to escape this foul place. I can't believe she thinks that I'll fall for Ryn's tricks.*

Scarlet turned out of the bed and decided to get dressed. *It's time to show Ryn just how in control I truly am.*

CHAPTER 9

inger shook Nathan gently, whispering in his ear for him to wake up. Her warm breath smelled of eggs. He had been in such a deep sleep that it took him a moment to remember where he was—The Grocery Basket. He pulled his cheek up off the notebook he had been filling with his tales before he dozed off. Nathan was happy to have been able to fill at least ten pages before his eyes closed in sleep.

He sat up, his head swimming in pain. "Ah."

"Headache?" Ginger asked, setting a plate in front of him. With the light from his flashlight, he saw scrambled eggs, toast, and sausage links.

"Real food?" He glanced up at her, able to make out the pigtails on the sides of her head. She was a welcome sight after the night he had.

"I found it throughout the grocery store. The freezers were still somewhat cold, so I took a chance on the sausage. The eggs I made sure to double-check before cooking. I made them up on a charcoal grill I found near the cutlery aisle."

Impressed, Nathan found himself smiling. *It's the little things*, he reminded himself, *that make all the difference*. In the darkness, in risk of danger and death, Ginger had taken the time to prepare him breakfast. "Thank you," he said, picking up the fork and cutting into the eggs.

"You're most welcome," she said with a chipper tone. "I've already eaten, so once you're done, we can head out."

"Sounds good to me."

He devoured the food, his stomach satisfied to have something of substance in it. When he finished, he packed up his bag, ready to leave the grocery store. Before he could get out of the office, Ginger came back with a small transistor radio she said she found in the back warehouse of the store. The thought of her journeying back there by herself in the darkness panged him with worry.

Setting the radio on the desk, Ginger scanned through the static until she reached a barely audible station broadcasting news headlines from around the country. It sounded like the same station Nathan had come across back at the Westgate Plaza Mall, when he was residing with Absolute's Rebellion—before Legion interrupted his stay.

"…earthquake brought down three of the tallest buildings in Denver, wiping out multiple square blocks. Even though the city was never deemed a sanctuary zone, and was in fact ordered to be evacuated, many people stayed within the city limits, keeping residence in the city's housing structures and apartment buildings. Legion's attacks never decimated Denver as they did other cities, such as Phoenix or Sacramento.

"The tremors also destroyed one of the city's main power generators, cutting electricity to most of the area. This will in turn lead to spoiled food and other ailments."

I wonder if the earthquake was random or if more will occur in other cities as well, Nathan thought before returning his attention to the newscast.

"Now I'll repeat the biggest news of the day, something we've been announcing every half hour today. If you haven't heard yet, President Stone is said to be alive and well."

Nathan's eyes widened. He felt his stomach churn with Ginger's breakfast.

"No way," she whispered.

"After the assassination attempt on her in Echo, and Nathan Pierce's escape from her administration, she was taken by ambulance to a hospital in Echo, where, incidentally, evidence revealed a faction of Daisy's Defiance had been staying. The group had already evacuated by the time President Stone arrived at the medical facility. Reports from there have been conflicting. One witness claimed to have seen President Stone flatline. Another reported that some of her administration demanded to be alone with her, forcing all medical personnel out of the room. It was shortly after this supposed incident that President Stone walked out of the room, unscathed.

"Related to this event is the confirmed death of Daisy Pierce. After a harrowing escape from President Stone, Nathan Pierce allegedly took Daisy to the same medical facility that treated President Stone. The president arrived there less than a half hour after Daisy was pronounced dead and was carried off the premises by her brother.

"We're going to free up the airwaves now in case those who oppose the facts are attempting to track us. The Underground News Coalition will be back in a bit."

Nathan plopped down in the comfy chair, speechless.

"What the fuck?" Ginger punched her fist through a wall. "I shot her! I saw that bullet go through her fucking skull!" She pulled her hand out, her knuckles bloody.

"I don't know. But if she is still alive, it's the work of something else."

She grimaced. "Meaning what?"

"Meaning something worse than Legion is working with her."

"Satan?"

Nathan nodded. The idea didn't sound as absurd as it would have weeks ago when Legion was just beginning its attack on Earth.

"If a potential end to this conflict is really in Providence, then we need to get there as soon as possible."

Ginger nodded, rubbing her wounded hand. "I just don't understand. It seems no matter what we do, we keep getting pushed back. We try to save your sister; she dies. We assassinate the president; she gets right back up. We try to create an alliance to fight this cause, and our entire team dies, except you and me. It's tiring."

"I know."

"But I won't give up. We've lost too much to not fight back."

They said their goodbyes to the grocery store and headed toward the main street leading out of town. After four failed attempts at finding a working vehicle, the twosome straddled a motorcycle, and Ginger drove them down the dark highway, headlamp lighting their path toward Providence.

How is all of this going to end? Nathan wondered. *The president's still alive—and probably more powerful than anyone could imagine. I have no idea if we're heading into a trap, the middle of a war, or a reunion in Providence.*

Ginger pointed at the sky ahead of them. "Do you see that? Looks like a falling star." She stopped the motorcycle momentarily, and he saw a large twinkle against a black backdrop, like a gem in black velvet. A long, bright tail strung out behind the star in marvelous shades of teal, forest green, and light blue.

"That doesn't look like one of Legion's vessels. At least not the ones that landed weeks ago."

"No, it doesn't."

CHAPTER 10

Scarlet marched to the doors leading into Ryn's throne room. The faceless guards extended glowing blue rods from the sleeves of their cloaks, weapons meant to deter her from proceeding any farther.

"I demand to speak to Ryn," she growled. If Ryn wanted to call her a princess, if he wanted to give her a title in this dark and dreary cathedral, she would live up to it.

She had managed to scrounge together a gorgeous black gown, its train trailing behind her like a stream of dark water. The dress fit perfectly, unlike the corset she wore the day before. She felt like she was in her element in the gothic dress, like the royalty Ryn was trying to pass her off as.

The guards didn't waver.

"I am the Princess of the Black Cathedral. I demand to speak to the king."

The double doors opened. The guards withdrew their weapons into their sleeves and allowed her to pass. She carried herself with strength instead of grace, stomping her heels hard against the black rug leading to Ryn's throne. She marched up the steps, refusing to allow the statues or the brilliant tree behind the throne to distract her. She was here on a mission—one she intended to fulfill.

She approached the throne and found Ryn sitting, seemingly staring at her with the same blank face and distorted air around him as the day before.

"I am appalled at your demanding disposition today," he said.

"I don't care. I want to leave this place. I'm not happy nor content here. I want to go back to my world."

Scarlet allowed the air to grow tense between them before she let out a long breath.

"You want to leave?" he asked.

"Yes. I don't care how. I just...I can't stand this place anymore. Release me."

"Release you? But you are not a captive here. You came here of your own free will."

"And it was a mistake."

"Oh? A mistake? Yes, I can see that. A mistake. So you do not wish to be my princess?"

She shook her head slowly, her instinct warning her to be cautious.

"I see." Ryn stood. "I am...sorry...you feel that way. I will send you back to your world."

Her heart leaped, but she quickly reminded it to be wary. "You will?"

He nodded. "Of course. I do not want you to be unhappy. I want to bring you comfort and solace, not loathing."

"Okay."

"Yes." Ryn raised his arm up, and the double doors opened. "I would like to show you something first, before you part from the Black Cathedral. Please, just hear what I have to say, see what I have to show you. If you do not like what I present, I will send you home to your dying planet."

Scarlet nodded.

A collection of men and women walked into the room and gathered at the bottom of the steps leading up to the throne. At first glance, Scarlet didn't recognize any of them.

But as Ryn led her down the steps, closer to the crowd, she recognized each person—male and female—as someone from her past. And she knew somewhere on their bodies, either exposed or hidden, almost every one of them wore the symbol of her iniquities—a pink rabbit.

"Do you remember?" Ryn asked. "Do you remember your trademark? Your brand? Your calling card?"

"I do," she whispered, glancing down at the tattoo on her left breast. Each person looked her straight in the eyes, no expression on any of their faces. They looked like dolls. Dolls she had at one time enjoyed collecting for her private shelf. Like trophies. Proof of her talent and skills.

"These are your achievements, Scarlet. You gave each of them your gift—your gift to the world, your gift to yourself."

"Yes...my gift."

"Yes, your gift." He passed her on his way down the steps and approached a young man who she already knew was not stamped with the pink rabbit symbol, although he probably should have been.

Christmas Eve, Scarlet remembered. *Before Legion's vessels fell. I wore one of my favorite outfits: red underwear and a bright red bow. I was going to break Freddy of his virginity. Instead, his parents came home, ruining everything.*

Ryn turned to her. "You remember, don't you?"

"Yes." She remembered the pride she felt when she strutted her body in front of that sorry sap and watched him nearly keel over from a heart attack.

Freddy stood near a woman. "Her?" Ryn asked. "Do you remember her?"

Scarlet nodded. *Brittany Hail. The first female I ever experimented with, in the restroom at school.* The act had done what Scarlet hoped it would—skyrocketed her status at the school.

Ryn went to another young man. Then a woman. Then an older gentleman, one Scarlet remembered quite well. *A businessman who worked the stock market. My experience with him netted me a thousand dollars. He's the first person I ever did things with who wasn't in my high school, and because of that, I learned something about older men—they have experience.*

Ryn went through the ranks, reminding Scarlet of the people she had impacted—sexually speaking, of course. She found herself more and more aroused as he went through the names and circumstances under which she knew each individual. She also found herself growing in pride.

"These aren't mistakes, Scarlet, as your old world would have you believe. They are your greatest achievements. What is sex, but a tool used to bring pleasure into someone's life? Correct?"

She nodded. "Yes." *They* are *achievements. My greatest.*

"Yes. A tool. Sex is a tool, a gift. And just think, this crowd here is just a fraction—a very miniscule fraction—of those you've used your wonderful gift on. You are a goddess of the night, of fantasies and forbidden things. You must understand, Scarlet, that that is why I brought you here. My sight reaches beyond this realm to yours, and I have seen so much potential in you." Ryn drew closer to Scarlet. "I want to understand your sexual nature more. I want to understand why you gravitate toward both males and females, why you indulge in such carnal acts of pleasure, why you trade everything for mere moments of ecstasy."

Shadows suddenly engulfed him, and moments later, Ryn emerged from the pillar of darkness as a female with a visible face, and clothed in black feathers. The female's stunning eyes reminded Scarlet of deep oceans of blue and green, portals of peace and comfort.

Ryn reached out to Scarlet, cupping the girl's chin in a gentle hand. "My dear servant," Ryn said in a female voice. "You have traveled so long. You have been through so much. I could not see you turn to dust like the rest of your kind. I wanted you for myself. I wanted you here, where you can dwell in safety, unaffected by the crumbling world. You are a sparkling jewel who should be put on display, not buried under rubble."

Scarlet felt her heart beat faster. She wanted to close her eyes, to put the darkness and the demons of her past away. She wanted to open her body, to give herself to this gift, this lowly spark within her that Ryn had been working to fan into a brilliant flame. Her gift was her purpose.

"Yes," Ryn hissed. "Yes, your gift is your purpose. I ask humbly that you give your body, your flesh, over to me. Say you will stay here, that you will continue to be the Princess of the Black Cathedral." Scarlet took a deep breath as Ryn removed his female hand from Scarlet's chin and turned away toward the crowd. Black hair spiraled down his back like a staircase spanning the height of his slender build. "I don't have much time left."

"For what?"

Ryn turned back around and pointed at the tree behind the throne. "A symbol of my life—rather, what is left of it. When the last leaf falls, I will perish. Part of my banishment here. I simply want to live out the rest of my days watching over my kingdom. It would give me great joy to watch you live out your destiny properly, Scarlet. And I don't believe you can do that in the old world."

Scarlet stared up at the tree, at the glowing blue leaves, and then turned back toward the crowd of people amassed at the base of the steps. Each person had the ability to scratch her where she itched, both in terms of her sexual needs and to feed her pride. "I would like to stay here," she answered truthfully.

"Make a commitment to me then. Promise me, with those exquisite lips of yours, that you will stay here and not go back to your world."

Scarlet looked into Ryn's colorful eyes and nodded. "I promise."

"A woman's word is her bond," Ryn said, clapping his hands together. "Now," he motioned to the crowd before them, "partake of the fruits of your labor. They are yours to do with as you please."

"For me?"

Ryn whispered in her ear, "You may have them. All of them. Every individual you rose above will once again be under your heels. You can do whatever you want with them. You can be the master you seek to be."

Scarlet looked out on the crowd. Her crowd. *A plate of pleasure from which I can pick whenever I want. I can devour as slowly or as quickly as I want. I will be their master. I will be in control.* Then she remembered her lack of restful sleep. "I've been meaning to ask you something. About my room. I can feel a presence there…touching me."

Ryn looked confused, then waved Scarlet's concern away, like he would shoo a bird from a windowsill. "I am sure it was your imagination. I built that room myself. For you. I knew you couldn't resist coming here to stay with me, so I crafted the room, brick by brick—every piece of furniture, every little detail—just for you. I know nothing of a phantom residing in there, but I will check it out for you and rid the room of this presence you speak of."

"I don't want that presence touching me or talking to me or writing things on my mirror. I want to move to a different room."

"No, no. I will rid your room of the presence."

"Do it soon."

Ryn reached a hand out, and Scarlet felt fingers tighten around her neck. "You once again forget whose domain you're in." He let go promptly. "Make sure not to make that mistake again. I am still—and always will be—the king."

Scarlet rubbed her neck.

"Now, pick one."

Scarlet scanned the crowd. Blank stares greeted her. But behind those blank stares, she saw memories. Memories from her adolescent life.

"Remember. This is only a fraction. If there is someone else you would like, someone you do not see in this crowd, let me know, and I will summon them as well."

Scarlet couldn't help but feel giddy. *A group of those I've mastered in the past. Here to be mastered again. And again. I can try out new tricks. I can do what I always wanted to do but was too afraid to try. This is my moment to shine.*

Soft caresses trickled across her shoulders. "This will be your grand opus, my dear servant."

Scarlet pointed to the businessman. "Him." She started down the steps, parting the crowd with her presence. She grabbed the hand of the businessman—his palm warm in hers—and led him to her sleeping quarters for *another* moment in time he would never forget.

CHAPTER 11

Mira ran through the hallways, her mind racing ahead of her, calculating the strategy she and some of Sil-verTech's staff had devised. It was mutiny, and poor old Mr. Silver had gotten stuck in the middle. A victim of his own creation.

Think you can control me? Think again, bastard.

She ran into security guards at a couple points, but easily took them down with bullets or hand-to-hand combat. Her arm had forced the bullet out of itself—a positive attribute of the immortality serum that Mr. Silver had introduced into her system—and was almost completely healed.

Mira turned down another hallway, where she knew she'd find a stairwell, and took that down to the third floor. She made her way to a small room where a trio of scientists in black SilverTech lab coats had gathered.

One of them, a dark-skinned man she knew as Des, smiled when he saw her. "You did it!" he shouted, his gaze fixed on the blood stains covering her outfit. "You really killed him?"

Mira nodded. "We need to get out of here."

"Agreed. This is Sharon," he said, motioning to the fe-male scientist next to him. Her blonde hair went straight up in a ponytail and curved down like a boomerang. "And this is Larry." He motioned to the other scientist, with thick glasses and a bald scalp.

Mira noticed dark smudges on the man's glasses. *How can he see through those things?*

"What about the suit?" Sharon asked.

"I couldn't get it off him" Mira answered. "It's protected."

"Electric shock?" Des asked.

She nodded.

"Dr. Reeves probably did that in case something like this happened."

"If we run into the good doctor, remind me to kill him," Mira growled.

"We're heading for the tenth floor," Des said. "The shuttles are down there."

"Shuttles?" Mira couldn't remember anything about shuttles.

"Things have gotten worse since yesterday. I've been listening to the radio broadcasts and rumors circulating around the country. Legion's presence is thick, and there's word of strange forces—armies—moving from city to city, destroying everything—including humans. If we want any chance of surviving, we'll have to get off Earth completely."

"My daughter..."

Des shook his head. "We don't have time for me to sugarcoat this. She's probably dead. If not, she'll be dead if she stays out there and doesn't have access to a SilverTech shuttle."

"You're probably right," Mira admitted. It pained her to think of her twelve-year-old daughter as dead. The saving grace was that her ex was probably dead too. *Justice.*

Larry cleared his throat. "We'll need to make sure we disengage the memory wipes on whatever ship we acquire."

"Memory wipes?" Mira asked.

"Yes," the man said, scrubbing the left lens of his glasses. "Mr. Silver programmed the vessels to wipe the memories of everyone traveling to Anaisha."

"What the hell?"

Des nodded. "He did that so he could easily convince everyone he was the true leader of Anaisha. Too bad for him we know otherwise. And he's dead, so it doesn't matter anyway."

"I would have killed that bastard sooner if given a proper chance. It's like trying to kill a Nazi cockroach."

"You aren't the first who's tried," Des said. "But right now we need to get out of here. Take the el—"

An alarm crowed, and the room's lighting turned red.

"We need to get to those shuttles," Des urged. He hurried to a lab counter and picked up a pistol. "We were only able to get our hands on one weapon. Otherwise, security and Mr. Silver would have gotten suspicious."

"We can protect the four of us," Mira said, motioning to Des and herself. "We just need to get to the elevator, and we'll be fine."

"Elevator is too risky now," Des said. "We need to head to the stairwell. We have security access, but I don't know how long that access will last. With Silver dead, it will only be a matter of time before security locks the building down."

"We really should have put forth more effort in obtaining Mr. Silver's suit," Larry said. "I would hate to see that data bank fall into the wrong hands—or worse, be destroyed."

"You're welcome to go back there if you want," Mira snickered, "but I have only one intention right now: to get out of this building."

"Agreed," Des said. "Let's go."

They exited the room and entered the hallway, awash in red light. Mira let Des lead the way down the corridor. Other scientists and SilverTech personnel scurried around them, making it easier to hide from the eyes of security. When the group reached the stairwell, they found it guarded by a half dozen guards. Des led his companions back down the hallway. They traveled the floor, weaving in and out of groups of scientists, passing distracted security guards.

"I really don't want to go through here, but we have no choice," Des said when they reached a set of doors painted in orange and red stripes. "There's another stairwell—an emergency stairwell—at the end of this section of the building. If we can get to it, it should take us all the way down to the shuttles." He entered a combination of letters and numbers into the code panel, and the latches on the doors slid aside with a thunk. The doors swung open, allowing the group inside. Once in the vacant corridor, they heard the doors slam shut behind them and latch back into place.

Like the doors, the hallway they entered was painted in orange and red stripes. Mira found her eyes wigging out at the striped decor combined with a checkered pattern of orange and red tiles on the floor. She felt nauseated. Part of that could have been because she hadn't eaten since the night before.

Thick steel doors with viewing ports lined one wall. Des steered the group to the other side of the hallway, an unspoken warning that they didn't want to mess with whatever was in those cells.

"Hey!"

All four stopped in their tracks at the sight of security guards ahead of them. The guards had flashlights and guns—all pointed at the escapees. Mira fired two shots, extinguishing one of the flashlights and hitting one of the guards in the leg. Des went to fire his gun, realized the safety was still on, and panicked as he took it off. A bullet in the head sent him to the floor.

Larry picked up the pistol and fired, bullets filling the hallway. He managed to hit some of the security guards before taking a dozen bullets himself, his body flailing in the gunfire.

Mira grabbed Larry's gun and handed it to Sharon, firing off four shots of her own gun—and crippling two more guards—to give Sharon time to adjust to hers.

Two remaining guards ran down the hallway toward the women, firing bullets. Sharon fired a shot. The bullet sailed over the guards' heads. Mira ducked as bullets hit Sharon in the chest, dropping the woman to the floor. Mira picked up Sharon's gun and charged down the hallway firing both weapons, emptying her clips into the last two guards, killing them.

Mira took a breath, reached into her pack, and pulled out her extra ammo. She refilled both guns, put the remaining ammo back in her pack, and then scooped up a walkie-talkie from one of the fallen guards, clipping it to her skirt. Listening closely to the device, she gathered that security was swarming each floor in search for her, no doubt dedicating their lives to finding Mr. Silver's killer.

She grinned, listening for more tidbits of information. Someone confirmed that the elevators were locked, but she didn't hear any word about the stairwell in the area, which gave her hope. She realized she would have to hurry, though, if she wanted to get to it before the other guards learned about those who had been killed on this floor.

Mira stripped one of the fallen guards of his Kevlar vest, slipping it on over her blouse. She took the security keycard from Des's corpse, stuffed it in her pocket, picked up her guns, and started down the hallway.

She stopped when she noticed a glowing light leaking out from one of the open viewing ports. A sign on the door read "Eden's Tree." Against her better judgment, she peered inside the cell.

Within the confines of the cement walls, someone had planted a giant tree. It looked as if the seed had been planted underneath the cement floor because the tree's trunk originated from the floor itself, rising up through the concrete, its roots breaking through the ground in certain places like the back of a sea serpent.

The leaves of the tree were a brilliant green, but the cause of the light Mira had seen was the glowing fruit—in colors of violet, red, and yellow. Different shapes, different sizes.

The branches of the mammoth tree punctured the walls, cracking the cement, giving just enough leeway to the locking mechanism in the steel door so that Mira was able to slide it open without any trouble.

The cell felt cool and fresh, unlike the warm, stuffy hallway. The scent of sweet rain filled the air. She slipped her bag off, shoved her guns into it, and reached up and grabbed one of the leaves. Its surface felt velvety under her fingertips.

The walkie-talkie squawked, telling her that security was heading toward her location.

She went to turn and leave when she felt compelled to investigate the fruit hanging from the tree's elephantine branches. Mira opened her sack and picked pieces of fruit off the tree, setting them gently inside. She managed to fit three pieces in before she ran out of room in the bag. *I could empty out the knife box to make more room, but I really don't want to.* Instead, she dumped out the American money and managed to fit in another two pieces of fruit, happy to have five—even though there looked to be dozens still on the tree.

Instinctively, Mira slammed her back against the wall and cautiously peered around the doorway. Her ears had picked up the sound of scratching, but she saw nothing that would have caused the sound. Then she noticed the body of one of the fallen guards—

the one from whom she had taken the Kevlar—disemboweled, his entrails strewn about his gutted abdomen.

Mira pulled the guns from her bag, slipped her bag back on, and raised both guns as she peered into the hallway in both directions. *Nobody.* The scent of blood filled her nostrils. She slowly inched her way into the corridor and saw that two of the other cell doors had been torn off the wall.

The first cell she approached was empty. The same with the second, but the second had an odd smell pouring out of it, like burned firewood and fecal matter. She backed away and nearly tripped over the door lying on the floor. A sign on it read "Demon Species."

Demons? Here in SilverTech?

She found "Chaos Matter" on the label of the other door.

What was Mr. Silver doing in this place? What is chaos matter? Did the demon interact with the chaos matter? And if so, what could have happened?

She caught movement out of the corner of her eye and dodged just in time for something to lunge past her. She fired shots, hitting it. It skidded to a halt on the tile, red eyes fading in the dark. *It must have been the demon that had been contained in the cell.*

In the red lighting, the creature's skin looked almost black. And its eyes—its eyes that at one point glowed like embers and died when she shot the creature—lit up again. The creature suddenly broke into two creatures.

"Shit."

Mira fired her guns at both, and they died, only to turn into four creatures moments later.

She ran down the corridor, realizing she had overstayed her welcome within SilverTech Industries.

CHAPTER 12

The motorcycle sputtered and came to a slow stop along the dark highway. At first, Nathan and Ginger thought the vehicle had run out of gas. But then Nathan noticed that the atmosphere on this section of highway seemed significantly thicker than the atmosphere they had passed through up to this point. He felt as if he were breathing through a thick comforter.

Nathan let go of Ginger's waist and pulled his flashlight out of his bag—sure its battery would die as a result of him leaving the beam on while he slept in Sterling. It gave enough light to expose the eerie scene. All around them was living darkness, swirls of shimmering black moving in the air like puffs of smoke from a campfire.

"I've never seen anything like it," Ginger whispered.

"Neither have I. This has to be the work of Legion, though."

"I agree. But what do we do now? Whatever this stuff is, I think it's what gummed up the engine. We aren't going to get anywhere on this thing now."

Nathan turned his flashlight off and looked out in each direction, straining to see a light somewhere in the distance, a beacon they could head toward. But only darkness awaited them out there. Only darkness and terror.

Ginger slid off the bike.

"What are you doing?"

"We don't have time, Nathan. Whatever significance that plane crash has, we need to get to it before things around here get any worse than they already are. I'm not going to sit here and wait to be rescued. We have to leave this vehicle behind and get to Providence."

Nathan felt as if he had been slapped in the face. *Ginger, of course, is right. We can't afford to make complacency or fear our companions at a time like this.* He felt foolish for wanting to do so. *Why would sitting here in the darkness or giving up do us any good?*

Nathan slid off the bike as well. *Whatever's in the air is thicker than what I see with my eyes,* he noticed. Moving his hand through the air, he felt like he was cutting through bath suds. However, when he stepped forward to pass through the darkness with his whole body, he felt pressure, like he was moving through a gentle waterfall.

"This is really strange," Ginger said, drawing close to his side, flashlight in hand aimed at the ground in front of them. The light never reached the terrain under their feet, but instead revealed moving mist.

Nathan grabbed Ginger's hand and pulled her closer to him. *She's the last person I have with me. If something happens to her, I'll be alone and without anyone.* He couldn't bear that thought. He shined his light on her and saw that her normally bright and bubbly persona had turned fearful. Her frown and her trembling hand told him she was just as afraid as he was.

They moved forward together, hand in hand. The mist skated across his skin like moving water, nearly suffocating him in darkness. He stopped every few seconds to take a breath. When he stood still, the mist did as well, swirling around him, sweeping past his ears and the nape of his neck, revealing enough of its presence to let him know it was a malevolent force.

"It's not a coincidence," Nathan said.

"What do you mean?"

"This. This isn't a coincidence. I've never heard of this happening anywhere else. I've heard of all sorts of things that happen in the darkness, but I haven't heard of nor experienced anything like this. It's almost like a wall was put up in our path just to keep us from reaching Providence."

"I think you're right. That just means we have to make sure we get past it."

"Yes," Nathan said. *Who put the wall up? It looks like the work of Legion, but my gut tells me it might actually have nothing to do with Legion.*

He and Ginger moved forward, a foot at a time. To Nathan's dismay, he found the waterfall texture of the darkness shifting to sand as they progressed. A thick wall of dark sand pushed against his whole body as he inched forward, straining his muscles, restricting even his neck movements. *Am I in quicksand?* He didn't feel himself sinking. *More like nearly drowning.*

Standing still in the mist, Nathan heard Ginger breathing heavily. "It's like we're moving through wet sand," she said.

"I know." *How are we going to get through this?*

Their flashlights dimmed and then faded out.

"Hold on. I have batteries I grabbed from the grocery store," Ginger said. She let go of Nathan's hand, and he heard her rifling through her backpack. The sounds seemed to trail off, as if she were walking away from him.

"Ginger?" Nathan reached out to where she had been standing. *Is the darkness just too thick to reveal her presence?* he wondered, but he was greeted only by mist. He fumbled toward the ground. *Maybe she knelt to go through her backpack.* But she wasn't there. "Ginger! Ginger, where did you go? Are you there? Where are you?"

No response.

"Ginger!!"

He stumbled in the darkness, reaching his hands out, grasping for the girl. He tripped and tumbled into asphalt, scraping his arms, dropping his dead flashlight. He heard the lens crack somewhere in the distance. He struggled to his feet and tore to the left, to the right, clawing his way through walls of mist, panicking.

She's all I have left! "You're all I have left, Ginger. Where are you? Ginger? Ginger!"

This mist grew thicker, tougher, but he continued to carve through it. Each step took him deeper into it, until he could go no farther. To his left, right, behind, and in front, he was trapped in a cage of darkness so thick he couldn't even move his fingers through it.

Nathan fainted.

CHAPTER 13

The jingle of the businessman's belt woke Scarlet from her deep, restful slumber. When she turned her head to see him off, he was already dressed and halfway out the door, saying nothing as he departed.

Just the way I like it, she thought. Her time with the businessman had been more than a little intense. Their first encounter in her past had been all about money. It had been mechanical, rehearsed. This time she did things out of pleasure, and it made all the difference. What were once stifled moans were now screams of ecstasy. The rough play that once felt awkward and shy now came out in an explosion of unbridled foreplay. The sex felt natural, wild, intimate, and alive.

It was only because she had grown tired—physically and sexually—that they stopped. Within seconds afterward, she fell asleep.

I feel proud, whole. Most importantly, I feel in control.

Scarlet sighed contentedly and stared at the violet canopy over her bed, wishing for a cigarette. She felt so at peace. *Could this really be where I spend the rest of my life? Did I really agree to leave my old world behind? Old world. It really is the old world to me. The people there, the darkness that swallowed that world—none of it means anything to me now that I have my own paradise here in the Black Cathedral.*

A hunger stirred within her. Hunger for another playmate. Another pawn in her game of ecstasy.

Scarlet slipped out from under the covers and quickly dressed into another gown—this one striped in red and black—and left for Ryn's chamber. Before she got halfway down the hall, she ran into Olivia.

The young girl simply bumped into Scarlet and kept walking. Scarlet turned and shouted at Olivia, summoning her to stop and acknowledge the princess.

Olivia stopped and turned, slowly, deliberately. When she faced Scarlet, the girl smiled sarcastically. "I see you've fallen in headfirst."

"Fallen in? You still think Ryn is tricking me?"

"Of course I do," Olivia replied. "How in the world can you trust a dark magician like that? Do you really think you'll be able to control what is happening to you? What you're becoming? Even now, you may be too far gone, although if you were to turn around at this point, there might—might—still be a chance to salvage what's left of your dignity."

"Fuck you, you little bitch."

Olivia just stared at Scarlet, showing no reaction to her outburst.

"I didn't mean that," Scarlet whispered.

"Of course you did. You meant it. You mean everything you're doing. You have become the epitome of sex. You might appear to be in control now, but I've seen things. I've seen the chains you'll wear. I've seen the sacrifice you'll make. You have no idea what's coming."

"You see visions…of me?"

Olivia nodded.

"That's what you see? Chains? Sacrifice?"

Another nod.

"I'll tell you what I see." Scarlet struck back. "I see power. I see control. I am master over these sorry saps. I'm the ruler over them. Princess over this kingdom. Royalty."

Olivia grinned. "You think you are. But you're wrong.

Ryn has given you the illusion of power, of control. He's the only one with control right now. He's pulling your puppet strings. Just because you get to pull the strings of some of his puppets doesn't make you master over them or him."

"I don't have to listen to this!" Scarlet shouted.

"No, you don't. But I know my words will echo in your ears when the chains are cutting off your last breath, and Ryn unveils what he is up to."

"He is dying."

"What do you mean?"

"The tree. He told me the tree in his throne room is a symbol of the life he has left. When the last leaf falls, he will perish."

"Tree?"

"Haven't you seen his throne room?"

"No. He hasn't taken me there yet." Olivia put a finger to her chin. "Do you think you can get me into that throne room? To see this tree? If he has a weakness, it would be wise to exploit it as soon as possible."

"I have no interest in destroying Ryn."

"You think he has your best interest in mind?"

Scarlet brushed her hair from her shoulders, her hunger for another playmate burning in her abdomen. "I think your hatred for him is unfounded and exaggerated."

"His tree may be the thing preventing me from teleporting out of here."

"That's not my problem."

"Your great fall is coming. Unfortunately, I will be here to see it."

Scarlet huffed. "I suggest you leave."

Olivia smiled and then turned and headed down the hallway.

Scarlet stood there in the corridor of black walls, on the black floor, and decided it was time to cure her appetite.

CHAPTER 14

Mira ran without looking back. Her feet moved so fast, she felt as if she were floating across the tile floor. Through SilverTech Industries she traveled, cutting through security forces, destroying doors, and passing through access panels with Des's card. Determination rose up in her like a phoenix, prompting her to run with one vision, one goal—to get out of SilverTech at all costs. *I don't care if I leave the building or the planet, but either way I'm going to get out of the bowels of this disgusting hell and get topside.*

Red lighting filled every hallway she entered. The alarms had stopped. *Is it from electronic exhaustion or because someone got tired of hearing them?* She had droned them out long ago.

She managed to find a stairwell, but the door's access panel wouldn't budge with Des's security keycard. She scanned the card multiple times. The access panel just beeped, and the red light stayed red. She fired bullets at the panel, but the metal shielding over the doorplate simply absorbed the ammunition. The doors were made of a special material Mira had learned of many years ago—Plexis— flexible paneling originally created to build homes to withstand hurricanes.

Cursing in a few different languages, she continued through SilverTech—her gun in one hand, security card in the other, bag on her back. *How am I going to get out of the building? I don't want to backtrack if I'm only going to run into the multiplying demons again. Where did those demons come from?*

Mr. Silver is evil, Mira thought. *Beyond evil. Beyond Hitler. Beyond Vlad Țepeș. Beyond Grigori Rasputin.* Not necessarily for his cruelty, but for his sick and twisted mind, which had the potential to destroy humanity if he was given the chance. He had to be stopped. *After failing twice in my assassination attempts, I finally managed to accomplish my goal.*

But now, seeing these experiments, or whatever they were, Mira knew Mr. Silver deserved to die long before he was even born. *SilverTech Industries has the potential to destroy the world. Possibly all of creation. I, too, am an experiment of Mr. Silver's creation. Imbued with immortality, I was, for a time, his lab puppet.*

But now I'm free. And he is dead.

Mira reached the end of a corridor where a door leading into a restricted access area stood. She passed Des's card through the access panel and, to her surprise, its light turned green. She heard hissing, like an airlock, and the door popped open. She pulled it toward her and passed through into the largest laboratory she had seen within SilverTech.

Large refrigeration shafts hung from the ceiling of the warehouse-sized room, which she surmised were keeping the room at what felt like a cool thirty degrees. She shivered in her skirt, scolding herself for not taking the pants off one of the security guards. Aisles of glass columns lined the room, reaching up from the floor roughly nine feet. Within each, she saw a mass of sparkling blue matter. *Energy field,* she assumed.

She found what hovered within the energy fields most interesting—and disturbing. One contained a variety of parts from what she assumed to be a human body: a skull, arms, heart, fingers. She saw artifacts in other tubes: a cube, its surface covered in glowing blue lines; a spear, its tip drenched in blood; a key, the blackest black she had ever seen.

She turned and shut the door behind her, then walked between the columns, astounded at Mr. Silver's collection. *The only place he would have been able to keep these things preserved like this is SilverTech Industries.*

At the end of the room stood a large circular platform, with stairs leading up all around. She went up the stairs, glancing behind her to make sure nobody—and nothing—had followed her into the room. *If the multiplying demons ran into any of SilverTech's security, and the guards shot at the hideous beasts, the demons would eventually grow large enough in number to destroy this entire building. And if they mix with any of the innumerable chemicals, artifacts, or experiments lying around SilverTech, who knows what will become of this building, or this planet?*

At the top of the steps, she reached the circular platform. Three circles—possibly lights—formed a triangle within the platform's surface. Ahead of her, at the other end of the large platform, Mira saw a computer array. The monitor rotated through screens of graphs and numbers. She drew closer and examined them, disappointed that she couldn't gather any understanding from them. One of the graphics showed a map of the United States. A red dot blinked over the state of California, over the word 'Providence.'

She looked back at the platform, wondering.

Mira set her gun and Des's card on the computer monitor and then sat down in the office chair in front of the computer panel. She hit the Enter button on the computer's keyboard. The flying seagull screen savers stopped, and a window came up, prompting her for a password. Mira attempted a variety of passwords, each of which she remembered from the files she had perused during her brief stint as Mr. Silver's assistant.

She finally gained access using the one password that should have been obvious in the beginning: L. The name of his late daughter.

"Get away from that!"

Mira turned to see a short young woman in a black lab coat standing on the other side of the platform, pointing a gun at Mira.

The woman took careful steps around the center of the pad and approached the computer terminal. "Get away from that. Now!"

Mira put her hands up, quickly glancing at her gun on top of the computer monitor. *Can I draw fast enough—grab the gun, and tear this woman to pieces with lead before she can get a shot off? From what I've seen, most of the SilverTech scientists have no idea how to handle a firearm.*

"Stand up."

Mira stood.

"Over there," the woman demanded, motioning toward the pad. Mira obeyed. "Trying to get out of here without the rest of us?"

"What are you talking about?"

The woman tilted her head toward the computer. "You have no idea how to run it, do you?"

"I don't even know what this is." *The Kevlar vest will protect me from a bullet—heck, even my immortality will do that—but if this woman shoots me point blank, even in the Kevlar, it will hurt.*

"This is a teleportation machine."

"Bullshit."

"Why do you think I'm here?"

"You want to get out of this hellhole as much as I do."

The woman nodded. "You're the one who killed Mr. Silver, aren't you?"

"And proud of it."

"Hmm. I hope you made sure he's really dead. That man is like a cat."

"I made sure to take out all ten million of his lives."

She smirked. "It doesn't really matter. Help me, and you and I can get out of here." She lowered her gun. Mira breathed a sigh of relief. "I'll set the controls."

"Where is this teleportation machine going to teleport us?" Mira laced her words with sarcasm, not entirely believing that Mr. Silver had created such highly advanced technology. She had seen the portal that Hush had fallen through, but that didn't seem like something created by technology—it was more supernatural in nature. *But then what do I know?*

The woman took a seat at the computer and let her fingers dance across the keyboard as a variety of screens popped up on the monitor. "Mr. Silver has always had all of his bases covered. ALL of them. Providence, a city he helped equip to withstand nuclear or other terrorist attack—even from our own government—is where this teleport leads."

"He has his own city?"

"No. He always had plans to build his own city here. Too bad the American public didn't want to give him that much control. So that's where Anaisha comes in. It's his way of building things…his way. Providence is where he was able to put some of his ideas into play. Only some of them. An Amtrak system runs through California, picking up those who want refuge in Providence. You see the energy fields his artifacts are contained in? Imagine a huge dome like that, over a city, protecting it from missiles, bombs, and the like."

Mira felt a surge of joy that she had killed him when she had the chance.

"Now we can take this teleporter to his laboratory in Providence. I know he has a private shuttle there he was keeping in case he had to make a hasty getaway from Earth."

"Wait a minute. He has a whole hangar full of shuttles in the bottom of this dump."

"Those are all for SilverTech staff. And they don't work."

"Seriously?"

"Mr. Silver has certain individuals telling all the rest of the staff that the stuff around here works. Some does, some doesn't. He has loyalists who work undercover here, among the rest of us, and he already made deals with them. He was going to bring them with him on his private shuttle and leave the rest of us behind to rot."

Mira stepped toward the computer monitor and grabbed her gun, placing it in her bag of fruit and other goodies. "Let's get out of here. I've had enough of this place."

"Of course." The woman continued to type commands into the computer system. Suddenly, the platform emitted a soft hum. The three lights in the floor illuminated, and bright pillars of yellow light particles rose from the circles. "That's it," she said, turning from the console with her gun aimed at Mira.

"What are you doing?"

"I'm making sure you don't do anything stupid. I'm going to go through first. Then you come in after me. This makes certain that you don't ambush me on the other side. Besides, I'm the only one between the two of us who knows how to pilot Mr. Silver's private shuttle."

"Is that so?"

"I designed it."

The woman walked across the platform. When her body

reached one of the light pillars, it disintegrated into small black particles that were swept up in the flow of the pillar's beam.

Mira took a good look at the room around her, wishing she could take more artifacts and trinkets with her. *I wonder if the building is filling with demons yet. If not, it will only be a matter of time. This is the end of SilverTech Industries. The end of Mr. Silver. And a new start for me, the woman who used to be known as Shaonna.*

She closed her eyes and stepped through the nearest pillar of light, upon which she immediately felt thousands of hooks dig into her skin. She screamed but did not hear her voice. Instead, a loud buzzing sound resonated through her ears, skull, and the bones of her neck and shoulders. Her head felt like it was going to break off from the violent noise, but then she felt the hooks pull away from her—still in her skin—and she blacked out.

CHAPTER 15

The pleasant aroma of freshly brewed coffee roused Nathan awake. He found himself slumped in a chair at a small table, a brown mug of steaming coffee in front of him. He sat up straight, recollection of his trudge through the darkness filling his mind.

"Don't worry, you are no longer in the cage."

Nathan looked up and saw a man sitting across from him. The man wore a black fedora, and his face seemed to be hidden in shadows. Black gloves covered his hands, which were folded on the surface of the table, and a dark suit enveloped him.

Nathan glanced around the café. He and this man seemed to be the only two people in the place. Even the front counter was deserted. To Nathan's relief, he saw his backpack resting against the leg of his chair. "Who are you? Where am I?"

"Where you are is of no consequence."

Nathan looked down at the coffee.

"Drink up. I'm sure it tastes better than that sludge you used to drink back in the mall. And no, it's not poisoned. My desire to kill you has passed. For now."

Nathan picked up the mug. He took a cautious sip. As the warm liquid ran down his throat, he remembered his coffee meetings with Serenity.

"You miss your friends. It's touching. However, we have an important matter to discuss, you and me."

Nathan set the mug down and rubbed his eyes. He felt somewhat rested. *Where am I? And where did Ginger go? One second I was*

in the darkness—in a cage made of thick darkness—and now I'm
sipping coffee with—

"I don't really have a name. If you want to call me something, call me the Infiltrator."

"The Infiltrator?"

The man nodded. "I brought you here so we could talk. Civilly. You have impressed—and outraged—a good number of powerful beings, and I feel it would be best if I attempted this approach to get your attention."

"You have it. For now." Nathan picked up the mug.

"Ah, you attempt to assert power you don't really have. I'll push your ignorant and blatantly disrespectful comment aside for the sake of peaceful conversation. And I'll boil things down for you. I want to give you a gift, Nathan. I want to give you back your sister, your parents, your friends. I want to give you back your life."

Nathan quickly set the mug back down without taking another sip. "What?"

"That's right. *Now* I have your attention. Trust me, I didn't just say that to get your attention. I really do want to give you back everything—everyone—you lost. I have the power to do so. I have the power to send you back."

"Back?"

"Back to when you first veered off the path laid out for you. Before the car accident."

"The car accident? Are you with the TPS?"

"You could say I created it."

"I thought Redford—"

"Redford is my pawn to head the TPS," he interrupted.

"You can send me back?"

"Yes. But there are conditions. If I send you back, you will then die at a time I deem appropriate."

"What is the point of sending me back if you're going to kill me?"

"I can send you back. Far back. Months, years, before the car accident. I will make sure that accursed driving instructor isn't replaced, and you won't get into a car accident at that point in time. In turn, events will play out the way they were meant to from the beginning. The benefit for you is that you will get to see your sister again—alive and well—along with the rest of your family. I will not simply send you back and kill you. I will give you the happiness you want. In return, you leave this timeline, allow me to send you back to the root."

"Why would you do this for me?"

"Redford already explained to you the ramifications of your actions. You were supposed to die at the church camp with Heather. Instead, you were spared, Heather learned of her powers, and everything has spiraled out of control. It is because of this that I will use my powers to restore things to the way they *should* be."

"It doesn't make sense. You only want me to go back so Legion can have the upper hand in everything."

The man pounded his fists on the table. "You humans aggravate me with your ignorance. Legion already has the upper hand. Has since the beginning. So has the Dark Army. You know nothing of the bigger picture, young man, so I will excuse your ignorance for lack of information. By not dying at the camp, you have altered the future of your entire species. Countless people have died—who would not have—because you live. Do you think that's fair to them? You were meant to die; they weren't. But they did anyhow, because you sit here having coffee with me."

"*You* brought me here."

"Yes, because I couldn't stand to see you implode with fright at the darkness in your world. That darkness is inevitable. Legion is unstoppable. Once you wrap your brain around that, maybe you'll take me up on my offer. Once you realize that your world is in peril one way or another—and that your death could save hundreds, possibly even thousands—maybe you'll reconsider."

"I didn't choose to get into a car accident that day."

"I am well aware of that. A rogue individual of your species decided to try to play the Hand of God and altered everything irrevocably."

Nathan slowly lifted his mug to his lips and took a long sip, pondering the man's proposal. *I'll get to see my sister again. And my parents. I can live out my life the way it was meant to be lived. Without the car accident, without Heather's scars, without the chaos at the church camp.* "What about Heather?"

"She will die, as will you. But again, under my terms, after the point of the car accident. It has to be that way so you won't try to circumvent your destruction again."

"How do you know I won't warn people ahead of time about Legion?"

"You can warn anyone of anything you want. You can spend those few months, few years that I give you, trying to come up with a way to destroy Legion—if that's how you want to waste the gift I give you. But it will still do you no good. Legion will win. Regardless of any and everything. If you haven't comprehended that, you are more foolish than I thought."

Nathan set his mug down, licking his lips. *His heart raced. I have the chance right now to go back, to see those I lost, to save my parents' lives, to meet Macayle ahead of time, to spend more time—precious time—*

with my sister. What would I do with that time? I would cut off all ties with my girlfriend, Shannon. I would tell Ryan—the man who would later betray me—to take a hike. And I would wait patiently for Pearl to return into my life. Yes, I could have Pearl back in my arms, and once that happens, I could enjoy the time with my sister, Pearl, and all of my friends.

And I would warn everyone of Legion. Of Legion, of Evanescence, of the coming attack on the world. I could change everything.

"And nothing," the man said. Nathan imagined him smirking underneath those shadows. "I'm not a fool," the man continued. "I'm not going to send you back if I think you have any chance of stopping us. This is simply my way of showing mercy."

Nathan rubbed his fingers around the rim of the mug. The caffeine was kicking in. His mind awakened, raced to find a way to figure this proposal out.

"You have five minutes to accept or decline my offer."

"I still don't see what's in this for you. Unless I'm getting close to something. Something that can change the tide. Something that can change everything." Nathan sat up. "The plane crash. Providence."

The man said nothing.

"You want to keep me from Providence. That's why you put the wall of darkness up. To keep Ginger and me from reaching the plane crash."

"Be careful, young Nathan. Your assumptions are starting to irk me."

"Why? Because I'm right? That's why you're offering me a chance to see my sister again. And my family. The fact that I didn't die—that Heather didn't die—has royally screwed up your plans. You thought killing my sister would put an end to things, would silence everyone. But it didn't."

"Be careful, young Nathan. You are skirting my distaste for humans."

"No," Nathan scooted his chair back and stood up. "I'm still alive, and I'm heading toward the end of this whole struggle. And we're going to win."

"You can't win."

"Says you. You don't have control over me, over any of my friends."

The man motioned with his arms to the rest of the empty diner. "What friends do you have left, Nathan?"

"You know that something is coming, something that will change the whole face of this attack."

The man stood abruptly, knocking his chair backward, toppling it to the floor. "You've crossed the line. I brought you here to have a civil talk with you, to offer you solace and retribution for what happened to you."

"Retribution? For what happened to *me*? My sister was wrongfully arrested, abducted, and then put on public display, killed for all the world to see. I watched a mall full of people get slaughtered by a monster. I was there when Legion annihilated a room full of police officers. I was there when Evanescence, the Great Witch, abducted her own daughter, Pearl, against her will. I was there when a building vanished in plain sight, possibly with a little girl in it! I don't need retribution for what they went through. I just want to save our future, to stop Legion, to stop the Dark Army, from destroying the human species."

The man tipped the rim of his fedora and then folded his hands together in front of him. "So you refuse to accept reason. That is unfortunate. If I sent you back, it would restart everything we are currently in, you know? It would set the clock back, it would save everyone who has died because of your journey to save your sister. The darkness would be rolled back—for a short time—and those souls who have been imprisoned would be free. For a time. Since they are captive for all eternity, don't you want to give them a little freedom? Don't you—"

"Stop talking," Nathan snapped. "I don't want to hear any more of your lies."

"Very well, Nathan. Nobody can say I didn't give you the chance. Remember this meeting. Remember the opportunity I put in front of you when you yearn for Pearl in the darkness."

"Whether Pearl comes back or not won't decide whether I will keep fighting or not. To go back in time, to send me back there, would make no difference in anything. It would simply give you the upper hand."

"You don't even know who I am."

"It doesn't matter. You are tied with Legion. That's all I need to know. And because of that, I *must* fight against you. I must. I don't…I don't know what else to do. I will keep fighting, even if the odds look stacked against me."

"Touching. But a fruitless endeavor. The forces you are up against cannot be stopped."

"So says the man on the other side of the line that divides this war."

"You know nothing of war, young Nathan. Not yet. But you will. This is the end of you…and your species. The end of your planet. And once we're done here, we will move on to the next planet and eradicate it as well. And then the next. And the next. Until the entire universe is ours. Speaking of which, it is time to move forward. I am disappointed in you. I had hoped we could come to an arrangement. I truly want you to be happy, and I figured allowing you access to your past, the past you cherish so much, would have given you some degree of joy, or at least some comfort."

"You don't want anything to do with my happiness. You only want to win. And I'm not going to let you do that."

"You won't be able to do anything about it when you're snared by the darkness."

Within the blink of an eye, everything went black, and Nathan found himself trapped once again in the cell of dark mist.

I should have accepted the man's offer. No, I will stay the course, even if it means I will be in the darkness until everything is destroyed. He felt his pack was on his back. *Nothing in it will help me escape.*

Then he remembered the mask.

He took the pack off, unzipped it, and pulled the stone mask out, putting it up to his face…

He found himself sitting on a toilet surrounded by white expanse. Slowly, a bathroom materialized around him. Once the tub was in place, it filled with water, and the woman from before—the one whose soul was trapped in here—appeared in the water, mostly covered in a froth of bubbles. She turned to him, her long black hair wet and matted to the top of her head, and sunk a little deeper into the liquid.

Nathan turned away. "Sorry, I didn't know this is how—"

"I imagine you have no control over *where* you appear in this prison, do you?"

He turned back to her. "No."

"What are you doing here? I usually don't get the same visitor a second time."

"I need your help. You seem to know more about Legion

than most people where I come from."

"We both come from the same place, moron."

He sighed. "That's not what I meant."

"Sorry. As you can guess, it's pretty miserable here. I...I take baths to try to relax, only because I know there's no escape from here."

Nathan turned toward the door and saw that it was locked. "You don't want the Tormentors coming in."

"The one resembling my husband tries to...initiate things whenever he sees me in the bed or tub. I can't bring myself to succumb to that. There are too many real memories tied to...I'm sorry, that's probably a little too much information for you. Listen, kid, why did you come here? I'm sure there are better things for you to be doing."

"Is there anything else you can tell me about Legion?"

"I told you how I was imprisoned. How my soul came to be in this mask, this other world. I don't know much beyond that."

"How was Legion able to capture you?"

She shrugged. "I just...I woke up and found myself captive."

"What were you doing before you slept?"

"I...I don't remember."

A dead end.

"Look," she whispered, "I know you probably don't want to even think of hurting me, but destroying the mask—finding a way to destroy the mask—is the best thing you can do for me now. Do you really want me stuck here, being tormented day and night by ghosts of my past? Do you know how many times I've tried to kill myself? It doesn't work. I'm not able to free myself from this place. But you can. Destroy the mask. Let my soul move on."

"But you won't go where you think you'll go."

"You think I'm going to Hell?" She laughed, splashed some

bubbles around, and then leaned her head back on the edge of the tub. "Kid, I've lived a fairly long life. I have yet to see proof of this God you mentioned. Don't get me wrong, you're entitled to believe what you want to believe, but to try and force that on me…I don't think that's right. I've already told you I don't believe God exists. And if I did believe He existed, I'd have to say He'd be just as screwed up as the one you call the Devil. One hurts people; the other stands by and watches people get hurt. Who is better? In my opinion, neither."

Darkness quickly replaced the bathroom. Nathan found himself back in his prison, surrounded by darkness, alone. He carefully stuffed the mask back in his pack and pulled the pack up on his back.

Why would the woman reject God after being tortured in the mask for so long? I want to help her, to explain to her that God lets some things go for a time because it's all part of a bigger plan, but I don't think my words will fall on ears that want to hear what I have to say.

He didn't want to destroy the mask if there was a chance he could help save the woman. *If I destroy it, and she was rejected by God, it would mean an eternity of torture worse than what's going on within the mask.*

Nathan sat on the ground, which felt soft with the mist gliding across it, and closed his eyes. By closing his eyes, he could trick himself into believing that he was the one bringing darkness upon himself, and not an outside force over which he had no control.

God, if you're there, I could really use your help right now. I was given a chance…a chance I'm not even sure would have been possible. Does that man, the Infiltrator, have power to send me back, to restart time? I refused, and now I'm trapped within this darkness. And I have a mask containing someone's soul? A woman, Margaret. I want her to turn to you, but she refuses. Do I have the right—or the responsibility—to free her from her torturous prison?

Without warning, Nathan's right wrist caught fire. He fell to the ground, howling, trying to put the flame out, but he couldn't quench it. It burned brighter, hotter, in shades of blue and green and violet, searing his skin. The flames reached an intense climax and then died. Nathan sat up and leaned against a wall of darkness, clutching the elbow of his damaged hand.

Looking at his injury, he saw burned into his skin, branded into his flesh, a symbol: three horizontal lines parallel to each other, a dot piercing the center of the middle line. That dot glowed a brilliant display of colors, while the lines pulsed with a bright white glow, illuminating the darkness around him. Strangely enough, the mark didn't hurt, although the flesh around it felt hot to the touch, like he had held his hand over a stovetop burner too long.

"What is this?"

The darkness began to move. At first, Nathan heard murmuring as the dark wall he had been leaning against moved away from him, dropping him back to the ground. He got to his feet and listened as the murmuring turned to shrieking. He noticed fire leaping painlessly from the new symbol on his wrist, scorching the darkness, pushing it back.

Moments later, a path had been burned straight through the wall of darkness. And in the distance, at the end of the road he stood on, Nathan saw the glow of a city, illuminating the otherwise dreary horizon.

CHAPTER 16

S carlet watched as Brittany, now a little older—and more experienced, it seemed—than she was the first time she and Cynthia had their romp in the girls' restroom, buttoned her blouse and slid her feet into the black heels Scarlet adored so much, the ones with the little red flowers adorning the buckles.

This time, instead of a clumsy rendezvous in a rancid bathroom stall, Scarlet explored sex in such a profoundly intimate way that she almost considered turning herself over to females completely. Scarlet's lower stomach pulsed with the pleasurable imprint Brittany left on her. The princess almost thought to ask Brittany to stay longer, to settle her head on Scarlet's chest. But before Scarlet's mouth could find the words, Brittany had already left the room.

Scarlet stared up at the canopy over her bed. *Is this all a dream? Here, I can indulge in my deepest sexual fantasies without consequence. Without judgment. Without refusal. I am denied nothing, and everything seems ready for my taking. And I will take.*

A knock on the door startled her from her thoughts. Her heart jumped at the possibility that it could be Brittany, wanting another session of unending passion.

Instead, Olivia walked in with a tray full of sandwiches and fruit. "Ryn wants to see you. He'll be coming here shortly." She set the tray of food on the dresser and turned toward Scarlet, frowning. "It's already started."

"What has?" Scarlet asked, pulling her comforter closer to her chest. She felt so uncomfortable around this girl.

"Your bondage."

Scarlet giggled. "Get out of here."

"Look in the mirror," Olivia said before leaving the room.

What is she talking about? How can I be in bondage and feel so much pleasure at the same time? Scarlet stumbled out of bed and slipped into the black robe hanging over her nightstand. She went to the mirror, thoughts of Brittany still dancing in her mind. When Scarlet glanced at her reflection, she couldn't discern what Olivia referred to.

Scarlet's skin had grown darker, tanner than its usual pale hue. Her eyes sparkled like black jewels. Her hair seemed longer than when she arrived at the Cathedral. *I'm beautiful.* She did notice dark imprints along her arms and neck, but she dismissed them as reminders of the horseplay between her and her playthings.

"Stupid girl," she muttered, referring to Olivia. Scarlet glanced down at the food Olivia had brought in. *I'm famished.* Scarlet picked up a beef sandwich. Etched in the silver platter under it, in glowing light, she saw another message, scrawled in the same handwriting as the one that had appeared on the mirror earlier: *My heart breaks for you.*

"What the fuck?" she shouted, knocking the tray to the floor. She spun around and glared at the walls around her. "What do you want with me? Huh?"

The door opened, and Ryn—in his male form—entered the room. "Is there a problem?" he asked.

Scarlet saw the mess she had made on the floor. "No. Just this…this room."

Ryn helped her pick up the food and place it on the platter on the dresser. If he saw the glowing text etched in the platter, he didn't react. And Scarlet didn't want to tell him about it. *If he's behind it, I don't want to give him the satisfaction of knowing it's unnerving me.*

129

"I see you are enjoying the fruits of your gift."

"I am," she said, suddenly hungry for another partner.

"That is good news. I came here because I want to discuss something with you. Something personal. Something very sensitive." He sat on the edge of the bed. Scarlet watched as the four posts and the violet canopy became distorted within his presence.

"Go on," she said, as if she had control of the conversation.

"I sense there is someone in this cathedral who is not what they seem to be. I do not know who, but I sense—this cathedral senses—someone is within my domain who has nefarious intentions for me and the Cathedral itself."

Scarlet brushed her hair away from her shoulders and leaned back against the dresser, crossing her arms over her chest. "Do you know who? Or why?" Secretly, she knew the building and Ryn were most likely reacting to Olivia's attempts to destroy him. She refused to let these thoughts surface for fear Ryn would sense them and take away her toys as discipline for hiding Olivia's true nature from him.

"The why is simple. There are many who would like to see my demise. They want to see me crushed to dust. It is futile for them to strive for my destruction. I will be eaten up by that tree soon enough. But the whom…I am not sure. I have some guesses—which I will not reveal to you yet—but I do not know for certain."

"I'll keep my eyes open," she said truthfully.

Ryn stood to his feet. "I am happy to hear that. I would love to eat the next meal with you. We can talk. I have not talked to anyone in a very long time. Even with so many servants and guests within this place, I still get lonely."

Scarlet nodded, feeling a sudden desire to talk to Ryn. The conversation between her and her playmates was strictly confined to the realm of sex, and that was only when they decided to talk. She had had no luck trying to converse with the other residents of the Black Cathedral.

Ryn opened the door and started to leave when he turned and looked—with that blank slate of a face—at her. "If you do recover any information regarding an enemy of mine within this kingdom, please let me know as soon as possible. I wish to root out any weed before it has the power to strangle the other plants. Including you, my flower. I am always willing to reward loyalty. Perhaps you would like some new toys to play with. Exotic toys."

Scarlet watched him leave, and then glanced at the platter on the dresser. The glowing words had disappeared. *Good*, she thought, as she headed out of the room to find another playmate.

CHAPTER 17

The warm air reminded Nathan of Arizona summers. He found it hard to breathe—to the point that he had to stop every now and then to rest and catch his breath.

The heat in the air around him was nothing compared to the heat radiating from the symbol in his wrist. The three lines of brilliant white light guided him forward. But the circle in the center of the middle line, in its continuing cycle of mesmerizing colors, caught Nathan's attention the most. He asked God what the mark was—seeing how it appeared during his last conversation with Him—but Nathan received no response.

Every time Nathan stopped to rest, he peered into the darkness using his wrist to light up the areas beyond the highway, in search for Ginger. He was careful not to wander off the asphalt path for fear of stumbling into another dark trap. He couldn't find any sign of Ginger, even though he yelled out her name.

He crested a hill and stopped at the top. About a half mile in the distance sat a twinkling city nestled in the midst of a low valley. Tall buildings reached into the dark sky, the light from their windows turning the structures into beacons. From where he stood, Nathan could see an archway lit up in bright white spotlights—an important difference from the red lights signifying the president's sanctuary zones.

How has the city avoided the president's bombs or Legion's attacks or any of the other threats from the darkness? Then he spotted, vaguely outlined against the metropolitan's glow, a large wall stretching all the way around the city.

A colorful object descended from the sky, headed in the direction of the city. The colorful ribbons of flame behind the object glowed brightly against the black sky. *Maybe it's another different type of Legion vessel, but why would Legion need more presence here when it's already gained the upper hand over Earth? And why would it land more vessels now, weeks after its initial attack?*

Everything is coming together, God said.

Nathan took a deep breath. "God?"

Courage. That is what you need. That is what I will give you.

"Courage? What's going to happen?"

No answer.

Nathan huffed. *I hate how God starts a conversation only to stop when I ask the wrong question.* But he took comfort in the fact that God was still with him. *It's foolish to think that God would just ignore this planet as it falls into darkness, but the silence is brutal. More brutal than Heather's harsh words when she ripped into me about sleeping with Cynthia.*

Heather. Nathan started along the road again, the light in his wrist revealing the path into the valley. He smiled when he remembered Heather's bright face, but the memories of her comforting touch made him ache deeply. *I miss her so much. I miss her like I used to miss my sister when she was captured but still alive. But not the same way I miss Pearl. Or my parents. Or Macayle.*

She is ahead of you, God said.

Nathan stopped. "Is she okay?" he asked, not really expecting God to answer that question.

Yes.

Nathan's shoulders relaxed. "Good." He decided to be bold. "What about Pearl?"

You love her.

"Very much," he said, surprised at how quickly tears gathered in the corners of his eyes. He started walking again, hoping the movement would help him progress past the emotion. "Will...I ever see her again?"

You've put her inside your heart, in a place only I can see her. Safe from harm.

Is that supposed to be an answer or a statement regarding what I already know? Nathan wondered. "I love her because You gave her to me."

Silence.

Nathan stopped walking, the glow from his wrist lighting a sign on the shoulder of the highway.

PROVIDENCE

The end. And the beginning, God said.

"I don't understand what that means. Is this where the world comes to an end?" Nathan asked.

Silence.

He huffed and continued walking, glad he had almost reached his destination. *I'm eager to see how everything pans out, but at the moment, even more eager to get behind the walls of this city. It feels like the darkness is attempting to close in around me again.*

Rain began to drizzle down from the sky. The fresh scent swept into his nostrils, along with other scents—ones less memorable. He could smell rotting flesh, but the direction of its source was almost impossible to pinpoint. He also thought he caught a whiff of oil.

And then he spotted by the glow of his wrist the train tracks a few feet to his left, running parallel to the road he walked. He continued toward the city, cutting through the cold yet refreshing rain, which let up once he arrived within yards of the archway—double archway, now that he was close enough to see it clearly. He confirmed that the train tracks ran under one arch while the road stretched under the other. Large iron gates blocked passage through both archways. Illuminated flags stuck out of the pillar between the archways, flying in colors of gold, white, and red.

Above the flags hung a megaphone speaker, out of which roared a rough, baritone voice. *"Stop where you are, please."*

Nathan stared up at the speaker, suddenly eager to get within the city walls. The smell of fresh paint drifted through the rain.

"Who are you?" the speaker boomed.

"I would like to enter Providence," Nathan answered.

"I asked your name, traveler. Not why you're here."

If I reveal my identity to the wrong people, I could wind up dead—or worse, under the president's torturous thumb only to wind up like my late sister. He glanced back at the highway behind him, into darkness.

"Your name, traveler, or you won't stand a chance of getting inside."

"Nathan Pierce."

Silence.

"Repeat that."

"Nathan. Pierce."

Longer silence.

The sharp screech of metal on metal made Nathan's ears nearly bleed as the iron gate blocking the road slid down into the road itself, allowing him passage. Without hesitating, Nathan walked inside the boundaries of the city. Almost immediately, the metal screeching sound returned, and the iron gate went up behind him without pause.

Before him, the road extended through the city. The entire

area was lit up in street lamps and neon signs. Tall buildings stretched high on either side. Vehicles of various brands and types littered the curbs, most of them appearing to be in decent shape, but idle. The train tracks ran through the city as well but went underground in the middle of the street through a tunnel that looked big enough for a steam engine to fit through. People walked the street and sidewalks, seemingly without a care in the world. It felt like Phoenix before Phoenix had become a casualty of this supernatural war.

Though the rain had let up, Nathan couldn't stop shivering.

Something grabbed him from behind and spun him around. A man in soldier fatigues stood before him, the fingers of the man's right hand wrapped around the shoulder strap of Nathan's backpack. "I need to see what's in your bag, kid."

Nathan pulled out of the man's grip and stumbled backward. "I don't think so."

The man shook his head. "Son, I need to see what's in that bag if you want to get inside the city. I don't have time to play games with you."

"I'm not playing games. A ship crashed here a while ago. I need to know what part of the city it crashed in."

"A ship?" The man thought for a minute, his bushy gray eyebrows tilting up like the flippers of a pinball machine. "Oh…the ship. Look, I'm not authorized to answer any of your questions just yet. You say you're Nathan Pierce? *The* Nathan Pierce?"

Nathan nodded.

"Hmm." The man examined Nathan with suspicious eyes. "You certainly look like him. Okay. Come with me. I'll take you to the mayor."

The man led Nathan to a small one-story building nestled between the massive wall surrounding the city and a multi-story high-rise that reached so far above Nathan, he couldn't see its top before it vanished into darkness.

Two more soldiers, each armed with a rifle, guarded the front double doors. They watched Nathan and his escort pass through. Once inside, Nathan assumed the building had at one point been used as a telemarketing call center or an insurance company. Dozens of vacant cubicles filled the room. Small offices—simple rooms with large glass panes revealing their barren innards—lined the back wall.

The man in camouflage led Nathan toward a separate office off to the right. When the soldier opened the door, he saluted the suited man sitting behind the desk. The soldier waved Nathan in and left him there, shutting the door.

Nathan stood in front of the desk and watched the suited man finish scribbling words on white paper. His black hair was parted to the side, and the top of his left ear had a chunk missing from it.

When the man finished his writing task, he set his pen down and stood, fastening the middle button of his Navy-blue suit jacket. "I don't mean to be rude, but I have to ask myself why a man of your status—if you are indeed the same Nathan Pierce for which the president of the United States issued a death warrant, the same Nathan Pierce who is rumored to have fought Legion and lived to tell the tale, and the same Nathan Pierce who lost his sister—has decided to devote part of his very brief life to journey here to Providence and demand to be let inside these city walls." The mayor glared at Nathan, saying nothing more and doing nothing, not even fidgeting. He simply kept his hands behind his back and revealed nothing of himself, aside from his partial ear.

Nathan fought the temptation to sit in one of the comfortable-looking leather office chairs. "I need to see the plane that crashed here."

"That was days ago."

"I know."

"What would you possibly have to do with a crashed plane?"

Nathan debated on holding all of his cards close to his chest. "I was told to come here."

"By whom?"

"That's a long story."

"Unfortunately, Mr. Pierce, I don't have time for long stories. This city is about to fall under siege, and I have to do my very best to make sure everything that has been put in place is executed on time and in the way intended."

"Under siege?"

The mayor nodded, turning his back to Nathan to pour himself a glass of alcohol from a glass bottle. Nathan thought the man might offer him some, and then felt a little disappointed when that didn't happen. Nathan wouldn't have accepted it, but the offer would have been a token of friendliness. "The president. She sent out creatures—or rather, soldiers—called Brinks to destroy those who haven't taken her mark, and to decimate this city."

Although Nathan had heard the same radio broadcast Ginger had, stating that the president had indeed survived the assassination attempt, he refused to believe it. "The president is dead."

The mayor took a sip of alcohol. "It's obvious you've been wandering the Broken Lands for a while."

"What are you talking about?"

The man turned toward Nathan, swirling his glass as if it held another ingredient that hadn't quite mixed completely with the spirits. "President Stone is very much alive."

"That's impossible. I was there, on the stage, when she was assassinated!"

The mayor licked his lips. "She's alive. And she used the assassination 'attempt' to pass the last of the Falling Star Directives—deployment of her units. Her Brinks, which are huge, hulking monsters with tubes coming out of their backs, are heading here to annihilate Providence. To destroy me, really. We have some defenses, but maybe not enough to repel this grand opposition. We'll sure try, though. Providence won't go down without a fight. You can't see it, but there is an energy field—courtesy of SilverTech Industries—over the city, like a dome. It should keep out most projectiles, like missiles and bombs."

"Where is the plane?"

"I'll have some of my men escort you to where it crashed, on the other side of the city."

"I don't have time to be escorted. Just tell me where it is."

The mayor sighed. "South end. You can't miss it."

Nathan turned to leave.

"There were no survivors," the mayor informed him.

Nathan stopped mid-stride. "What?"

"There were no survivors. From the crash."

"They died? How many? Do you know who they were?"

"No. Actually, there wasn't anyone on board when my men finally got to it. Plane went right into a building. You'll know what I'm talking about once you see it. Nobody could have survived that crash. Nor did we find anything particularly useful inside the aircraft, so I'm not sure what you're hoping to find when you reach it."

So you're just assuming, Nathan thought bitterly. He left the building and rushed onto the main street, heading south. He didn't pause to talk to anyone, didn't bother with being amazed at the well-preserved environment around him. He knew that if the president was still alive—clearly an act of Legion or Satan or any number of other supernatural phenomena—that she would stop at nothing to kill Nathan, if she could find him.

It has to be more than coincidence that she's set on destroying this city when I've only just arrived. Then he remembered what God had said shortly before Nathan arrived at the city wall: *"Everything is coming together."*

Nathan's thoughts went back to the woman with blue eyes, the one who had interjected herself into his life on at least two occasions. She had told him, on the last occasion, that it was time to fight.

And now the president's army is on its way here. I don't want to fight, he told himself and God. *I don't think anyone stands a chance, especially if Legion joins the fray.* Legion had already shown Nathan that it was a powerful and highly dangerous foe, one he didn't want to tangle with if he could avoid it.

It is time, God said.

Nathan kept walking. He had no question for God after an answer like that. God could have meant it was time to fight, or time for things to end, or time for Pearl to return, or any multitude of other things. Nathan didn't care. He focused on finding the crashed plane, on where the path was taking him. Something told him the enemy was already a few steps ahead of him, though.

"Shit!"

Nathan turned to see a group of teenagers all staring up at the sky. He followed their gaze, and his heart almost fell into his stomach. A vibrant sphere of colorful flames had entered the city's atmosphere and barreled into the top of a skyscraper, cutting it apart in an explosion of shattering glass and breaking brick. A loud boom signaled the sphere's impact, but Nathan had no clue how close it had been.

The teenagers dispersed in a frenzy. Other onlookers hollered and howled as they broke out in mad dashes away from the crumbling building. Nathan held tightly to the straps of his pack and ran as fast as his feet would take him. He heard bricks crumble and metal buckle behind him. He glanced over his shoulder and saw thick smoke sweeping toward him.

Nathan continued running, moving forward as others ran alongside him, everyone hoping to get away from the awful destruction. Some headed down into the train tunnel under the street, while others took cover in nearby buildings. It reminded him of Phoenix and the tidal wave of asphalt and cement, the bloody dust, the heat. Legion's vessel landing. *But is this Legion?*

He turned down an alley with a crowd of those fleeing the dust flood, unsure of where he was heading. Dirt particles swept through the alley, blinding everyone, filling the narrow corridor with thick haze barely dispelled by the street lamps. In the commotion, someone slammed into Nathan, sending him into the nearest alley wall. Nathan turned toward the brick, closed his eyes, and held his breath as the dust moved around him and the others.

God, what is going on? What is this?

Minutes passed, and Nathan pulled away from the wall. The dust had settled enough to allow him to breathe and see somewhat. He maneuvered through the panicking crowd to the end of the alley, where the air was a bit clearer. He found himself in a parking lot that stretched toward a wider building, which looked like it had once been a department store...before the object that had fallen—a large sphere—crashed into it, surrounding the structure and part of the lot in a strange yellow fog, which moved slowly like wisps of smoke under the amber-colored parking lot lamps.

Nathan stood in the parking lot staring at the department store, half listening to the murmuring of confusion behind him, half pleading with God to save him from this nightmare.

"What happened?" a young girl asked as she drew to his side.

Nathan started to walk through the lot, curious as to what had crashed into the department store. An alarm wailed in the distance, no doubt the city's alert system in action. As Nathan drew closer to the crash site, he was able to see more clearly through the yellow haze. The sphere had collapsed the roof and two of the department store's four walls. The vessel—which is what Nathan assumed the sphere was—had to be at least six car lengths in diameter and four stories tall.

"Hey, man! Hey! Where are you going?" the young girl shouted from behind him.

Nathan suddenly stopped, something inside him warring with his inclination to get closer to the sphere. His stomach somersaulted, and he felt as if he was about to vomit, so he dropped to his knees and took a few deep breathes until the nausea finally passed.

The sphere lit up in a kaleidoscope of colors.

From where Nathan stood, which was only about fifteen car lengths from the building, the sphere looked to be formed from innumerable hexagonal panels. Half of the sphere rose up out of the destroyed department store, crudely mimicking Epcot. It would have been a surreal scene had Nathan not seen other, more outrageous things in the weeks since Legion had initially attacked Earth.

He stood, and the colorful array suddenly ceased, leaving the hexagonal plates shimmering black—the same material that formed Legion's original vessels. A sound like that of carbonation breaking free from a soda bottle hissed from the sphere. Each hexagonal plate burst away from the sphere at once, in perfect sync. From the openings the plates left behind, black capsules flew in every direction. Some soared hundreds of feet, crashing into the asphalt of the parking lot. Others disappeared behind buildings.

One of the pods crashed a few feet from Nathan, embedding the bottom half of itself into the asphalt, rumbling the ground under his feet. The pod's surface glimmered like all of Legion's machinations did. Nathan estimated the capsule to be at least seven feet high.

The front slid open, and a shadow crawled out.

Nathan recognized the creature at once—the human-shaped figure in black skin dotted with tiny elements of light, like the stars the sky once held, was the same as the creature that had tried to kill him in the gas station mart before angelic beings intervened.

Nathan stepped back as the creature struggled to stand on two feet. When its glowing blue eyes focused on Nathan, they widened, as if the creature, the otherworldly being, was surprised.

Nathan held tightly to the straps of his bag, unsure of which way to run.

The creature blinked, and the lights in the parking lot flickered and went out, leaving Nathan in darkness. He looked down toward his right wrist and saw the lines glowing a soft white, just enough to light up his immediate area.

"Human," the creature's raspy voice snarled. "You should have perished long ago. How are you still among the living? Why do you still breathe?"

Nathan refused to answer. His arm grew warm, and he noticed fire rise up from the mark on his wrist. *I can probably find my way back to the alley between the apartment buildings and get back to the main street of the city.*

"My kind should have destroyed you. I was told…we were told…that you had been annihilated."

"I'm alive and well."

The creature laughed. "So you think. You may be alive now, but you are not well. You are fooled into thinking you stand a chance against mighty Legion."

Behind the creature, behind its seven-foot-tall pod, Nathan spotted more pairs of cold blue eyes moving in the darkness.

He bolted toward the alley, using his wrist to light the way across the parking lot. When he reached the main street, still lit by the city's electricity, he ran south, hoping to find the crashed plane, the weapon rumored to kill immortals, and a friend or two.

CHAPTER 18

The steak tasted bland, but Scarlet managed to wash it down with wine in an attempt to enjoy the meal. Sitting across from her at the long, shiny, black metal table, Ryn ate. Scarlet watched him, trying to figure out how he did so without a mouth. She squinted toward the end of the table as he lifted his fork to his face. The food dissolved within his distortion field.

Her attempts to hold a conversation had failed. The table was so long, and he had chosen to sit at the very end, opposite her. She found it awkward to shout across the distance.

Servants brought them food in stages, just like at a five-star restaurant in her old world. Their dead eyes looked upon her like those of deceased fish that floated to the surface of a dark lake. Despite that, she found her desire to sate her sexual needs to be far greater than ever. Scarlet finished her meal and leaned back in the cushioned chair, staring up at the dazzling chandelier hanging above them. *Who created such a magnificent building?* she wondered, curious about the origins of the supernatural realm in which she found herself and of the Black Cathedral.

"Are you satisfied with your meal?" Ryn shouted.

"Yes," she answered in a loud tone.

"Good, good."

Silence ensued. Scarlet glanced down and noticed that the dark imprints on her arms were growing into shapes—ovals. She chose to ignore them. They didn't hurt, strangely enough, and they almost looked like tribal tattoos, which she wouldn't mind having decorate her bare flesh. She hadn't noticed the marks anywhere else on her body except her neck and ankles. She secretly wished some would show up on her lower back. That always enticed the men.

When Ryn finished eating, he escorted Scarlet back to her sleeping quarters.

"I enjoyed our meal together," he said as they approached the door to her room.

Scarlet said nothing, only nodded.

"Is something troubling you?"

She shrugged. "No, why?"

"I can sense that you are blocking me from something."

Her heart raced, but she kept her cool. "What do you mean?"

"Ever since you arrived here, you have been more than open with me. I've made it plain to see that I can read not your thoughts but your feelings. I can sense fear, courage, anxiety, sexual pangs. You have been filled with the first and latter of these the most. Anxiety sweeps in now and then, but I have yet to see true courage emanate from your being. Lately, though, I have sensed an influx of anxiety. This tells me you are worried about something. Something—or someone—is distressing you."

Scarlet did her best to keep thoughts of Olivia at bay. She didn't want to expose the girl just yet, if ever. "It's these marks," Scarlet said, thinking quickly. She showed Ryn the black ovals on her arms.

He reached out with his presence—again, she didn't see his arms move—and took hold of her wrists. She felt his stare burrow through her skin. "You are reaching your true potential. These are the marks of the Lover, and they will fully materialize once you've reached the apex of your gifting."

Scarlet breathed a sigh of relief. "Is there a way to hurry them along?" She didn't like not knowing exactly what they would turn into.

Ryn let go of her and shrugged. "They will adapt to your growing gifts."

"Okay."

"Is that all you've been worried about?"

She nodded.

"Very well. I must attend to other matters." He left.

Scarlet entered her room and shut the door behind her.

Olivia stood near the dresser.

"What are you doing in my room?"

Olivia pulled on Scarlet's arm, tugging her to the mirror. The girl forced Scarlet to look at her reflection. Black ovals—more prominent than before—marred the skin of her neck, and thin metal wiring weaved between strands of her hair. Though unusual and unexpected, the new additions to Scarlet's appearance didn't bother her. Quite the contrary. She found that the more adornments she collected, the more stunning and exotic her appearance.

"What are you trying to prove?" she asked Olivia.

"You're changing. You're transforming. You're falling."

"Stop speaking in riddles. It's annoying."

"The marks. They are marks of bondage. I saw them on another woman who showed up here long before you did."

Jealousy struck Scarlet like an arrow. "Another woman?"

Olivia nodded, running her fingers across Scarlet's wrist and arm. "She turned into—"

Scarlet pulled away from the girl. "I'm tired of your lies!"

"Lies? I'm the only one around here telling you the truth."

"Fuck you, you little pint-sized brat."

"What?"

"You heard me." Scarlet brushed her hair off her shoulders and adjusted the top of her black and red sleeveless dress to boost her cleavage. "I need you to leave now."

"I am now fully confident that I have done everything to help you, Cynthia."

"Scarlet! My name is Scarlet!"

"Your name is Cynthia Scarlet Ruin. An appropriate name for the path you've chosen."

Scarlet grabbed Olivia's arm and shook her. "What the hell do you know?"

Olivia pulled herself out of Scarlet's grip and took a step back, her eyebrows arched inward in anger. "This is your last chance to turn back! I've tried to warn you of my visions, but you've spit in my face at each attempt." The girl's eyes shimmered bright blue. "I need you to understand where you are. An extension of the Depths, in a cathedral made of sin. This is a place for demons and other spawn of Hell, not humans. Not any species."

Scarlet took a deep breath and calmed herself. "I am the princess of this cathedral. Of this kingdom."

"You are nothing but a puppet. You should never have come here. You should find a way out and take it."

"Why? My world is dying. Here, I have shelter, food, and as much...fun...as I want."

"Your fun is about to run out. Nothing comes without a price."

"My fun does. I think you need to leave. I order you to leave. Now!"

Olivia nodded. "Goodbye, Cynthia Scarlet Ruin." She

148

turned and left the room.

Scarlet stood there, her senses awakening to her desire to play. But something else snuck in—a sudden desire to please Ryn. He had become a guardian to her, taking her in, feeding her, sheltering her from the dark world she left behind. She felt loyalty rise up, and she realized what she would have to do to prove that loyalty to Ryn.

CHAPTER 19

Nathan went as far south as the main street would take him. When he realized he was approaching the south gate leading out of the city and into the dark valley beyond, he began to lose hope that he would find the plane. But then he passed a building blocking half the view of a taller building, and he found the crash site.

It's definitely a Vector ship, he thought. *It has the same stealth bomber design and black paint, similar to the ship Jasper, Hush, and Heather left Los Angeles in. It looks as if it crashed head-on into the fifteenth floor of the skyscraper, carving through the glass and building frame.* The back of the ship jetted out the side of the building like a splinter in a giant's finger.

He noticed, through glass windows still intact in the building, floors where lights illuminated the still-standing rooms. *The fact*, Nathan concluded, *that bodies have not been found is a good sign. The fact that the ship is still intact, and that the building hasn't come down, is a good sign as well.*

Quickly, he entered the tall office building through glass doors. The lobby was lit, yet void of people. *Probably in fear of the building collapsing.* Once at the elevator, Nathan pressed the call button, curious if it would work. To his lack of surprise, it didn't. He found the stairwell and started up toward the fifteenth floor.

Pacing his climb, Nathan traveled the concrete steps, lit by the dim lamps affixed to the walls of each floor, his memory replaying the trek he and his sister had taken up the burning Phoenix Summit building in Phoenix to search for his parents. As much as he wanted to grieve their deaths, he crammed the grief deep inside of him, deciding instead to cherish it, to wear it as a necklace—much like the ichthys he wore around his neck—to remember them by. If he couldn't have them in their physical form in this reality, he would cherish the memory of them and wait until the day he could see them again in Heaven.

He deliberately kept Pearl out of the equation, holding tightly to a shred of hope that she could very well return to his side.

Each step took him higher, until he finally reached the fifteenth floor. He opened the stairwell door and headed down the hallway. He passed a receptionist desk for the realty firm that took residence on the floor, and he burst through a set of double doors at the end of the hallway, entering a mess of cubicles and desks, all haphazardly strewn about due to the black ship pushing them aside.

He approached the aircraft—which was the size of a small private plane—and struggled to pull the door open. He heard glass bits crunch while sliding the door to the side. Nathan managed to open it wide enough to crawl inside the vessel. He found the interior of the ship warm and musty, and stinking of oil and smoke. Glass and burn marks covered its plush seats. Clearly, a fire had engulfed the cockpit and its instruments.

He didn't find anything significant, nor did he find evidence of Heather. Frustrated, he went over the interior of the ship again, looking for any clue, anything that could help point him in the direction he was supposed to go from here. He finally crawled out of the ship empty-handed.

Nathan wandered to the side of the building the ship had torn through. Cool air currents moved through the building's wound, sweeping the heat from his hair and face. He looked out on the streets below. Toward the other end of the city, he saw lights flicker and go out in one section. Then another.

Legion's forces must be advancing. If you want me to fight, God, I need something to fight with.

Your friend has it, God replied.

Has what? What friend? Heather? Where is she?!

No answer.

Nathan rushed into a nearby desk, sliding it toward the opening in the wall. It fell over the edge and tumbled down the side of the building. It hit the ground with a loud boom and broke into pieces.

He restrained the curse words approaching the tip of his tongue and instead poured that anger into raising his voice. "How am I supposed to do this?! How am I supposed to fight the enemy if I don't even have a weapon? Why do you send me to these places with no answers? Why do you allow me to fall into Legion's clutches all the time? Why do you allow my friends to die? Why?!"

Nathan fell to his knees as bitter tears poured down his cheeks. He didn't bother to wipe them, knowing more would come. And they kept coming.

"Is this where it ends?" he wailed, rocking on his knees as he watched darkness engulf the city in portions. "Why did you lead me here? Where is Heather?" He shouted his questions, aimed them directly at God, assuming he wouldn't receive an answer. He couldn't stand the riddles, the silence, the half-answers that made no sense until they came to fruition. It was too much.

He fell flat on the floor, images of his sister and his friends plaguing his mind, conjuring up memories like ghosts that haunted the deepest parts of him. He felt like a shell, like a vessel that floated through the world with no real direction, taking in more and more residents—ghosts—who wanted him to take them somewhere.

He knew that darkness was coming for him, that Legion wanted him dead and would stop at nothing to make that happen.

And then something gentle—someone's hand—grasped his shoulder and pulled him to his feet. His face was placed in the crook of a warm neck, and he felt solace there, tenderness— where everywhere else was only darkness and despair. The hand ran softly through his hair, massaging his skull with light caresses, and he fell at ease, at peace. He sobbed.

A melodious humming—a song he had heard before in church—vibrated pleasantly in his ears, sung by the girl who now embraced him: Heather. And that song, that hymn, pulled together his broken parts, healing his shattered spirit.

"Your mercy stirs my heart to sing, a melody I was taught in creation's womb,

Though the stars fall to the earth, and darkness plagues the land, Your love will remain,

The flowers of the field will sing Your praise, and all the world will dance for You.

You, oh Lord, give me light to battle the shadows,

You, oh Lord, give me healing with the pain,

You, oh Lord, give me shelter in the storm,

Oh Lord, I live to give glory to Your Name."

"I missed you," he whispered.

"I know," Heather whispered back. "I missed you, too."

He sank into her soothing voice for what seemed like decades before she stopped singing and they just stood, enjoying one another's embrace. He felt foolish briefly, but then realized he was now more whole than when he had first entered the city.

When he looked at Heather, he noticed—although it could have been his imagination—that she appeared more mature than when he had last seen her. Her face still looked full of youth, but her scars—the airbag burns from their tragic car accident—had buried themselves underneath layers of new skin. Her wounds weren't completely gone, but they had subsided enough so that Nathan almost didn't recognize her. Her beautiful green eyes sparkled, though not with youth but with heartache and the wisdom that comes with it. Her once shoulder-length brown hair—a few blonde streaks here and there—had been cut just above her neckline.

She wore a black skirted trench coat, black pants, and black boots. A black scarf wrapped around her neck like a shadowy boa constrictor. She smiled at Nathan. Not an immature, young girl sort of smile, but a smile that told him she was overflowing with confidence, with a plan. But he sensed she was also teetering on the edge of losing that confidence, of crashing and burning like the ship that sat before them.

"I'm glad you're alive," she said.

"Barely," he replied.

"I knew you'd come."

"How did you know I'd come here?"

She hesitated and then said, "God told me."

"Where is…what happened?"

She glanced at the ship behind her. "We crashed once we cleared Echo."

"You were there?"

She nodded. "We tried to join you, to help you with your sister, but we arrived too late. My plan was to circle the city until we could find a safe place—and time—to land. But something hit the right engine, and we went down here."

"We who?"

"Jasper and Hush."

"Where are they?"

"They were both with me up until a few hours ago. We were hiding out in another section of the city, but we were found out. I separated from them so we wouldn't all get caught."

"A bunch of us saw your ship go down. And then I was led—instructed, whatever—to come here."

Heather took a deep breath. "You and I have to fight, Nathan."

He remembered what the woman with blue eyes had told him would happen next. "The mayor told me the president is alive. She's about to set siege to this city."

Heather nodded. "We have no choice but to fight."

"We can run. Do you think there are SilverTech shuttles here? Do you—"

"Does it matter if there are?" Heather asked.

"We can leave the planet before the president's army reaches us."

"No, we can't."

"Why?"

"We have to defend this city, Nathan. That's what you and I have to do."

"What's so special about this city? Why is the president even wasting her time with it?"

"She knows you and I are here. She knows the last of the resistance is here."

"The last of the resistance? That's ridiculous! There are others out there. We can't be the only ones left."

"True. There are other survivors. But most of those still in the United States have either been captured by Legion—"

"You know about that?"

She nodded. "Most have either been captured by Legion or killed—or they're hiding in the sanctuary zones. Between the president's bombings, the creatures roaming the darkness, and Legion, not many are left. Before you arrived here, scores of people made the journey here, most on the tracks that run under the city and back around half the state of California.

"Once Daisy was executed…" She gave him a caring smile. "I'm sorry for your loss, Nathan. Once she was killed, most of those who were following the president couldn't stomach the president's regime. When she survived the sniper bullet—it terrified a lot of her supporters. It terrifies me. Anyway, they rose up against her, and most were killed. Those who weren't killed fled here. You see all these buildings? Most of them are filled to the brim with people."

"I didn't see that many people when I arrived."

"I know. There are a couple reasons for that. The city itself is an example of proactive tactic. The mayor was in a national paper a while ago for building the wall around the city."

I remember Ericka telling me something about that, Nathan thought.

Heather continued. "He knew an attack was coming. At

156

least he assumed it and prepared for it. I don't think he truly knew it would be from his own government. So he has a lot of the people in this city trained for an invasion.

"The other side of the coin is that many of those who fled the president's tyranny and came here for refuge aren't prepared for a fight. They don't know how to use weapons. They aren't accustomed to violence. That's the main reason they fled the president once she called everyone's bluff and killed your sister. Some of them are families, with children."

"What's going to happen to them when the president's army attacks the city?" Nathan asked.

"I haven't had a chance to speak with the mayor. But if I were in charge, I would send the families and those who can't—or don't know how to—fight into the valley to the south. Those who can fight can stay in the city and oppose the invading units. If worse comes to worse, we can move the defenseless from the valley to the mountains. That will at least give them a chance to hide. Although they won't last long out there without supplies. But this is worst-case scenario.

"The other problem," Heather continued, "is the type of enemy we are fighting. To be honest, we don't know what's going to come at the city. We know the president is sending her Brinks, but what else? If she's in line with Legion—which I don't doubt she is—there could be a lot more coming our way than just her army. Which brings us to another issue—many of our traditional weapons won't work on Legion. You and I know that firsthand. Sure, if those demons flood the city, we stand a chance against them. But not the Legion females or whatever the heck we were fighting against on our way to Los Angeles."

She had a point. A frightening point.

"We don't have much time, Nathan. Hush and Jasper are off on their own—maybe looking for something that can help us. But you and I can't just leave. We may be the only hope these people have. Me with my powers and you with *Shadowbanish*."

"*Shadowbanish*?"

Heather smiled. "Yes. It's a sword we believe can kill immortals."

Finally, an answer! "The sword has a name?"

She nodded. "And you're the only one who can wield it."

"What? Why? How do you even know that?"

"Those questions don't matter anymore. I hid the blade in the city. I'm sorry, but I had to. I couldn't risk getting caught and having it taken from me, not after everything we went through to get it."

Nathan glanced out the opening in the wall, his brain putting pieces of the larger puzzle together. *The president somehow knew I would be here. And I came here because God led me here. So I'm meant to fight with the sword against the president's forces. Whatever forces those may be. But the blade is said to kill immortals, so are Evanescence or others like her destined to show up? What about Chaos, the man in the red suit?* "How long do we have?" Nathan asked.

Heather pushed back the sleeve of her jacket and glanced at her pink Indiglo watch. "I don't know, to be honest. Right now, we should go get the blade. Once you have it, we'll stand a better chance against whatever is going to come at us."

Her gave her a half-hearted smile. "Can it really kill immortals?"

"I don't know much about the sword. I haven't seen it in use, and nobody has really explained to me its true potential.

But right now, we need to use all the cards we have. You're dealt this card, while I was dealt another—my powers—which I'll use to the best of my abilities."

Nathan's right wrist itched. He scratched it, then remembered the mark. He showed it to Heather. The lines were dark, but the circle sparkled faintly under the light. "I don't know what it is, but I think—"

Heather showed him her wrist. The same mark had been imprinted in her flesh. Her little circle sparkled faintly just like his did.

"What do you think it means?" he asked her.

"Remember the president's mark? The bar code? This is God's mark. It came to me after we crashed. The three of us went exploring in one of the lower floors of the building, where there was no light. I...I was scared. We all were to some degree. We were in the dark, wandering, lost. I called out for help..."

"And that's when the mark appeared," he finished. "And it cut through the darkness."

She nodded. "Yes. Jasper and Hush don't have one, though. I've seen some people here and there in the city with it, and others without it. I can't say for certain that everyone who follows God has it yet. It seemed to appear for me out of necessity."

"I was trapped in the darkness," Nathan said. "I had coffee with someone...the Infiltrator—that's what he called himself. He wanted me to trade with him."

"Trade what?"

Nathan's eyes stared off listlessly. "He said he'd send me back. Back to a time before the car accident. He'd let me have more time with my sister, with my family." His gaze turned back to Heather. "With you. He said he would do that if I just quit."

Heather put her hand on Nathan's shoulder and grinned, like

the way his sister used to when she was proud of him. "I'm glad you didn't give in. We can't afford to quit right now. Not when everything is at stake."

"I know. When I returned to this world, to the darkness, my mark appeared in a blaze of fire so that I could escape."

"Mine came in a melody."

"What?"

"A song. I heard a song playing around me—Jasper and Hush didn't seem to hear it—and while the song played, the mark slowly appeared in my wrist."

"No flames?"

Heather shook her head.

"So it appears in different ways for different people?"

She shrugged. "I don't really know much about it. But c'mon. We need to retrieve *Shadowbanish* before that darkness reaches us. I bet half the city is already in a panic."

"Not hardly." They both turned toward the voice, which originated behind them, near the door leading to the main hallway. A man stood there, shotgun in one hand, flashlight in the other. "You two brought them here, didn't you? You led Legion to Providence."

"Legion was already on its way here," Heather answered as she stepped in front of Nathan. "As is the president's army."

The man stepped toward them. Nathan dropped his pack to his left arm, ready to pull the gun from it. The man slid his flashlight into his back pocket and held his shotgun in both hands. "Not so fast, young one. Put your bag on the floor."

"No," Nathan replied, drawing his pistol from it. He slid the bag over his shoulder and pointed the gun at the man. "Back away and leave us alone."

"As soon as you entered our city, that thing came from the sky. The darkness will engulf this whole area, leaving us blind."

"It's Legion," Heather explained. "Do you want to sit here and argue about who led it here, or do you want us to help you rid the city of it?"

The man's gaze shifted from Heather to Nathan, then back to Heather. He lowered his gun. "We've taken too many precautions to protect this city."

"I understand that, but right now we need to fix this problem of the electricity going out. There's a siege about to take place on the city, and if we're left in the dark, we won't stand a chance."

"The Legion that crashed here is different," Nathan said. "It has the power to cut electricity. And like the rest of Legion I've come across, it can't be killed with regular weapons."

The man shifted his weight from his left foot to his right. "Then what are we supposed to fight them with?"

Nathan waited for Heather to reveal information about the sword. He didn't know anything about this city that Heather hadn't told him, and he didn't know if this man could be trusted. The man could be Legion for all Nathan knew, although he doubted it.

"We need to go," Heather finally answered the man. "You should make sure everyone has flashlights or candles or some source of light."

"Where are you going?" the man questioned. "You just gonna leave the city? Leave us all to die by the hand of the enemy you led here?"

"No, I'm going to find a way to save this city so it stands a decent chance at fighting the army that's coming." Heather took Nathan's hand and led him into the stairwell. But instead of traveling down—where Nathan assumed they were going—they went up.

161

Nathan listened for the stairwell door to open behind them, expecting the man with the shotgun to run in, firing on them. But nothing like that happened. In fact, Nathan didn't hear the stairwell door at all. Apparently, the man had decided to let them go.

As they approached the top floor of the building, Nathan stuck his gun back in his pack and followed Heather through an unlocked door leading into a darkened penthouse apartment. The only light they had was the light shining from their wrists. It lit up the bed—neatly made—and the dresser, which had been cleaned and organized with a collection of jewelry boxes on its surface. Heather led Nathan to the living area, toward long, black drapes. She pulled them back, revealing a sliding glass door. She unlocked and slid open the door, pulling Nathan out to the patio.

A rectangular pool stretched out before them—dark, murky water inside. "It's in there," she said, pointing toward the water.

"What?"

"The blade fragments, in a metal box at the bottom of the swimming pool."

"Why would you hide it in there? What if someone came up here?"

She shook her head, flipping a light switch on the patio wall. A white strand of Christmas lights flickered on around the patio alcove. "I found this place yesterday. Nobody bothers coming into this building. Even if they did, they wouldn't think to come straight up here. I don't know whose place it used to be, but she was female and had a good taste in jewelry and clothes." Heather spun around to show Nathan her skirted trench coat and scarf.

"Those were hers?"

Heather nodded. "Yes. Don't worry, the place is abandoned. I'm sure of it." She walked over to one of the alcove pillars and flipped another switch. A light burst on inside the swimming pool, piercing the cloudy water.

"What's in there?"

Heather shrugged. "I'm not sure. When I put the box of sword fragments in the pool, I found the water like that an hour later."

Nathan approached the edge of the swimming pool. He glanced out on the city, realizing they were on top of the tallest structure in the whole area. He could see the roofs—mostly abandoned—of all the other buildings.

"It's a nice view, huh?" Heather asked.

He watched darkness engulf the city, closing in on them like the flame on the end of a bomb's fuse.

Heather sighed. "Would you mind?"

Nathan followed her stare to the center of the pool. "Mind what?"

"Getting the sword?"

"I have to go in there?" He knelt and dipped his finger in the water. Ice cold. "You have to be kidding me."

"I'm not. Please, I don't…"

"Don't like the dark," he finished.

She gave him a fearful look.

"There isn't a net around?"

She shook her head. "I looked for one. And the water is at least eight feet deep."

He stared into the murky water, debating on jumping in. He couldn't do it in the clothes he wore—he would freeze. He'd have to strip down and leap in.

"We have to hurry this along, Nathan. The darkness is going to be here soon. As soon as the electricity goes off, you'll be jumping into a pool full of darkness. I'm not sure anyone would want to do that."

She's right. She's always right.

Nathan took off his backpack and jacket and set them on the ground. He took off his socks and boots, unbuttoned his pants, and warily slid them down. To his relief, Heather had her back toward him and was looking out at the city. He slid off his shirt and stood in his boxers. *I'd be better off just jumping in than being timid about it.* So he leaped in. The water hit his flesh like ice. He went under, refusing to open his eyes for fear of damage to them from the murk. He headed straight toward the bottom and felt around its surface for the box of blade fragments.

When his fingers felt what he thought might be a metal surface, he lifted the small box into his hand and rushed toward the surface. He crawled out of the pool and stood for a moment, dripping, clutching the box.

He felt soft hands touch his shoulders and move down his arms. He turned to find Heather close to him. "Uh...hi," he said.

She grinned, but he saw sadness in her eyes. "I..." she forced her hands to her sides. "I still love you, Nathan."

His heart pounded at her admission.

"I was mad at you for a season. Very mad. Angry, really, if there's a difference. Angry just sounds more mad. When you slept with Cynthia—"

"I don't want to talk about her."

"I know," Heather said. "I know. I know there wasn't

164

really anything going on between you two. I know she used her sexual wiles on you. That's not excusing you. I just...I've had lots of time to think, you know? I know you didn't do those things out of spite. I know you didn't *want* to hurt me."

"I didn't." The air between them grew thick.

"I've always loved you. That didn't go away when we were separated. It just...it just became solidified. More mature, I guess. And..." She reached out and took his hand. "I know you have Pearl," she put her hand on his chest, "in there. I wanted to be in there, you know? I wanted to have a place in your heart. But I know that place is for Pearl. Wherever she is. Whether or not she's coming back. I know she's in there now, and I don't want to upset that."

Nathan grabbed Heather's wrist. "There's a place in there for you too, you know? You and I may never be together—like that—but you're in here, in a different fashion than Pearl. I love you, Heather, in ways different than I love Pearl. In ways different than I loved my sister. But I love you."

Heather smiled, tears dripping down her cheeks.

"You and me. We're going to get through this, to—"

She drew closer to him, wrapping him in her arms. He felt warmth in her embrace. Warmth and love.

"I love you so much, you know?" she whispered. "I don't know if you'll ever really know how much I love you. Like a brother, like the man I wanted to marry, like the friend I would give my life for."

"Well, let's hope it never comes to that, huh? The giving your life part. We'll get through this. Then we'll find some way of getting off this planet."

"Together?"

He hugged her tighter. "Together."

She pulled away from him. "C'mon. Let's get you dressed and get that sword put together. The darkness is going to…" Her gaze wandered to a point behind him. He turned and watched the building across from them dim like a blown-out candle.

Nathan hurriedly dressed. He and Heather sat at the poolside table and opened the metal box. He found multiple shards of black steel and two pieces of a hilt contained in black velvet cutouts. He carefully pulled each item out, placing each shard—which felt light as feathers—on the surface of the table.

The lights suddenly went out, leaving Nathan and Heather in the glow of their wrists.

Nathan turned toward the penthouse. Through the sliding glass door, in the darkness, he caught sight of dancing blue marbles. Glowing eyes. The eyes of Legion.

We know your plans, Nathan Pierce of Earth. And you will not succeed.

CHAPTER 20

carlet stood before the mirror—the one the Mirror Man held for her—and carefully painted her eyelids with black eye shadow, thick as midnight. As she stared into her pupils, she noticed they shined like obsidian.

"Y-y-you are very b-beautiful, princess," the old man said.

"I know I am. Now hold that mirror still. You're trembling like a damn leaf."

"S-sorry your ma-majesty."

Scarlet finished applying her makeup and then puckered her lips at her reflection. "I'm finished."

The old man took the mirror and left the room. Scarlet sat on her throne, alone with her thoughts and the oval marks consuming her flesh. They were starting to itch.

The double doors at the end of Scarlet's throne room opened, and she watched Ryn make his way across the black carpet. When he reached the bottom steps of her throne, he waited.

"Come up here," Scarlet said. "I have something to report to you."

"You are mistaken if you believe you can give me orders. You will come down here. You will bow before me, and you will acknowledge me as your king."

Scarlet wanted to lash out at the man. *How dare he impugn my authority!* But she held her breath and stood, making her way down each step, cooling her temper completely by the time she reached him. She bowed halfway toward him, and something suddenly grabbed hold of her hair and pulled.

"Ah!" She toppled to the floor. Ryn kicked her in the side and then put his foot on her back, pressing her hard against the floor.

He held her there. Neither said anything for a while.

Finally, Scarlet spoke up, her voice cracking. "I'm sorry, Ryn. I just...I just got a little too comfortable in my position."

"Yes, that's always been your problem, hasn't it?"

"What?"

"What did you summon me here for? It better be important."

"I wanted to..." She second-guessed if she should tell him or not, but then decided to. "I wanted to reveal the traitor to you."

Ryn lifted his heel from her back and helped her to her feet. He had transformed into his female form, wearing the slender build of a woman dressed in black crow feathers. "My dear, you found the traitor?"

Scarlet nodded. Ryn put his hand on Scarlet's cheek and stroked it gently. "Who?"

"Olivia."

Ryn retracted his hand. "Olivia? She is mentally gone from this realm."

"She only wants you to think that. She told me herself. She's been attempting to find a way to destroy you. I've tried to talk reason into her, but it's pointless."

"My, my, my. A clever child, Olivia is. I never would have guessed she was faking, although it should have been plain to me. I tried so hard to bring her here, to rip secrets from her, but when she arrived, she feigned mental incapacity." Ryn looked at Scarlet, an evil crimson smile spreading across his angelic face. "I'll have to do something about this, won't I?"

Scarlet shrugged. "I don't know. I don't know if she's capable of harming you."

"I will see. Go back to your sleeping quarters. I want to give you a reprieve. Get some rest."

Scarlet wanted to ask him again about the marks forming on her, but Ryn was already walking away, transforming back into his male form as he headed toward the doors. *Besides,* Scarlet thought, *it doesn't matter what they are. I have given myself to him. He is the one I am loyal to. Not Olivia. Nobody but Ryn.* If the marks somehow proved that Scarlet was his property, she would be content with that.

She headed back to her sleeping quarters. When she arrived, she climbed into her bed and took refuge under the covers. She fell into a deep sleep, one she would never have woken from if she knew what awaited her.

Hours after betraying Olivia, Scarlet felt phantom hands caressing her cheek, and cool lips kissing her forehead. She refused to open her eyes at first, wondering how far this phantom assailant would go. Nothing went past the cheek caresses and the kiss. A tender kiss, one not filled with sexual lust but with compassion. Sadness.

When Scarlet did open her eyes, nobody was there with her. But she saw pages scattered across her room—pages from her awful biography. They had been ripped from the spine, torn from the base, which still sat on the edge of her nightstand. She stumbled out of bed, fumbling to pick up the pages. Her heart raced as she swept them from the floor, gathering them close to her chest, terrified at the thought of anyone getting their hands on them. These contained her darkest secrets, her darkest moments, and only she could know the deepest parts of her psyche.

When she gathered as many pages as she could find, she set them in a stack on top of her dresser, wondering who had done such a thing. When she picked up the spine, she found it had been emptied of all the pages. All but one.

It was that fateful day, within the Black Cathedral, that Cynthia Scarlet Ruin—or rather, Sin...or rather, Scarlet—realized exactly what she had agreed to give to the one she adored: Ryn, the man/woman who had taken her in and given her the desires of her heart. Unlimited sexual pleasure, a chance to best the achievements of her past, an opportunity to prove her loyalty.

Ryn was so proud of her. Proud of his fallen angel.

It was a shame that his fallen angel had passed from freedom and true royalty into bondage and depravity. And so, while the One who loved her the most pleaded with her to turn from her erroneous way, Scarlet fell...

The oval marks across Scarlet's arms and ankles and neck bubbled, blistered, and broke open, leaking thick black ooze across her skin. She fell to the bed, clutching her arms, hoping to rub the black substance away.

But it was no use.

Within seconds, the substance formed into physical chains, black links with the shimmer of new metal. They wrapped around her wrists, pulling her arms behind her back. They tangled around her ankles so she couldn't move her feet, and they twisted around her neck, cutting off some of her airway.

She forced herself to stay calm, to conserve her air and

not to panic. "What's happening?" she called out. "What are you doing?" she asked the Cathedral.

She heard no answer.

The chains grew longer, heavier, swarming her bed with metal. She felt the foundation of the bed creak, and then it collapsed to the floor with a loud boom. Chain links spilled all around her, and she felt her flesh pulling, ripping from her bones. She screamed, wasting precious oxygen as the chains around her neck tightened, cutting off her airway completely. As the room filled with interlocking metal loops—destroying the dresser and mirror, her nightstand, knocking over the pages of her life—she looked up at the violet canopy overhanging the bed and saw the words written there in white light: *It is not too late.*

Darkness filled her vision, and the Black Cathedral swallowed her whole.

CHAPTER 21

*W*e *know your plans, Nathan Pierce of Earth. And you will not succeed.*

Heather reached into Nathan's bag and grabbed his pistol. She fired three shots at the sliding glass door, shattering the glass with the second bullet. The Legion entity that stood there moments earlier had left, and now they were down three bullets.

As patiently as he could, Nathan took the gun from Heather's hands and stuck it back into his pack. "They can't be destroyed with guns."

Heather sunk into the poolside chair. "Sorry."

Nathan turned his attention to the sword fragments. "How does this go—"

Before he could finish, the pieces of blade began to rattle against the surface of the table. They slid against each other and interlocked, piece by piece, forming a short blade, the blade of *Shadowbanish*. The two hilt pieces joined with the blade—one a black metal cross guard, the other a black grip with rounded pommel. When the sword was complete, Nathan grabbed the handle with his right hand, lifting it with almost no effort at all.

Heather let air escape her lips. "It really is you," she whispered.

Nathan tilted the blade left, then right. The black metal had been etched with glowing white lines, lines that made symbols he hadn't seen when the sword was in fragments: an ichthys, an oak tree, a meteorite, and a coffin.

Symbols of his life.

"What is it?" Heather asked, moving around the table so she could see the blade up close.

"Nothing. It's just…these pictures on here…they're pictures of things from my life."

"All I see are straight lines in the blade."

That's weird. I wonder why, he thought. The sword felt comfortable in his hand, as if it was always meant to be there. *Will it do any good against Legion? If not, what is it good for—especially if Evanescence and Chaos refuse to make an appearance while the president and Legion attempt to destroy Providence?*

Heather started toward the penthouse.

"Where are you going?"

She turned but didn't stop. "We have to go. We have to get to the gate before the attack starts. You and I have a job to do now that you have the sword."

Nathan grabbed his bag and headed into the penthouse with Heather, her wrist light shining across the walls. "There's no sign of that thing in here," she said.

"I don't think it came to fight us. I think it's an advance party of some kind. Here to wipe out the lights."

Heather opened the dresser's top drawer and pulled out what looked like a black cloth. It was, in fact, a sheath. "I made this," she whispered, handing it to Nathan. "For *Shadowbanish*."

The sheath gave off the heavy scent of new leather. He slid *Shadowbanish* inside it. The fit was a little snug, but her estimate of how big the sword would be when assembled had been nearly perfect. "Thanks."

She reached out and took the sheath, turning it over in her hands. "It has a strap, so it can go on your back. With your bag."

She helped him take off the backpack and slide the sheath strap onto his shoulder. She then helped him put the backpack on over the sheath. The weight felt steady on his back.

Now I just need a holster for my gun, Nathan thought, *and my weapon ensemble will be complete.*

An alarm echoed throughout the city, startling him. It reminded him a tornado warning alarm.

"C'mon," Heather said. "We need to go."

They made their way back to the stairwell and headed all the way down. When they exited the building through the glass doors, they found the street full of people and flashlights. People flooded out of nearby buildings, most in an organized fashion. Nathan spotted some with wrist lights—the mark of God—that both he and Heather had, but not everyone had them. *I wonder what the mark really means.*

That you are mine, God answered.

"Yours?"

"What?" Heather asked.

"What?"

"Yours? What do you mean?"

"Never mind."

"C'mon." She pulled him through the crowd, toward the north gate. Smells of sweat and dust filled the street, clogging his nostrils. When Nathan and Heather were a few blocks from the gate, beams of bright white light coasted all along the street, reaching the north gate and slipping between the iron bars into the Broken Lands beyond. Nathan and Heather looked behind them—as did most of the crowd—to see where the light originated from. Large spotlights—the kind used to promote large city events—had been set up near the south end of the city, streams of light weaving in and out of the crowds of people.

The city had light again. At least a good portion of it.

Everyone in the crowd turned off their flashlights. Nathan was amazed at how organized the city seemed to be.

But then the true enormity of the situation rested on Nathan's shoulders. Looking around at the people, at each face, Nathan saw hundreds—possibly thousands—of people within the walls of Providence. And they were all united. United in one purpose—to dispel the president of her want for power over Providence. United against the darkness and Legion and any other forces that would dare to cross paths with them.

The bright glow of fire soared over the gate and struck one of the high-rises across the street from them. Chunks of brick and mortar crumbled to the street, injuring and maiming those caught underneath the debris. The building caught fire.

Nathan pulled Heather off the street into a nearby Laundromat.

"What was that?" Heather asked. They watched through the windows as the flaming building slowly fell apart.

"I don't know, but they're here."

Another flaming cluster—Nathan could tell it was a cluster of fiery wood—soared over the gate. This time it fell in the middle of the street, scorching a dozen people before anyone could react and get out of the way. Nathan watched as bodies dropped to the ground and rolled to avoid burning. Fellow city folk jumped in to help extinguish the flames of their fallen companions. As Nathan watched the destruction, he also watched a well-oiled machine.

The crowds moved faster and moved toward the sides of the street, realizing that the middle was too exposed, too vulnerable.

Whatever was shooting the flaming wooden boulders over the wall would have to be taken out soon, or the city would fall under flame alone.

Nathan grabbed Heather's hand, and they rushed toward the north gate. Another cluster shot over the wall but soared well past them, crashing into another building elsewhere in the city. *It's a good thing*, Nathan thought, *that the spotlights are at the far end of the city.* He realized that, ironically, even if the spotlights were taken out, the fire would keep the city aglow for a while.

They got within a block of the gate. Crowds of people filled that block. Many had weapons—guns and metal bars and sticks of wood, whatever they could get their hands on, but a good portion of them remained defenseless. Camouflaged soldiers stood post near the gates, keeping the crowds back and doing their best to keep whatever was on the other side out.

Flaming wood shot straight up from the other side of the gate and hurled down toward the block of people. Heather reached her hands out and erected a violet light shield over her, Nathan, and the rest of those around them. The wood hit the surface and disintegrated. As she dropped the shield, stares fell on her and Nathan.

A high-pitched screeching sound echoed from the iron gates ahead of them. Nathan peered through the crowd and spotted someone cutting through the iron bars from the outside.

"Stop him!" Nathan shouted to the soldiers as he grabbed Heather's hand and pulled her through the crowd. "Stop him! They're cutting through the fence!"

Another wooden fireball sailed over the wall, drowning his voice and capturing the attention of those around him. He didn't give Heather a chance to stop it, seeing how it sailed clear over the city. Instead, he yanked her arm, almost out of its socket, and dragged her through the crowd until they came out of the sea of people a few feet from the bars of the gate. They were too late. The creature—the Brink—holding the cutter was the same type of creature Nathan had seen back in Echo: thick armor, faceless helmet, tubes running from the helmet to the base of its spine.

"No," Nathan whispered.

The Brink dropped the cutter and stepped through the iron gate. Behind the creature, Nathan could only see darkness. But he knew—somehow—that in that darkness lay the city's destruction.

Soldiers opened fire on the creature. Bullets pierced the thick armor, and fluid leaked from wounds. But the Brink neither seemed phased by nor halted from the attack. Nathan reached back and drew the sword—*Shadowbanish*—from his back, wielding it in his hand as comfortably as he would a butter knife for his morning toast. It felt...organic, as if the sword was a part of him.

The Brink—and the soldiers—stared at Nathan. Well, Nathan could only assume the Brink stared through its faceless helmet. Whatever was happening behind that armor, Nathan knew that his drawing the sword had caused a reaction.

Small embers glowed in the darkness behind the armored Brink. Eyes. Red eyes. The eyes of a demon. Or dozens of demons. The Brink stepped back behind the iron gate, walking backward until it disappeared into darkness, leaking fluid as it went.

Demons moved forward, hunched over, teeth shimmering in the glow of the spotlights.

"Get back!" Nathan yelled.

The soldiers raised their guns as the demons leaped from the darkness into the city.

177

CHAPTER 22

athan swung the sword, splitting a demon in half. It fell to the ground in parts, blood running under his feet. Killing it had been so easy, like slicing through a banana with a finely sharpened butcher's knife. Only this was a demon and a sword. *Shadowbanish.*

Before Nathan could grow confident in his sword-wielding prowess, the demon swarm reached the crowd and filled a quarter of the block, forcing Nathan and Heather back into the crowd. Heather grabbed Nathan's arm and tugged him back farther, saying something he couldn't understand over the screams from the crowd.

Members of the crowd fired guns, swung weapons, and killed demons. Demons killed as well. Heather had her arms extended, erecting a shield over those in her general vicinity, but Nathan could tell the effort was taxing on her. Before Nathan knew it, Heather lowered her shield, and they returned to the Laundromat.

He slid *Shadowbanish* back into its sheath and pulled his backpack off, offering the pistol to Heather. She took the gun happily, saying, "We're going to need more weapons. At least I am."

"Do you know where there might be some around here?"

She pointed across the street. "The bank. They had security in there at one point. Should have some weapons—shotguns and pistols."

"Okay. How long can you shield these people?"

"Not long," she huffed. "I don't have an unlimited amount of power, but I can at least give some of them a chance to fight back."

When Heather and Nathan ran through the crowd, demons chased them, maneuvering through the mass of people. One leaped into the air to catch a ride on Heather's back, when a shot fired, splintering the demon into bloody chunks. Another demon lunged at Nathan's feet, grabbing his leg before another bullet took it out in a crimson mess.

Nathan glanced over his shoulder but saw nobody near them with a gun aimed toward them.

"A sniper," Heather said. "Building behind us, fourth-floor window."

They reached the front doors of the bank but found them locked. Screams from the crowd turned to grunts and growls. Gunshots rang out like firecrackers on the Fourth.

Nathan drew his sword and slammed its rounded pommel into the glass, shattering it. He and Heather stepped into the bank's lobby. Beyond the front desk stood large metal detectors. Beyond those, a number of desks. Heather led Nathan toward a door that said "SECURITY." Locked. Using the butt of her pistol, she destroyed the handle, and they entered a narrow hallway, which they lit up with their wrist lights.

The two found an unlocked room at the end of the hallway. Once inside, Nathan shut the door and lodged a chair underneath the handle to keep out intruders. Heather found lockers along one wall—most of them locked, although the ones that were open were empty. To avoid wasting more bullets, Nathan used the sword to destroy the combination knobs. The locker doors swung open lazily, revealing rows of shotguns and dozens of boxes of ammunition. Also inside were smoke bombs, tear gas canisters, and a couple of rectangular ballistic shields.

"I think we have what we need," Heather said, half joking. She loaded a shotgun and then dropped some boxes of ammo into Nathan's backpack. The extra weight added tension to his shoulders, but he quickly passed it aside to focus on what was happening in the city. He debated on taking a gun, but Heather handed him back his pistol, which he stuck in his bag—satisfied with that and *Shadowbanish*.

He moved the chair away from the door, and they made their way back down the hallway. They reached the end and opened the door to the main banking area, halting abruptly. Hordes of demons were pouring through the front doors of the building.

Nathan pushed Heather behind him and shut the door. "There are too many."

"We have to kill what we can," Heather answered. "And we need to get back outside and help the people hold the front gate."

Nathan thought for a moment. Then he ran back down the hall to the security room. He grabbed some of the smoke grenades from the lockers and then lifted one of the ballistic shields, just to see if he could make use of it. He found the shield too heavy to be helpful.

He ran into the hallway where Heather stood, her wrist light splashing white on the walls around her, and they returned to the door of the main bank lobby. He opened the door cautiously, pulled the pin on a smoke grenade, and tossed it into the middle of the room. Demons scurried across the tile, some sliding haphazardly, crashing into desks and décor. Others leaped onto light fixtures, watching Nathan with glowing eyes.

Smoke filled the room in a matter of seconds. Nathan rushed into the room swinging his blade, slicing through a half dozen demons before he had to stop and take a breath. *Shadowbanish*'s handle pulsed in his grip, as if the sword fed off the demon carnage, a heart inside of it beating for dark blood. Through the thick smoke, Nathan cut a path through the bank, killing demons as he went. Heather followed him, firing the shotgun, blowing demon innards around the room.

When they could see the front doors, Nathan realized they would have to go a different way. Demons filled the street—hundreds of them. People were fighting the creatures, but the swarm was too much. Nathan and Heather headed toward the bank's teller windows.

Demons were coming in through the vents, crashing out of the ceiling, flailing about. The smoke dissipated, leaving the creatures a clearer view of Nathan and Heather.

Nathan took Heather along the wall, toward the open vault. Then he realized what the demons were doing: cornering him and Heather.

Lacking choices, Nathan stopped in front of the vault, moving Heather behind him. Using *Shadowbanish*, he attacked, cutting down demons, splattering blood across walls and furniture, dismembering the pink creatures. He remembered the school—the little kid whose innards had been eaten by these disgusting abominations—and attacked with more fervor, swinging the blade in wide arcs, cutting down rows of demons as they leaped through the air, slid across the tile, and tried every which way to get at Nathan.

When one came too close, Heather's shield went up over her and Nathan, protecting them. The demons crowded closer to the two, pouring in from the street, from the vents, from every orifice in the building. They smashed windows, broke down doors, and seemed to fill the entire bank.

"I can't keep this up!" Heather shouted.

Nathan stopped for a second under her shield to catch his breath. He couldn't go much longer either, not at this pace. Demons piled up on top of the shield and slid down in a mockery of their attempts.

He had only one option. He sheathed *Shadowbanish* and grabbed hold of the vault door, pulling it with all of his might as it slowly moved toward Heather.

"What are you doing?"

He pulled the door shut and prayed the demons wouldn't figure out how to get inside.

CHAPTER 23

Nathan didn't know how much time had passed since he sealed himself and Heather inside the bank vault, but he knew it had been a while. They could hear nothing outside the vault. The thick door and walls kept all sounds—and the demons—out. He knew it was too risky to open the door. If the entire bank had filled with the filthy creatures, most would be waiting on the other side of the vault door. Waiting to feast on him and Heather.

He felt tired. Heather had already fallen asleep sitting beside him, her head resting on his shoulder, her wrist light glowing softly like a nightlight. Nathan looked down at his wrist, at the light spilling out the lines marked in his flesh, and tried to will the light to glow brighter or go out. Neither happened. *Does the light have a mind of its own, or does God actually control it?*

Nathan wanted to wake Heather but figured she probably needed the rest, especially after the crash of her Vector ship, and after her attempts to hide out in the city. For the moment, he decided to sit, rest, and pray that God would show them a way out of this mess.

He suddenly desired to venture into the mask...

This time he arrived in a white room on top of a bed. All around him, pieces suddenly came together to form a bedroom, dimly lit. The woman appeared underneath the covers to his right, leaning against a pillow, reading a book.

She bookmarked her page, shut the book, and set it on her

nightstand. "Do you get pleasure from other people's pain?" she asked.

"No."

"So you just drop in here whenever you want, with no regard for my privacy?"

"I'm stuck in a bank vault in our world. I just…I wanted to—"

She frowned. "That's why you came here? Because you're bored? I'm about to go to bed."

"Bed? You sleep here?"

"This is a world just like the one I was stolen from. Only here, I'm alone. There is nothing outside of this house, this prison Legion built for me. I'm trapped within these walls, with the fake family members who reside in the bedrooms of my memories. I sleep to make the time pass—to avoid the Tormentors, myself, and this world."

"I think there's a way out of this. I think God wants—"

She sat up straight, and her eyes lit up with rage. "You came here to preach to me? Really, kid? I already told you I'm not interested."

Nathan turned his wrist over and showed her the mark. "He's marking us. Making us His."

She glanced at his wrist but showed no visible reaction to the marks. "I don't give a shit. I. Don't. Care. Get that through your head. I have one request—destroy the mask. Give me freedom from this hell I'm stuck in. Please. If you love your God, you won't want to keep coming here to watch me suffer. I've suffered enough, and I'm asking you nicely—sincerely—to free me."

"What if I think you're going to go to Hell if I destroy the mask? Wouldn't it be my responsibility to prevent that and try to convince you to accept that God exists and that He wants—"

"Wants what? A relationship? Give me a break. Your responsibility is to respect my wishes. To stop visiting me like the Tormentors do. The last thing I want is more lectures and stories and speeches. I just want rest."

"What's your name?" he remembered to ask.

"What do you care?"

"Please, tell me your name."

"Margaret."

"I'm Nathan."

"I don't care. You have my mask. You have my soul in your hands. Just find a way to destroy the mask and free me. Please."

He struggled to form words, to make a compelling argument for her to receive salvation. Salvation from this prison. From the prison to come.

Tears rolled down her cheeks.

Nathan found himself back in the bank vault, the mask in his hands. Heather stirred for a few moments and then fell back to sleep. Nathan put the mask in his bag, still undecided about what he should do with it. *Destroying it would mean the end of the line for the woman—for Margaret. If I continue to visit her, she'll only continue to get angrier and angrier at me, not only for disturbing her privacy, but for preaching to her. Even though I don't think my actions comparable to preaching. Her soul is at stake—in my hands—and the decision I make regarding it will forever alter her future. For better or worse.*

He slowly and carefully took Legion's Machine out of his bag. Nobody knew he had it—other than Ginger, but he had no idea where she was. He missed her, but the odds of them crossing paths again were slim unless she had managed to make it to Providence herself.

The neon etchings on Legion's Machine illuminated part of the vault in a soft blue glow. *I wish I knew what this machine actually did. Is part of Viranda DelaCourte—the Legion rogue—inside it? Is it a machine that can be used to destroy Legion? If so, I have no idea how to work it.* He saw a button on the end but refused to push it, not knowing what it would do. *I wonder if the machine might be useful against the demon horde just outside the vault door.* It pained him to know he could be holding his and Heather's way out of this mess in his hands, but without the knowledge to work it.

Click.

Clack.

Click.

Clack.

Nathan shoved the machine in his bag and hurried to his feet, startling Heather in the process. He slid *Shadowbanish* from its sheath and moved toward the door.

"What's going on?" Heather asked as she rubbed the slumber from her eyes.

"Stay there," he whispered. "Someone is coming in."

The vault door opened, and a female's silhouette stood in the threshold, illuminated from behind by the burning buildings visible through the bank windows. Nathan tilted his wrist up and shined light on the figure.

Ginger stood there, her clothes bloodied, bruises along her cheekbone and arms, a smirk on her beautiful face, and a sniper rifle slung across her back underneath her pack.

"What are you doing here?" he asked, sheathing *Shadowbanish*. He noticed the demons had left. "What happened while we were in here?"

Without answering, she rushed toward him and wrapped him in a hug, just as Heather approached the two of them.

When Ginger pulled away, Nathan noticed Heather's crossed arms. "Who is this?" Heather asked.

"Ginger. She helped Macayle and me in Echo. We got separated in the Broken Lands."

Ginger reached her hand out to shake Heather's.

"Nice to meet you," Heather responded, shaking the girl's hand.

"Once we got separated, I found my way out of the darkness with this," Ginger said, showing Nathan the mark on her wrist. "And I followed the road here. I was the one sniping those demons off your back earlier. When I saw you run in here along with the hordes of demons—I waited. They left after they realized they couldn't get into the vault."

"What does it look like out there?" Nathan asked.

"The demons are running rampant. Everyone is fighting. That's about it. Those flaming balls keep getting shot over the wall. Some of the buildings are on fire. The north gate is still secure, and the south gate is still holding the line of spotlights. C'mon. Let's get you two out of here. I'm eager to jump in and kill a few more of those ugly things."

Nathan and Heather followed Ginger out of the vault and back onto the street. The scents of smoke and blood filled the air. A small portion of the city was on fire, but it wasn't enough to destroy Providence. Another flaming sphere coasted over the wall, slamming into another high-rise. This time, the fireball tumbled away from the building and fell to the ground below, catching a group of city folk fighting demons on fire.

"Has anyone been out there, beyond the wall?" Nathan

asked. "If we can stop whatever is shooting those things over the wall, we can save the city from being burned down."

"I asked one of those soldiers up by the north gate that same question," Ginger answered. "He said they don't have the manpower to head out there into the darkness. I believe them, too. But I agree: Something needs to be done."

Nathan drew *Shadowbanish* from its sheath. "I'm going out there. If you two want to come with me, I could use the help."

Heather clung to his side. "I'll protect you as best I can."

Ginger nodded. "I'll get to one of the higher windows and cover you."

Together, the three of them headed toward the north gate. When they reached it, they saw that someone had covered the breach in the iron fence with chicken wire. Nathan and Ginger worked the metal off, and all three of them slipped through, replacing the barrier behind them, as useless as it actually was.

The road leading out of the valley was void of everything but darkness. The three of them used the light pouring from their wrists and traveled the highway up to the top of the hill, only to find their worst nightmares realized.

The Dark Army spread before Nathan, Heather, and Ginger. Darkness retracted its hold on the land temporarily, through large moving pillars topped with massive stone bowls full of fire. As far as the threesome could see, as far as the horizon went, stood rows upon rows upon rows of the president's Brinks. Only now, Nathan got a hint that the Brinks had nothing to do with the president really. They were agents of evil—each in thick armor, a faceless helmet, and equipped with the strange tubes that Nathan could only guess contained their lifeblood. The creatures wielded no weapons, which Nathan found peculiar. They simply marched, the sound of their feet echoing through Nathan's ears like a drumbeat of doom.

In the midst of the army, the Brinks tugged along large, white egg capsules. Nathan didn't want to guess what those held. The large pillars holding massive bowls of fire stood parallel to each other, separated by yards, rolled along on carts with wheels. The pillars dotted the landscape all the way back to the horizon. Large trebuchets rose in their midst, though the ones Nathan could see looked empty of the wooden projectiles that had been shot into Providence.

At the front of everything, a glowing blue gem lit up the darkness. The necklace of a sorceress.

Nathan's heart fell into a dizzying spiral of despair. "We can't win this," he whispered.

Ginger gasped. "How did they get so many—so many of whatever those things are?"

"Nathan," Heather whispered, "we have to go back. If they spot us—"

The entire mass stopped moving all at once, in unison. The decrepit woman in rags, Evanescence, looked toward them. Nathan guessed at least a mile stood between his group and the army, but within seconds, Evanescence traversed the distance and appeared in front of them.

"Nathan. Heather. Ginger," the old woman said, her frail body clothed in a dark, ragged cloak. "Have you three crawled out of the city's walls to offer surrender?"

All three remained silent.

"What's the matter?" Evanescence asked, clutching the blue gem resting between her breasts. Her skin had turned an ugly shade of gray, and her fingers, clutching the gemstone, revealed a framework of jagged bone under a thin veil of what one might call flesh, but looked to Nathan more like translucent wax paper. "Did you not think we held such a grand army? I warned you," she looked at Nathan, "of the consequences of your actions. I warned you not to touch my daughter. I warned you that your world was going to perish. Did you think I was kidding?"

Nathan realized Evanescence was so close that if he drew *Shadowbanish* fast enough, he could cut through her. But he couldn't move. The fact that such a grand army existed— paired with the fact that it marched toward the gates of Providence—paralyzed him.

Evanescence clutched Nathan's chin with her rawboned fingers and moved her wretched face close to his. "This city is mine." Her breath reeked of rotting flesh. "I will destroy it. I will destroy everyone in it." She reached down and grasped his glowing wrist. "He has marked you, hasn't He? We knew He would. But it matters not." She dropped Nathan's wrist like she was letting go of a piece of trash. "He has abandoned your world. The proof is all around you." Before she pulled away, Nathan thought he saw maggots moving across her scalp, under the hood of her ragged cloak. The sorceress grinned at Heather and Ginger. "Go back to your city. Hide behind your pitiful defenses. We will be there shortly."

In the blink of an eye, Evanescence appeared once again at the head of the grand army, and the marching continued.

"Will *Shadowbanish* kill those things?" Ginger asked.

Paralyzed by fear, Nathan said nothing, only gawked at the approaching army.

Heather grabbed Nathan's arm, and they ran back to Providence with Ginger, back to the safety of the tall walls and the cover of the bright spotlights, as destruction marched toward them.

ricka and Marigold took another detour, this time into an abandoned check-cashing building. Marigold wasn't feeling well, and Ericka had no way of healing the wound in the woman's arm.

Marigold insisted on getting to the destination on her cell phone before Absolute found out she was accessing his satellite. She rested her head on the carpeted floor and closed her eyes. "Five minutes. Then we leave."

"You still haven't told me why my bracelet, which my dad gave me, is important to stopping Legion," Ericka pointed out.

"Coordinates. Absolute found coordinates to Legion's planet."

"Yeah. NASA knew where Legion's planet was long ago."

"No, these are *real* coordinates. The planet—it moves. If we can launch an attack—maybe nuclear—on that thing while we know where it is, we could destroy it. *Destroy* Legion."

"Save this planet," Ericka whispered.

"Maybe. It's worth a shot."

"What made you turn on Absolute? I thought you two were…were lovers."

Marigold's eyes opened, and she struggled to sit up against the wall. "He's gone too far with everything. He's more of a terrorist than he is a savior. And I'm not sure I still love him."

"I'm sorry."

"Whatever, I don't care. It's the end of the world, right? I have more important…Ah!" She cradled her arm. "I have more important things to worry about."

"We need to find a doctor."

"No. We have to get to the dot on that phone."

Ericka glanced down at the cell phone and realized they were only about a half mile from their intended destination. "Where are we going?"

"A house. A scientist…he can help us get the coordinates of Legion's planet to the right people. People who don't trust the president."

"Do you think this scientist can heal you? You're not going to last much longer."

"I'll last as long as I need to." Marigold put her good palm to the wall and tried to pull herself to her feet. She did so, but then slid down the wall. Ericka caught her before she hit the floor, and helped steady her on her feet.

They headed out of the check-cashing building and continued down the barren street. *I'm so glad there's still electricity in this area and that the street lamps are still able to illuminate the dark road*, Ericka thought. *Otherwise, we'd be in big trouble.*

The red dot on the cell phone led them into a residential community called Station's End. Their destination, 2348 Smokestack Way, turned out to be a one-story brick house nestled between a pair of two-story homes. Looking at the house, Ericka got the feeling that something about it was out of place. She noticed it was the only house in the neighborhood made of red brick. The rest of the homes on the block had been stuccoed and painted tan.

The women followed the cement walkway to the front door. Marigold went to knock but tripped on the welcome mat, barely catching her fall. So Ericka knocked. Minutes passed with no answer. The women took turns knocking some more.

Finally, the door opened a crack, and a young man with glasses peered out. "Can I help you?"

"She needs medical attention," Ericka said, "and apparently, there's information on this bracelet that can help you."

The man opened the door wider and examined the bracelet's four-leaf clovers. Black machine grease covered his hands. His thick fingers fumbled with the bracelet, but Ericka found his touch rather comforting. *It must be because the world is becoming a dark, lonely place that any type of innocent human interaction seems welcome.*

He moved his long brown bangs away from his eyes and looked straight into Ericka's before taking a good look at Marigold. "You're the reporter, Ericka Shane. And you're the girl who opposed the president on television."

Marigold's eyes fluttered, and she collapsed in Ericka's arms.

"I can take care of her in here," he said, opening the door wider.

Ericka entered the house backward, dragging Marigold's unconscious body in tow. The man closed the door behind them. The scent of teriyaki wafted from the kitchen to their right. The man helped Ericka down the hallway to their left, and then they descended a set of stairs to the basement. The man helped Ericka carry Marigold down the cement steps.

At the bottom, a pool table stood under triangular lights. It looked as if a game hadn't been played in months with dust caking the balls and the table's velvety surface.

"This way," he said, helping Ericka carry Marigold down another hallway and into a back bedroom.

Ericka felt leery venturing this deeply into a stranger's home. *He hasn't even had the courtesy to introduce himself. For all I know, he could be working with Absolute—or worse, the president. But I don't have time to waste on paranoia and superstition.*

Once inside the bedroom, the man directed Ericka to lay Marigold on the floor while he shut the door and reached over to a black filing cabinet, pulling open the third drawer. A doorway popped open in the surface of the wall.

They picked Marigold up, and the man took them through the new doorway down a very narrow spiral staircase into a machine shop cluttered with scrap metal, electronics, and what looked to Ericka like junk. The room stunk of oil and grease and reminded Ericka of the times she and her father tinkered with her mother's car to get it to run properly. It never did.

The young man led them to his workbench, on which rested a large metal ring covered in grease. They set Marigold on the floor, letting Ericka rest her arms. On the floor to the right of the workbench sat a small platform over which hovered a pillar of large metal rings, each about five feet wide. A large gap had been cut in the front of each ring so a person could walk into the center of the pillar and stand on the platform.

A small laptop graced the only clean spot on the workbench. Scrap metal, screws, nuts, bolts, tools, and other miscellaneous things Ericka didn't recognize cluttered the rest of the surface. Along the back wall of the workbench hung hundreds of photographs depicting various locations around the world.

"What is all this?"

The man sat on the stool near the workbench and held his hand out. "May I see the bracelet?"

Ericka hesitated. He reached over, grabbed her wrist, and unclasped the band. Setting it on his workbench, he popped open one of the bracelet links and stuck a thin wire into it. Then he typed in commands on his computer. The monitor screen filled with text. He scanned the words and then sighed. "Nothing I didn't already know," he mumbled.

"What?"

He unplugged the bracelet and handed it back to Ericka. "Junk. I already had all of this information in my own systems. Most of which I gathered from...well, I guess that's a long story."

"What? Look, can we get some help for my friend here?"

"Ah, yes," he said, adjusting his glasses so they weren't teetering on the edge of his nose. He helped Ericka carry Marigold to a metal table that resembled a gurney, and they laid her down on it. The young man pulled Marigold's jacket open, grabbed the front of her blouse, and ripped it apart, buttons flying across the room. He unfastened the tourniquet.

"What are you doing?"

He ignored Ericka's question, undoing Marigold's bra. He slipped her jacket and shirt off her arms and started working on her pants, sliding those off—*quite vigorously*, Ericka thought—and then pulled Marigold's underwear off without hesitation. Ericka stood and watched. She didn't get the feeling this guy was going to rape Marigold. *If he was, wouldn't he want her awake for it? Unless he's one of* those *people.* Marigold's arm wound looked gruesome— puffy, black and blue with blood oozing out. It looked like the bullet had gone clean through.

The young man turned and started typing commands into a small touchscreen panel which was affixed to the end of the gurney. Ericka noticed then that the gurney was really a machine of some sort. A metal bar extended from the side of the gurney and retracted over Marigold's head. Then a violet light shined from the bar, and the extension started to travel the length of Marigold's body, shining the light across her form and humming loudly. "There. Happy?" the young man asked.

"What do you mean am I happy? She was going to die."

The young man went back to his workbench and started tinkering with the metal ring.

"What are you doing? We came all this way to give you the bracelet. Marigold almost died. Not to mention—"

"She's not your friend. You didn't call her friend just now; you called her by her name. Marigold. So if she's not your friend, it means she is someone who was an enemy but whom you've taken into your graces to care for. If she was just an acquaintance, I'm not certain you'd be willing to walk for miles with her falling apart like she is."

"What does that have to do with anything?"

"It has to do with everything. She's not your friend. She's your enemy. But you're keeping her close because she has you convinced you two can do something about everything that's gone wrong in the world in the last few weeks. Well, you can't. Not really. Not now anyway. But maybe later." He moved the ring to the pillar of other rings and carefully placed it on top. It locked into place. He rubbed his palms together and smiled. "Done."

"With what?"

"Our ticket out of here."

"Our?"

"Indeed. You want to get out of here, right?"

"Out of this house?"

"No. Off this planet."

"You didn't really give me your name, you know?"

He typed commands into his laptop, and the pillar of rings hummed. Smoke poured out the base, but the young man smiled nonetheless. Minutes went by, and then the rings began to spin around counterclockwise. An array of bright, colorful light filled the middle of the rings. The man typed something into the laptop, and the light vanished, the smoke stopped, and the rings slowed down.

"What is that?"

"A teleport machine."

"Teleport?"

"Yes. Like in Star Trek."

She looked at him blankly.

"Stargate, maybe?"

She sighed.

"Okay, well, whatever. You'll see it in action soon. Once your friend is healed. Probably in a few minutes."

"I don't understand what's going on."

"You don't really need to. Do you trust me?"

"No. As a matter of fact, I don't. I never trust a man whose name I don't know."

"What about a woman whose name you don't know?"

"Well, I guess—"

"That's a trick question. I couldn't care less whom you trust or how you trust or any of that. Look, my name is Samuel Grey. To make things short and to a point you can comprehend, my grandson from the future—well, not our future now, but another future—came back to this time and mailed me a letter about things to come. Well, things to come in the future he came from." Samuel mumbled to himself. "Well, that future is gone now, but our future is still here, and that's the one he wanted to change by coming back from his future and..." He glanced up at Ericka. "Sorry, it would be hard trying to make you understand all of this."

"I don't understand any of it. Your grandson is a time traveler? You really expect me to believe that?"

"Doesn't matter if you believe it or not. Your friend is going to be healed. Then we're going to pack up some rations and take this teleporter to Mr. Silver's lab in Providence. There's a shuttle there that we can take to get off this planet."

"Mr. Silver? From SilverTech Industries? You think we're going to get away with taking his shuttle?"

"We have to. My future grandson sent me schematics for this teleport machine—a much smaller version than Mr. Silver's. I've spent the last couple weeks building it. And since my grandson also sent me the coordinates to Mr. Silver's teleporter in Providence—well, you can put two and two together."

"What about the coordinates to Legion's planet?"

Samuel typed commands into his laptop again, and a screen came up with a diagram of the universe. He pointed to one location. "This is where Legion's planet, Atrum, was, in the Orbis Galaxy, when Legion's vessels fell. Now? Nobody knows. The planet actually moves. It's a living entity. Probably the core of Legion's existence."

The machine scanning Marigold stopped humming. Samuel started toward her.

"What is she going to wear now that you ripped her shirt?"

"I'm not interested in either of you that way."

Ericka scoffed.

"Please, I'm not meaning that as an insult. I'm simply a man of science. Absorbed by the theories of existence and relativity and—well, you don't understand, so I won't get into it." He approached the computer near the healing machine and typed in some commands. The moving bar stopped, and Ericka saw that Marigold's wounds had completely healed.

"How is that possible?" Ericka asked.

"Some of SilverTech's technology. I simply borrowed his design and made my own." Samuel reached down and broke a capsule open underneath Marigold's nose. She jolted awake.

When she realized he was there, standing over her naked flesh, she crossed her arms over herself and screamed. Samuel shook his head and went back to his workbench.

"What the fuck?" Marigold shouted.

"Calm down," Ericka said. "His machine healed your wounds."

Marigold examined her arm. "How?"

"I don't know."

"C'mon, ladies." Samuel motioned to a refrigerator in the corner of the room. "I put some bags in there with rations in them. Get them out, and let's get going. That shuttle isn't going to stick around forever."

"Shuttle?" Marigold asked, picking up her undergarments, jacket, and jeans from the floor. "What the hell happened to my shirt?"

Samuel waved her away. "There are shirts on that shelf over there. They might be a little dusty, but they'll fit you."

Marigold fumed. "The next time you try to heal me, how about being a little more careful with my clothes? It's not like I come across a gold mine of fitting clothes every day!"

Ericka went to the workbench, watching as Samuel typed furiously into the laptop. "I still don't understand this whole time-traveling thing you keep talking about."

"But you're curious, aren't you?"

"Yes."

"My future grandson traveled here from an alternate future. In that future, Legion succeeds in destroying Earth and then, later on down the line, destroying Anaisha. There are heroes on Anaisha called the Lazerblades—a bunch of teens who think they can save the world—and they end up dying—correction, most of them die—in the alternate future, yet they are the only ones truly capable of destroying Legion once and for all.

"So, in order to save our future—our humanity—my grandson returned here to our time, got a job at SilverTech Industries, and gave his technology to SilverTech to develop pulse weaponry, which will help us defend ourselves against Legion in the future. That technology has already been transferred to Anaisha, so at the very least, my grandson achieved his primary goal.

"On top of that, he also sent me a letter explaining all of this and giving me much of Mr. Silver's research documents, which include NASA's coordinates of Legion's planet. That's how I already knew what the coordinates were. My grandson's data has helped me devise special algorithms to determine Legion's location anywhere in the universe. But even using it, I can't seem to find Legion's current location...outside of Earth, of course. I was hoping your bracelet—with the information Absolute hid on it—had Legion's current coordinates. No such luck. It almost seems as if Legion's planet has completely disappeared off the star maps altogether. But that would be highly improbable."

Ericka stared at Samuel while Marigold took one of the dusty, black shirts off the shelf and slid it on over her head.

"Anyway, humanity doesn't stand a chance against Legion right now," Samuel continued. "Our president, corrupt as she was, was one of our weakest links. She allowed Legion, or whomever her dark advisor is connected with, to take control of her puppet strings and steer all of us into our own destruction. None of the world's other countries have had much luck defending themselves against Legion either. So it's time to leave. I'll take my algorithms with me, and I'll do what I can to increase our chances of destroying Legion once and for all, even if it's years from now."

"Our future?" Ericka asked. "Why don't we fight back right now?"

"Don't you listen? We don't stand a chance. Do you want the last of the human species to go down fighting a pointless battle?"

Marigold approached them, knapsacks in hand. "He's right. We don't stand a chance right now. We should hit that shuttle and get to Anaisha. We can rebuild. Give our future a chance."

Ericka sighed. She didn't want to hear that solution to everything, but it made sense.

"There are others," Samuel said, cleaning his glasses with a washcloth, unveiling his soft gray eyes. "There are powerful others who will populate our future and do a fine job of making sure Legion's reign comes to an end. Until then, we need to preserve our species. That's our part in all of this."

Marigold handed Ericka one of the knapsacks. Ericka took it and strapped it over her shoulders.

"Let's go," Samuel said, typing commands into the laptop. He picked up a black satchel from underneath the workbench and slid it over his shoulder. "I set it so that once you step into the machine, it will start the rings and teleport you to the lab. I'm not sure what's going to be over there, so keep your eyes peeled."

"Why would you want to bring us of all people with you?" Ericka asked. "You don't really even know us."

"The journey to Anaisha is going to be a long one. And that's if we can get off this planet in one piece. Companionship is a commodity many take for granted. It seems the three of us can get along with each other just fine, so why not stick together? Besides, once we get to Anaisha, I'll need your help securing our future." He motioned for Ericka to step into the machine. "I'll be the last to go," he said. "I have a self-destruct sequence I want to initiate."

Ericka stood on the platform. "You don't want to bring any of this with us?"

He patted his satchel. "No. I have everything I need in here. I can rebuild anything you see in this place with simple metal and wiring. And maybe a little plutonium."

"Plutonium?" Ericka asked as the rings began to spin.

She felt her insides twist outward, and then she blacked out.

CHAPTER 25

Nathan did his best to keep his cool as he explained to the mayor of Providence, once again, the forces they were up against, hoping the man would initiate the plan that Nathan, Heather, and Ginger had suggested regarding moving the citizens of Providence to safety in the foothills.

"No," the mayor said again as he stood from his desk and folded his hands behind him. "I won't surrender. I don't care how great the army out there is. This city was built with an attack in mind, and I have other tricks up my sleeve."

"You don't get it," Nathan said between gnashed teeth. "We can't win against whatever is out there. We need to draw back, into the valley, and then start moving those who can't fight into the foothills. If we can get over the mountain range, we—"

"There is nothing for anybody on the other side of that range, Nathan. Another town or two, but nowhere that will provide the defenses this city has. We have to stand and fight. That's what I intend to do."

"That's fine that *you* intend to do that," Heather growled, "but what about those who can't defend themselves?"

"Look, I just received confirmation that the demon horde that swept through here has been obliterated. We won their first round. And we'll win the subsequent rounds as well."

"You got lucky," Nathan said. "And how many died in that first round? Didn't you hear us when we told you what's out there? That army is innumerable. The Great Witch is leading it, and they have those giant things of fire, which I'm assuming they intend to drop on the city. If that happens, this whole place will burn."

He waved Nathan away. "I'm not listening to any more of your pessimism. My job is to ensure the advance of that army ends here in Providence. I will do what I must to make sure that happens. Now, the rest of the city knows not to go beyond the north gate, to wait until the president's forces breach it. I hope you decide to be just as prudent. But if not, it's you at risk, not my city. Now, leave my office."

Nathan slammed his fists on the desk. "No! Don't you understand what's going to happen? They're going to march straight through your walls! They're going—"

The door opened, and the two soldiers in camouflage stepped in. "C'mon, kids. Get out of here."

Nathan took a deep breath and straightened up. It took everything in him to bite his tongue and stop the many comments in his mind from reaching his mouth. He, Heather, and Ginger left the office and were escorted outside, near the north gate.

"What do we do now?" Ginger asked. "The three of us could maybe take out small sections of their offense. But we'll be overrun within the first hour."

"My shields will only last so long," Heather added. "I could protect the two of you for half the time I could protect one. And that doesn't include protecting myself."

Nathan mentally kicked himself for not taking the chance to cut Evanescence down when he had it. *I may never get that chance again.* People crowded around the threesome in front of the north gate, waiting for a fight, not realizing—or not caring—that they would be destroyed in the next wave, if not the one after that.

God, what do we do?

Silence.

Parts of the city burned, casting a harsh orange glow over the street.

Fire.

"That's it," Nathan whispered.

"What's it?" Heather asked.

"Fire. The demons. Those creatures. They hate fire."

"That's right," Heather said.

"So?" Ginger said sarcastically. "They're sure okay handling it."

"Yes, when they control it. But what if we took that control away from them?"

"Set the city on fire," Heather stated, apparently aware of where Nathan was going with his thought process.

"That's crazy," Ginger laughed. "But I guess it kind of makes sense. And it's better than leading all these people to the slaughter."

Nathan glanced up at the high-rises flanking the north gate. "We could set those on fire. It would keep some of the army at bay."

"But to what end?" Heather asked. "I like your plan, but what is it going to do for us? We'll just buy more time. Time for what?"

"You and Ginger can get these people into the valley. While I go after Evanescence."

Heather glared at him. "Are you insane?"

"No. This is what I have to do. You said it yourself. I'm the only one who can wield *Shadowbanish*. And if it can kill immortals, that means I can kill Evanescence. She's the one leading the army. I wonder if I strike her down if it might stop their advance. If only temporarily, then so be it. You and Ginger can do your best to convince these people—at the very least those who aren't able to defend themselves—to fall back. I have a feeling most of them are at the south end of the city by now anyway."

Heather grabbed his arm, but before she could protest his actions, he took her hand off his arm and set it at her side. "I have to do this. If I can kill her—or at least wound her badly—it may turn the tide."

"You'll need my help," she whispered.

"These people need your help more. It'll take the both of you to convince them to draw back. When I'm finished…when she's dead, I'll return here and fall back with all of you."

Heather nodded reluctantly.

Ginger touched his arm. "Be careful. Who knows what tricks she has up her sleeves?"

"You two get started on setting these buildings—and maybe even the gate—on fire. It should hold the army back long enough for you to convince the city to retreat."

Heather and Ginger both wrapped him in a hug. He closed his eyes and imagined he was back home, with Heather and his sister and the rest of his family. The girls pulled away, and Nathan made sure his sheath and backpack were tight on his back before the group split up. Ginger and Heather headed toward opposite sides of the north gate to the skyscrapers while he bent back the chicken wire over the gate.

He glanced back at the mingling crowd. Everyone had their weapons at the ready, looking for a fight. He felt confident that if anyone could convince them to pull back, it would be Heather and Ginger.

With that settled, Nathan took a deep breath, *God help me*, and exited Providence.

CHAPTER 26

The air around Nathan felt unsettled. Charged. Full of electricity and evil and the end of things. When he had imagined the end of the world or the apocalypse in the past, none of this had ever come to mind. He always supposed the world—at least the United States—would be destroyed in a nuclear attack. Or Jesus would come down and wave His hand, destroying evil, chaining Satan in the thousand-year box, and taking Nathan and other Christians to Heaven to reside for all eternity. That scenario, though, he admitted, seemed less likely than all others, not because it seemed unbelievable—he had read something in that regard in the Bible—but because it didn't involve a fight, or pain, or any type of destruction.

What's war if it doesn't involve fighting? Or death? Or destruction on some level? It's no war at all.

Nathan debated on even dubbing this a war. *This is more like a hostile takeover, planned by different factions coming together for one purpose—to destroy the human species. Genocide.*

As he trudged up the hill, leaving the valley and Providence behind, he thought of the weight he carried on his back. *Shadowbanish* weighed next to nothing, but he still felt it against his back, beneath the weight of his backpack.

And it was inside that bag that he carried the most weight.

A pocket watch, previously owned by a man who took responsibility for Nathan, much like his own father had when he was alive.

A mask containing the lost soul of a woman named Margaret.

A woman who would rather die and vanish into what she thought would be nothingness than accept the love of a God who wanted to save her from her torturous prison.

Legion's Machine. A mysterious piece of technology from an alien race. It was a shame Nathan had no idea what it did or how to use it.

The beginning of a chronicle of Earth's last days. Something his children and his children's children could all read together some day. It would be, by far, the most interesting story he would probably ever read to them in their lives.

He also carried his past with him. The memory of those who had died—his sister, his parents, Macayle, and anyone he used to know who had been caught in Legion's invasion—and Cynthia, the woman he had given fragments of his innocence to. The memories all went with him toward the hilltop, traveled with him to face off against evil's dark messenger. Against Satan's dark lieutenant, Evanescence.

When he reached the top of the hill, a horde of demons approached him. He drew *Shadowbanish* and cut through the first half dozen within seconds, spraying blood and entrails across the road. The rest of the horde charged directly at him. He knelt, sword in hand, ready to fight. The first three went down easily. Two others flanked him and managed to get claws into his cheek and arm before he dispatched them. A dozen more tried to dog-pile him, but he spun around, blade out, and cut through them like a propeller blade would. He felt as a ballerina must feel, spinning and moving with grace, speed, and accuracy, his blade an instrument of death, a shield to those in the city behind him. He cut through dozens and dozens of demons, his face coated in demon blood, his arms covered by the insides of Hell's lowest denominators.

He fought with ease, swinging *Shadowbanish* as if it were an extension of his arm and hand. It responded quicker than his instinct, cutting and slicing through the air with precision and purpose.

It felt like a half hour had passed, but Nathan realized it had only been minutes before he finally stopped, took a breath, and saw that he had murdered the entire advancing horde. Yards in front of him, Evanescence stood, staring, her cerulean eyes piercing him with their gaze. Behind her stood the grand army, the weaponless Brinks—some carrying white egg capsules, some helping the fiery pillars along. Everything had stopped moving, and silence filled the air—except for Nathan's huffing to catch his breath. His lungs burned, and his side cramped with pain. But he still held *Shadowbanish* confidently, as if it were a good friend accompanying him on his crusade.

Nathan turned to see that Heather and Ginger had accomplished their goal. The buildings closest to the north gate had caught fire, as had the wall in which the gate sat. *We stand a chance now*, he thought. *At least a chance to save those who can't fight.*

He turned back toward the army.

Evanescence stood just outside *Shadowbanish*'s reach. "Dear child, you have to stop this. You think you are giving people hope, but all you are really doing is postponing the inevitable." She thrust her hands out, striking him with a gust of air that knocked him backward and cast *Shadowbanish* from his hands. He tumbled over demon entrails and crashed into the asphalt of the main road.

He heard not marching, but stomping. He looked up to see a group of Brinks charging toward him. He scrambled to his feet, his eyes searching frantically for *Shadowbanish*. He spotted the sword not more than a few feet from him, but the Brinks were already on him. He dodged the first one, evading it only to run into another. The second grabbed him in its beefy hands as another grabbed his bag and ripped one of its straps, pulling the bag off his shoulders. The Brink unzipped the bag and spilled the contents out across the asphalt.

Nathan felt a fist hit him point blank in the face, nearly breaking his nose.

More hands grabbed hold of him, pulling his arms, his legs, even his head. Tugging, pulling, yanking. He screamed, but his voice caught in the darkness, stripped of its familiar tone. Another punch to the face, and then a kick to his abdomen caused him to lose the contents of his stomach. The Brinks backed away, letting him catch his breath.

Evanescence stood over him. "Surrender, and I'll spare you your pathetic life. For now."

"No." This time, Nathan did not hesitate. He had *Shadowbanish* off the ground and in his hands before Evanescence knew what was happening. He thrust the sword into her chest quickly, but the blade refused to go through the woman's flesh. Her necklace, the blue gemstone, kept the blade at bay with an impenetrable force field.

When he pulled the sword back, she smiled a knowing smile. "You thought it would be so easy, didn't you?"

His side flooded with pain. He glanced down and saw her hand gripping a small dagger that she had slid into his abdomen. "You really thought you could come here and kill me with that fiendish sword, didn't you? I'll attribute some of that ignorance to your youth." She twisted the blade, and he felt his insides tear. When she pulled it out, he swayed, fighting to keep his balance, and then fell to the ground.

Evanescence knelt beside him. "You humans detest me. You think you're better than immortals? You think you have weapons that can destroy us? Gods that can ruin us? Who do you think you are? Who do you think I am?" She stood and looked out on the burning city. "Your little trick may have bought you a smidgen of time, but that is all. We will still march through those gates.

"Finish him," she told the Brinks. "Then we march into Providence."

The sorceress walked away. Brinks circled Nathan, mighty hands ready to crush him into dust. Blood oozed from his side, the pain growing. He didn't know if she had stabbed him in a vital organ or not, but he was sure he would die from the blood loss soon anyway.

He clutched *Shadowbanish* tighter, ready to fight to the end. He used the sword as a crutch and slowly got to his feet. One of the Brinks charged at him. He swung the sword sloppily and managed to strike the creature in the chest. The sword refused to penetrate the thick armor. He swung again, leering to the left as he did, so the Brink couldn't grab him. The sword struck the Brink's arm but barely caused a scratch.

Something rammed Nathan from behind, sending him to the ground in a wild tumble. *Shadowbanish* slipped from his grip and skidded across the asphalt, landing close to the scattered items from his bag.

Brinks appeared over him, and he realized he had lost more blood trying to fight. *Shadowbanish* began to rattle against the surface of the road, drawing attention away from him. It rattled and shook, actually moving toward one of the objects from his bag—Legion's Machine. When the blade touched the piece of alien technology, Legion's Machine shattered into dust which

Shadowbanish's blade quickly absorbed.

What just happened?!

His vision blurred into a dizzying spin, from which he fought valiantly to recover. A boot struck him in the stomach, and his vision threatened to black out. *God help me. Help. Me. Please.*

CHAPTER 27

Scarlet opened her eyes and found herself shackled to a pillar, naked. Many pillars filled the large chamber she found herself in, people—both men and women—chained and bound to each. Rags covered some people. Others were naked, their skin full of bruises and gashes. All hung by shackles, either asleep or dead. Smeared across the black floor, Scarlet could see dark stains—blood—leading toward a large pit in the center of the torch-lit chamber.

The room smelled of feces, blood, and a hint of urine. It was too much for Scarlet's nose, and she decided to breathe through her mouth.

The physical chains that had engulfed her had disappeared. But tattooed chains marred almost every inch of her flesh, wrapping around her abdomen, thighs, and arms. Black ink even marked her bare toes.

Ryn came around her pillar, taking the form of a woman in crow's garb. He touched Scarlet's chin with a long, pointy black nail and grinned. "Your word is your bond. You are now mine. You belong to me, of your own will, and you belong to the Black Cathedral."

"I—" Scarlet gagged and spit blood. It landed on the ground, near Ryn's feet.

The crow woman grimaced. "You humans are the most revolting species."

"You said I could stay here. That I was your princess!"

He grinned. "You are my princess. And these are my other

human princesses and princes, and whatever else they had to be told to surrender their devotion to me."

"Send me back."

"Back to where?"

"My world."

"Your old world, you mean? I hate to tell you this, but your old world is in the midst of war. And when the war is over, and the human species has lost, your planet will be destroyed completely. Nothing will be left of Earth."

"Who are you? Really?"

"I am Ryn." He turned and stepped past other pillars, making his way toward the center of the chamber. "You remember that tree, right?" He stopped in front of a pillar where a woman in dark rags hung by shackles. Ryn unfastened the shackles merely by touching them, and then he caught the falling woman in his arms. "She is so tired, Scarlet. Bone thin. Worn out from feeding her addiction to hate." Ryn carried the woman to the pit, holding her up precariously near the edge. He grinned at Scarlet and then pushed the woman over. She vanished over the edge.

Scarlet gasped.

Ryn strutted back to Scarlet's pillar, grinning seductively. "I gave you the chance to live out your desires, did I not?"

"You tricked me."

"Tricked? No. I was very honest with you. More honest with you than I daresay I have been to the rest of the humans residing here. I simply gave you an outlet for what you already were—a slut. Steeped in sex and a slave to your own impulses. You fell so hard, so fast. I thought it would take more time for you to release all of yourself, but you couldn't help it, could you?

I gave you an inch, and you took miles. But now, my little puppet, I am tiring of you." Ryn left the room without another word.

Scarlet did her best to hold herself up, but her legs hurt. Plus, the stench upset her stomach.

Minutes passed, and Ryn returned with Olivia. The girl looked up at Scarlet, clearly angry.

"I told her you were the one who betrayed her," Ryn said to Scarlet. "And please, don't think I don't appreciate your loyalty. You've taken a special place in my heart, Scarlet, and maybe that's why I haven't thrown you in there yet. I wanted to savor you just a little longer. But Olivia here..." He held Olivia's arm up. "She has two options right now: Help me with her powers of future telling, or feed my life like the rest."

Scarlet couldn't look the girl in the eyes. Scarlet knew her betrayal went deep—to offer such a young child into the hands of whom Scarlet knew now was the enemy. Regret wrapped around her like metal chains. Thick metal chains, from which there was no escape.

Ryn transformed into his male form, distorting the space around him, making his blank face and figure a blur. "Which is it, young Olivia? It would benefit me to know what is going to happen before it happens. I feel you might even be able to help me find a way out of this realm."

Olivia's eyes changed to a shade of gray. "The worlds are dyed in color, but the Cathedral only bleeds darkness. Your reign is at an end. These pillars of black will crumble into the sea, and—"

Ryn threw the girl to the floor. "I didn't ask for your riddles, brat."

Olivia scrambled to her feet. "I tell what I see in the manner I am able to." Then she looked directly at Scarlet. "He has been trying to communicate with you, but you've ignored Him. Blinded by your own ambition, your own carnal urges. You

215

soaked in Ryn's lies like a filthy sponge, leaving no room for the One who truly cares for you."

"Who?" Scarlet asked.

Ryn grabbed Olivia by her hair and pulled her toward the pit. "Enough! Refusing to assist me with your powers, I have no choice but to destroy you and take your life for myself."

"The One you've ignored your whole life. The Almighty. Nathan's God."

Nathan's God?

Ryn held Olivia at the edge of the pit. "You filthy humans continue to believe in your worthless deities. It makes you a weak species and is clearly one of your greatest weaknesses." He threw Olivia into the pit. Light burst out of the shaft. Olivia disappeared, and then reappeared at Scarlet's right.

Ryn stared into the pit, wondering where the light had come from.

Olivia turned to run.

"Wait," Scarlet whispered. "Wait. What do you mean, Nathan's God?"

Olivia turned her wrist over to reveal three lines etched in her skin, with a colorful dot in the center of the middle line. "God. The God of all creation. Christ, His Son. You know all this. You've always known all this, but you rejected it. The thing is," she whispered, "He never rejected you."

"But what do you mean He's been trying to comm—" She suddenly remembered the writing on the mirror, on the platter, on the canopy: *I long for you. My heart breaks for you. It is not too late.* "That was God? The same God Nathan worships?"

Ryn turned, spotted Olivia, and charged toward her. Olivia ran. Ryn went after her, leaving Scarlet alone in the large chamber, shackled to the pillar, naked and about to be destroyed in the Black Cathedral.

Why would God be communicating with me? I thought it was the Cathedral itself, or Ryn. Or something else entirely, something I should fear, something that wanted to violate me in every possible way. But now Olivia tells me it was God who was trying to communicate with me?

"Was that really you?" she asked in a hushed tone. "Did you send me those messages? You...you long for me?" The only ones who had ever longed for her had never really longed for her, but for her body, her sex. Her skills. "Your heart breaks for me?" *Why would God's heart break for me? I'm just another soul, another person who threw my hand up in the face of religion and 'the establishment'.* "What does that mean, 'It is not too late'?"

Scarlet closed her eyes, remembering the baby inside her. *If I did in fact stay here in the Black Cathedral, is this really the place I would want to raise a child?* She shook her head. She had been so fearful of what lay on the other side, what waited for her out there in the afterlife.

There is no reason to fear, she heard.

Her eyes opened. "Who said that?" Nobody seemed to be stirring. Ryn and Olivia were still absent. She knew Ryn would be back soon, and then it would all be over for her.

I've chosen you to be mine.

"But I'm already Ryn's. I gave myself to him."

You are not his. I have called you, Cynthia Scarlet Ruin, by name. I gave up my own child to restore relationship with my creation. I created you in my secret place. I am the One whose heart you continually break, yet I am the One who longs for you more than any other has ever longed for you.

She felt chills scurry up her arms and down her bare back as she stood in shackles, naked and bare, vulnerable and broken. *God—Nathan's God—is holding a conversation with me? He reached into this realm—wherever this is—just to get through to me? For what purpose? To prove I made the greatest mistake of my life? To remind me of all the times I turned on him, refused to follow after His calling?*

Come home, God said.

"Home?" She didn't have a home. Her world lay in ruins. And this cathedral was the darkest place she had ever been. Her mother had died. Her plans to lure Nathan into loving her had failed. Now it was just her and this baby—alone here in a realm outside the confines of space and time.

Space and time are mine.

Ryn returned, obviously vexed. "Rest assured, your little friend will be caught, and when she is, I will kill her. For now, I think I'll get rid of you and that child of yours." He unfastened her shackles, and her knees buckled, dumping her onto the grimy, blood-stained floor. "Get up!" he shouted, grabbing her under the arm.

As he pulled her along toward the pit, she wondered what was down there. *How far down does it go? Are there spikes at the bottom—sharp, blood-stained ones that will impale me?*

He took her to the edge, her body teetering over it as she stared into the dark abyss. "There is no end to this blackness. You will continue to fall for the rest of my existence—your life, your spirit, feeding my health, giving me the ability to live much longer than those who banished me here thought possible."

I want to come home, Scarlet—Cynthia—told God. She felt a strange scratching sensation on her wrist and looked down to see the same mark Olivia had on hers. The chain tattoos suddenly vanished, leaving behind unblemished skin, void of the Pink Rabbit mark and the president's bar code tattoo.

Disgusted and annoyed, Ryn grabbed Cynthia's wrist in

his hand and examined it. "What is this? Who gave this to you?"

The chamber shook as chunks of ceiling crumbled down into the pit, vanishing into the darkness below. Cynthia shoved her weight into Ryn, pushing him back, and then took off running in the direction Olivia had gone. Cynthia's knees almost buckled a few times before she caught a rhythm, but she managed to escape the chamber and make it to one of the Black Cathedral's long, black corridors.

CHAPTER 28

Thunder rolled through the sky above, like powerful ocean waves. Nathan's vision blurred, but he managed to sit up while the creatures standing over him glanced up into the sky to find the source of the noise. Directly above him, a spinning vortex of white and blue light—marvelous shades of blue, some of which reminded Nathan of Earth's blue skies—twisted into a funnel that opened in the dark sky.

Through the tunnel, a sparkle of light emerged, resembling the stars Nathan used to observe through his telescope. That sparkle, that miniscule light barely visible through his narrowing vision, came straight toward him.

At first, he figured it was Legion, casting itself from the sky to crush him in one final blow. Of course, Evanescence could have easily killed him, but she left it to her errand boys to do her dirty work. They had definitely begun that work but, for the moment, were too preoccupied with the object hurtling from the heavens to do any more damage to him. And this told him it couldn't be Legion, because if it had been, the creatures wouldn't have been so surprised.

Nathan turned and saw Evanescence, who had also stopped to look up at the falling object. Her face cast disappointment, possibly anger, as her eyebrows dipped down and the wrinkles in her decrepit face folded. Her fists, fragile and skeletal, were balled up at her sides. Whatever was coming down looked to be a threat—a substantial threat.

Whatever was coming down wasn't slowing down but

was speeding up. *I'll welcome it when it comes*, he decided. It would either put him out of his misery or put a stop to all of this. *Maybe*, he thought, *it's Jesus. Or more of Heaven's elite. Or*—

A violent gust of wind swept through his hair and across his face, scattering dirt and tiny chunks of gravel across him. The Brinks that had taken part in Nathan's beating were thrust into the air, only to vanish in the darkness.

Nathan managed to sit up. Off the road, in the dirt, a cloud of smoke rose from a small crater the object had created upon landing. But the smoke looked more like light than actual vapors originating from a source of heat. When the light parted, a woman stood on the edge of the crater, staring at Nathan with beautiful blue eyes.

"This is preposterous!" Evanescence shouted.

"Shut your mouth, Mother." Pearl's white blouse and white skirt accentuated her pale complexion but did not distract from the massive and elegant pair of cobalt wings jetting from her back.

Nathan sat breathless, his body wracked in pain, his blood loss critical. *Am I hallucinating, imagining things that aren't really there?*

Pearl strode to his side, her bare feet moving silently across the road. When she reached him, she knelt down and placed gentle hands on his forehead and chest, gently pushing him down so he was lying on the asphalt again. "Take it easy."

"What are you…where did you come from? Where were you?"

She grinned slyly. "You could say I was being remade."

"Remade?" Evanescence drew closer, almost stumbling in her frail form. "Remade? *I* made you! *I* created you," she held her decrepit hands out in front of her, "with these hands! *I* am your creator. Not the Nameless One."

Pearl closed her eyes and began to pray over Nathan, just as she had in the SUV on the way back from the lighthouse battle. Nathan felt the wound in his side closing, the scrapes and tears in his flesh sealing, and the bruises in his ribs and face vanishing. Within moments, he was whole again.

She helped him to his feet and then pulled his lips to hers, clearing the darkness from his mind.

When they pulled apart, he marveled at her wings. "Are you…are you an angel?"

She shrugged. "I don't really know what title you'd give me. But you can say I'm yours."

"What?"

"He gave me to you, Nathan. Not as an object of course, but as a gift."

"A gift."

"Stop this nonsense!" Evanescence shrieked. She thrust her hands out toward Nathan to knock him over again, but Pearl put her hand up and covered the both of them in a pearly white barrier that protected them.

"No more," Pearl stated.

"Kill them!" Evanescence screamed. The army that had been stationed a half mile from their location started moving again, the sound of their march echoing into the darkness.

Nathan retrieved *Shadowbanish*. Then he picked up the spilled contents of his bag, shoving them back in his pack. *What about Legion's Machine being absorbed by* Shadowbanish? he wondered. He glanced down at the black blade, the white etchings of the ichthys, oak tree, meteorite, and coffin. The edge of the blade seemed to glow a soft red, not with blood, but with light.

Evanescence leaped at him. Out of instinct, he thrust the

sword toward her chest, intending to move her back and dodge her attack. But the blade hit her necklace again—the blue gemstone she always had nestled between her breasts—and this time shattered it. The sword pressed through the fragments, reaching Evanescence's chest and carving through her brittle skin.

Nathan meant to lean into the blade to help push it as far as it would go, but the sorceress stumbled backward away from his weapon and fell to her knees, clutching her chest, where blue blood poured out of her. "You struck me. You struck…"

He stood, holding the sword, watching the colorful liquid drip from the tip of it. The red light in the sword glowed brightly and sucked in the blue liquid.

"You found *Shadowbanish*," Pearl whispered.

Evanescence tried crawling, reaching toward them, but instead fell face-first to the ground and stayed there, blue blood pooling around her.

Nathan went to plunge the sword into her one more time, to make sure she was dead, but before he had the chance, something grabbed him from behind and lifted him off the ground. Surprised, he shrieked and tried to struggle free until he realized Pearl was holding him as she ascended into the sky.

His stomach somersaulted when he realized how high up they were, Pearl's mighty blue wings flapping behind her as she lifted Nathan above the grand army. "We need to slow the Brinks down a bit," she shouted, flying him in close to one of the fiery pillars. Wind raced across his face and through his sweaty hair, cooling him, giving him a rush he had never experienced before. He closed his eyes, nearly terrified at the feeling of being so high, held up by a mere girl. He remembered, though, that this was no mere girl, but an angel of some sort.

My angel? Nathan opened his eyes in time to see Pearl closing in on one of the massive stone bowls.

"Grab it!" she commanded.

Nathan grasped the edge of the bowl, warm to the touch, and pulled while Pearl flapped her wings, lending strength to his effort. He tipped the bowl, and it toppled off the pillar, landing on the creatures below, smashing some, setting others on fire.

Out in the distance, far out near the horizon, Nathan could see two large black cages filled with shadow—each the size of a small skyscraper. They moved side by side and looked to be at the tail end of the army.

"What are those?"

"Those are the beasts I unleashed," Pearl said somberly.

"Take me to them. We can destroy them now before they can reach the city. That will take out a good percentage of their opposition."

Instead of following his request, Pearl swung around and started flying toward the burning city, passing another pillar. The same effort from before dropped the flaming bowl down on another portion of the army, knocking one of the white egg capsules over, breaking it open. Dozens of pink creatures scattered out, like insects.

Demons.

"Pearl, take me to the cages. Please. We can end this now."

"No. You can't defeat those things, even with *Shadowbanish*. We have to get back to the city and get those people into the mountains."

"We can fight those things. They're in cages right now. Let's set them on fire, or you can drop me on them, and I'll

224

get inside and carve them to pieces."

Pearl redirected toward the city, passing the front of the army and Evanescence's motionless body sprawled out on the asphalt of the dark road. "No. Your sword can't defeat them. Nothing can. They are indestructible."

As they neared the city, Pearl had to fly higher to clear the smoke rising from the burning buildings. No artificial light shined through the main street, only the glow of fire. *The spotlights must be broken*, Nathan thought. He didn't see many people down there, just small groups of those who apparently still wanted to fight whatever was on the other side of the north gate.

You don't want to fight what's out there, he thought. *Just run. Run far to the south and get to safety.*

Pearl landed on top of an intact building in the center of the city, releasing her hold on Nathan and retracting her wings into her back.

Nathan took a moment to regain his equilibrium and then used the light from his wrist to find a utility box on which he set his bag and sword. He sat down, his head spinning from the flight. "I think I might be sick."

"It takes some getting used to," Pearl said, her wrist glowing across his frame.

He took a few deep breaths, willing the nausea to subside. Then he asked, "Where did you go? What happened?"

"I went to see my Father. He took away my mark. He made me clean and whole."

"The key mark?"

She lifted her skirt and shined the light on her thigh. He saw no indication that a mark ever existed there—not even a scar or a bruise. She dropped the hem of her skirt and looked out into the distance, toward the north. "We're running out of time."

"For what? Will you tell me what's going on?"

"You killed the witch. That's something. But there are greater forces on their way here. We need to move to the valley and help escort people into the mountains. The city on the other side will have the supplies they need. And those creatures won't be able to pass over. They are too big—and yet not big enough. The people will be safe over there."

Nathan reached out and grabbed Pearl's hand, pulling her down to his level.

She took a seat across from him, folding her legs at her side. "Nathan, this is the end. He told me it's the end. And I came back to make sure you make it through everything."

"Like a guardian angel?"

"That's ridiculous," she grumbled. "I'm far from an angel. These wings were a gift from Him, to help us do what we can to slow down that army. But we can't stop them. Only He can stop them, and He has chosen not to for reasons I don't entirely understand. So for now, we need to head into the south valley."

"I'd like to find Heather and Ginger."

"If you want, I can fly us near the street below. Once. That's all we have time for."

He nodded, and then he slid his bag over his shoulder and placed *Shadowbanish* in its sheath.

Pearl stood and extended her wings. She grabbed Nathan from behind, lifting him into the sky. Then she dove toward the street, soaring between the rows of buildings, some of which continued burning into the darkness.

A violent gust of wind struck Pearl and knocked Nathan from her grip as they both spiraled down toward the street.

CHAPTER 29

When Nathan came to, he found himself in the middle of the street, the man in the red suit standing over him with a quizzical look. "I have a score to settle with you and your kind."

Nathan realized that *Shadowbanish* and his bag were nowhere near him.

Chaos held the bag up in one hand, the black mask in the other. "You've taken things that are not yours."

"That's a woman's soul," Nathan whispered, his eyes searching for Pearl. He saw her lying on the ground behind Chaos.

Chaos cursed as he threw the mask across the street. Nathan heard it slam into a metal garbage can in the nearby alley. "What do you humans know about the soul? About eternity? About anything? You are all so ignorant, it sickens me—me and my sister, the one you slaughtered out there beyond the city walls. That was retribution, wasn't it? Retribution for taking your sister. So you took mine."

"I didn't know she was your sister. But I knew she had to die."

Chaos's eyes glowed with fury. He turned toward Pearl just as she began to stir. He grabbed her by the hair and sat on her back, straddling her magnificent wings.

"What if I took her? What if Pearl was my retribution for your retribution? My sister's daughter. My own niece. I could slice her up right in front of you. Then I wonder how heroic you would be. You and that stupid sword and your stupid ideals. They are all meaningless." Chaos hopped off Pearl, pulled her to her feet, and then shoved her toward Nathan. She fell into his arms.

"I am finally tiring of this game." Chaos stepped back into the middle of the street. Then he got on all fours and knelt his head down until the top of it touched the surface of the asphalt. His body slowly began to mutate. First into a series of lumps, which stuck out from his back, arms, and legs, tearing through his suit, shredding all of his clothes. He shifted into an animal—a tiger. He growled, his eyes dark red and glowing, his stripes the colors of darkness and blood. His tiger shape bulged, and he transformed into a black rhinoceros, his horn covered in ice and stained in blood. From a rhinoceros, his body changed into that of an elephant, the trunk of which formed the neck of a brontosaurus, his next transformation. Extending his neck up over the buildings of Providence, his elongated form bulged and swelled into his final form—a towering, monstrous dragon.

Black metal plating covered his mass, the same material—Nathan guessed—that made up the bulk of Legion's mysterious vessels. Chaos's tail extended out far behind him but hovered over the back half of his mass and tapered to a point, where black spears jetted out its sides. Wings spread out on both sides of him, crashing into the surrounding buildings, eclipsing the fiery buildings to the south. Eyes—glowing red orbs set deep into the face of the dragon—pierced Nathan, and three pairs of horns twisted out from the creature's snout—each horn tip splashed in red.

Not only has the Dark Army created an alliance with Legion, but Legion has somehow integrated itself within the Dark Army, Nathan realized. Shadowbanish *gobbled up Legion's Machine, and only after that, was it able to destroy Evanescence. It somehow consumed the alien technology and then used it—to kill anything associated with Legion.*

"Where is the sword?" Nathan asked, frantically searching the city street for it.

Pearl stood in front of him, her wings spread wide, addressing Chaos when she said, "Finally, you reveal your true form to the humans."

Chaos laughed heartily, his long mouth displaying razorblade teeth. "It's time to end the reign of the mortals," he said in a snarling voice. Black mist sprayed from the dragon's mouth, traveling through the air toward Nathan. Instead of engulfing him in darkness, the fluid was absorbed into Pearl's bright blue wings, which she used to shield him from every drop of filth Chaos expelled.

Something broke up out of the concrete near Nathan's right foot. He recognized it as the black grip of a sword—*Shadowbanish*, as if going to him by its own free will. Nathan grabbed the handle, and the sword came up out of the street with little effort.

Chaos screeched and then swung his tail around, slamming one of its spears into Pearl, lifting her into the air on it. The dragon thrust his tail with a high arc and hurled her into the side of a building.

Nathan stood before the dragon, *Shadowbanish* in hand.

Chaos, his glowing red dragon eyes emitting enough heat to scorch the surface of the sun, faced Nathan. "You have certainly come far. You surprised even me. But you can't go any farther than this. Even with the sword, you cannot stop what is coming. You can either surrender or succumb to the darkness!" The tail swung to the left, forcing Nathan to roll to the right. But at the last minute, the tail shifted right and slammed down toward Nathan.

He drew his arms up in a feeble attempt to protect himself from the fatal impact. Instead, the large mass of black plating struck the violet shield that now enveloped him. Catching his breath—and confirming he did not in fact wet himself like he had done in Los Angeles—he turned and saw Heather standing behind him, her arms outstretched to hold the shield over him.

He got to his feet. "Boy, am I glad to see you!"

She grinned. "I know." Dropping the shield, she drew to his side, and they both faced the dragon together.

Chaos snorted. "A human wielding *Shadowbanish* and a Wedge are no match for me. I have destroyed entire civilizations."

"Where's Ginger?" Nathan asked.

Heather pointed up toward one of the skyscrapers. "She's around, somewhere. She has her eyes on us. I'm just glad you made it back."

"If it wasn't for Pearl, I would have died out there."

The dragon swung his tail again, its impact deflected by another shield erected by Heather.

Chaos snickered. "You cannot keep that up forever. I know your Wedge powers are extremely limited."

"Cover me," Nathan whispered to Heather. With *Shadowbanish* in hand, he rushed toward Chaos. His heart pounding in his head, Nathan leaped up when the dragon swung its tail again, this time in a vertical arc. Nathan jumped out of the way at the last minute as the jagged black spears struck the asphalt, digging into the surface of the street. Nathan grabbed hold of one of the spears and rode the tail back up, dropped off, and landed on the dragon's head.

Grasping tightly with one hand to one of Chaos's horns, Nathan plunged *Shadowbanish* down, forcing the blade between the black plates of armor protecting Chaos's head. Nathan felt the flesh give before he was tossed off the beast. His body crashing into the side of a parked van.

Struggling to his feet, his ribs aching, Nathan held tightly to *Shadowbanish* and watched as the dragon tossed its head about, black liquid spewing from the shallow wound. Heather threw a shield up over Nathan, protecting him from the goop. Pearl dove from the sky and landed on Chaos's head, digging her nails into his eyes, pulling at the top of his jaw to try and snap it open.

Nathan heard a loud boom, and then crumbling stone. He glanced down the street and saw that the north gate had been breached. Brinks and hordes of demons entered Providence. But those still in the city, those with weapons and a fighting spirit, rushed out of the surrounding buildings, heading off the demonic horde.

Nathan hurried toward the dragon and struck the sword into what looked like a good fleshy spot in one of its feet. The foot came up, its claw scraping across Nathan's face, bringing a fire of pain to his eyes and nose. Unable to see, he stumbled backward and tripped, falling to the ground, dropping *Shadowbanish*.

A shield went up over him again before the dragon's foot could come down on him.

Nathan rubbed the blood from his eyes. He heard Pearl scream and then something crash through glass. He heard the metal clang of his sword behind him and swung around to find Jasper trying to lift it off the ground. He rushed over, took hold of the sword, and pulled Jasper to the side, out of the way of the dragon, to give Heather a chance to rest her powers.

"What are you doing here?" Nathan asked.

Jasper, in blue jeans and a brown jacket, motioned to Hush, who stood beside him. She wore a green sleeveless gown that had ripped and torn in areas, damaged by what Nathan presumed might have been scuffles with the demon horde. The iridescent swirl marks on her skin, including the teardrop mark under her left eye, lit up her worn appearance. "Hush thinks she found a shuttle we can use to get off this planet. Underground, at the end of the tracks." Jasper turned toward the multitude of creatures advancing into the city. "We can't fight all of them and win."

"I agree. We need to kill Chaos, though. I already finished off Evanescence."

Jasper's eyebrows arched upward. "She's really dead this time?"

"I don't see how she couldn't be. I stuck this sword straight through her chest."

"Let's do this then," Jasper said, glancing up at the dragon. "Hush, you know what to do."

She moved to the center of the street, directly in front of Heather, and closed her eyes. She held her arms out in front of her, and Nathan watched as water began to drip from the crooks of her elbows, her wrists, and her fingertips.

Chaos roared. Pearl peered out of the broken window she had been tossed through. Nathan watched as a fountain of water shot out from Hush's palms. When the liquid hit Chaos's outer shell, it created a loud sizzling sound. The black armor began to bubble and warp, as plates fell to the ground, crashing against the asphalt.

The dragon thrashed around, swinging its tail wildly, nearly missing Jasper, ramming into the shield that Heather put up over Hush at the last minute.

Nathan charged at the dragon, *Shadowbanish* in hand.

Each panel of dragon armor Hush struck with her acidic

fluid dropped off, revealing the dragon's vulnerable soft tissue. Nathan carved his blade through the exposed red flesh, engrossed in slicing up Chaos, striking at every point he could, making sure blood flowed from each wound. He didn't realize when the group of demons and Brinks managed to break through the crowd of fighting residents and reached his group in the center of the city.

Shots rang out, and one by one, demons fell by way of sniper bullets. Chaos finally tromped back a few feet as black bile spewed forth from his mouth again. Hush stopped her attack, instead turning to grab a demon that leaped at her, tearing its limbs from its body. Jasper teleported in front of Heather, grabbing hold of a demon that would have torn her to pieces without his intervention. He swung the demon into a nearby car. The creature exploded in a mess of blood and entrails.

Pearl landed near Nathan, fluttering her wings to create a giant windstorm that blew some of the demons back toward the north gate.

The Brinks weren't so easily stopped. They approached the group, and one took Jasper in its hands, breaking Jasper's fingers before Hush went berserk and managed to rip the creature's arm off and strike her fist through its chest, pulling out a mechanical orb that acted as its heart.

Heather retreated near Nathan and Pearl, throwing her shield up wherever she could, even over Jasper, who had his own shield up over Hush.

Nathan used *Shadowbanish* to dispatch the demons easily. The Brinks took some work. With Hush in a frenzy, Jasper used his power to suck the dark Legion core from the faceless Brinks, disintegrating them in a colorful flame within his palm. Heather shielded whom she could in tactical bursts, and Pearl dug her claws into the necks of the Brinks, pulling their heads off. The group finished off their enemies in little time.

Shadowbanish cut through the last two demons with ease, but with his attention on the battle, Nathan didn't see the dragon's tail come down, its black spears threatening his victory. Heather rushed into him, throwing him to the ground as the spears impaled her chest and abdomen.

Confusion filled Nathan's mind. He watched as Chaos's tail lifted Heather's body into the air.

Chaos hung her there, his exposed flesh pouring black blood into the street, his body slumped over, all of his strength devoted to holding Heather up like a trophy. "And this is my retribution, Nathan."

Heather's body slid off the spikes and hit the street with a sickening slap. Without thinking, Nathan rushed toward Chaos, *Shadowbanish* guiding his path. The dragon slammed its tail down toward him, but Jasper already had a shield up protecting Nathan. Hush projected a line of acid toward the beast's head, knocking the plate protecting its brain away. Nathan leaped into the air, and Pearl flapped her angelic wings, pushing air under his feet, giving him the lift he needed to reach the dragon's head.

He didn't think his moves out ahead of time. He didn't wallow in the sorrow of losing Heather, his best friend. He simply took the sword and dug it straight between the fading red eyes of the dragon, piercing flesh and brain matter. He slid *Shadowbanish* all the way through.

He struggled to pull the sword out, and then he jumped down to the street as Chaos collapsed behind him, the dragon mass shaking the street as it fell.

Nathan sheathed *Shadowbanish* and rushed to Heather. Her skull had cracked open from hitting the street, and blood escaped from various wounds in her body.

Nathan lifted her into his arms. Her eyes stared at him, open and unblinking. *Is she breathing?* He pressed his face into her moist scarf, despite the repulsive taste and scent of blood. "Heather? Heather, why did you do that? Why did you—"

Someone pulled him up off the ground and took him into the air. He realized Pearl had swept him up, but before he could protest, he noticed another wave of the Dark Army had entered the city, and he understood. More people spilled out of the surrounding buildings, attacking the opposition.

As he looked down on the burning city—on Providence—his eyes blurred with tears. The reality that he wouldn't be escaping with Heather, the girl who had become a sister to him, broke his heart.

CHAPTER 30

Cynthia found Olivia waiting in Cynthia's room. After throwing on a black blouse and skirt, Cynthia followed Olivia to Ryn's throne room, knowing they had only one option left: to destroy Ryn's tree.

On the way to the throne room, Cynthia wondered aloud about the symbol in her wrist. "Where did this—"

"It's God's stamp, placed on you to show you're His."

"What does it mean?"

"It means you can't be thrown down that eternal pit. It also means you have a reason to leave the Black Cathedral and move on from here. I'm hoping that by destroying Ryn's tree—and in turn, destroying him—maybe this cathedral will come crashing down, and we can all get out of here."

They turned another corner, passing through the hallways, Cynthia keeping her eyes peeled for the dark-robed, faceless guards. When the two finally reached Ryn's throne, Cynthia was surprised to find the doors unguarded and wide open.

"It's a trap," Olivia said, stopping before they could enter the room. Through the doors, on the other side of the room, Cynthia could see the blue-leafed tree towering over Ryn's throne. Leaves fell, slowly drifting to the grass surrounding the trunk.

"We have to do this before he comes back," Cynthia said. "Now." She rushed through the doorway, her eyes focused squarely on the tree.

As soon as she passed the threshold, Olivia fell in line beside her. Together, they rushed between the statues of naked species, climbed the steps to the throne, and approached the tree.

"How do we destroy this thing?" Cynthia asked.

Olivia looked up at the umbrella of branches overhead. "The leaves."

They both reached up and yanked glowing blue leaves from the branches of the giant tree, tossing them into the grass where the others had fallen into small piles.

"No!"

Cynthia refused to turn around. Olivia glanced over her shoulder and yanked the leaves off more furiously.

Wings flapped, and Cynthia felt the pointy beaks and sharp claws of low-flying crows attack her exposed flesh and tear at her skirt and blouse. She fell into the grass, beating the birds away while Olivia continued to pull the leaves down. Cynthia managed to grab hold on one bird's neck, and she twisted without any regret, feeling the crunch of broken bones. She tossed the dead animal to the side only to grab another. A sharp set of talons scratched her under the left eye, and a beak pecked her nose, drawing blood.

The birds split into two groups—one group dove toward Olivia, attacking her back. She continued to pull at the leaves, but Cynthia knew that Olivia wouldn't finish in time. Cynthia grabbed a branch and began to pull herself up. She felt an all-out attack on her hindquarters, the birds' beaks like sharp needles pricking her rear. She managed to pull herself up onto the branch and start picking at the higher leaves while Olivia took the lower ones.

Gathering together, the birds coalesced into Ryn's female persona.

Cynthia ripped entire branches down, refusing to look at Ryn, refusing to check and see if Olivia was all right. *This is our only chance to defeat him.*

"He's dying," Olivia said.

Cynthia stopped and turned to find Ryn on the floor of the throne room, on his knees. "You…" he gasped.

Olivia pointed up, higher into the tree, just above Cynthia's head. "Get the last of those leaves."

Cynthia reached for them, but lost her footing and slipped off the branch, landing in the grass on her arm. She heard—and felt—a crack.

Olivia ran to her side and helped her sit up. Ryn stood slowly and started up the steps toward them, his female avatar reverting to his male persona. Dust poured from the sleeves of his black garb. "I gave you everything," he wheezed. "I gave…I gave you life."

Cynthia tried to move her arm, the pain confirming its broken state. She couldn't climb to the remaining leaves. Ryn's clothing dropped to the floor as a murder of crows flew out of it, attacking Olivia. The girl screamed and tried beat the birds away, but she was no match for the amount of fowl pecking and biting and scratching her young, tender skin.

Cynthia used her good arm and the tree trunk to get to her feet, realizing what she would have to do to stop Ryn and save Olivia. She moved toward the girl, grabbed her, and pulled her out of the bird frenzy. She pushed Olivia toward the tree, motioning to the remaining leaves.

Then Cynthia rushed into the tornado of crows before they could break apart and go after Olivia.

The crows pecked and prodded. They scratched and slashed.

They tore a fingernail clean off Cynthia's finger, yanked some of her hair from its roots, and shredded through her clothes to get to her vulnerable flesh. Cynthia endured the pain, glancing up through the flock of black feathers to watch Olivia climb up onto the main branch, reach up, and start picking the last of the leaves.

As the glowing blue foliage coasted down from the top of the tree, Cynthia closed her eyes and accepted her fate.

I want to end this charade. I want to go home.

A sharp talon dug into her eye, ripping it out. Cynthia screamed. Another bird wrapped its beak around her tongue and bit down. Her mouth gushed blood as she buried her head in her arms and prayed for God to end this.

Rescue me. Please.

The birds ripped flesh from Cynthia's back and clawed nails off her bare toes. They tore off pieces of her ears. She felt something crawling across her breast and looked down with her remaining eye to see maggots burrowing up from the grass to crawl across her flesh. She went into a frenzy and tried to get to her feet, but the malevolent birds severed her Achilles tendon and ripped apart a finger, and then started on the rest of her.

"Done!" she heard Olivia yell.

The birds halted.

Cynthia's heartbeat slowed, and everything grew quiet.

***

Olivia pulled the last leaf and leaped down from the tree branch, nearly twisting her ankle upon landing. The birds vanished, and the Black Cathedral shook.

Cynthia lay nearly dead—or completely dead—Olivia

couldn't tell for sure. Cynthia's body had been mutilated beyond recognition.

Closing her eyes, Olivia teleported herself out of the crumbling kingdom, redirecting herself through time and space toward the destination in her latest visions—Anaisha.

CHAPTER 31

athan and Pearl waited on the small Amtrak platform underneath Providence's main street for Hush, Jasper, and Ginger. Nathan opened his bag and pulled out his pistol, aiming it at the nearby soda machine. He fired the gun, shattering the lock. As it fell to the ground in pieces, he sighed. He knew it was a waste of a bullet, but he was thirsty. He opened the door of the soda machine and reached in, pulling out a semi-cold can of Coca-Cola. He popped the tab and took a sip, enjoying the cool liquid as it traveled down his throat.

Hush and Jasper agreed to go back for Ginger, who had gotten trapped in the building she was sniping from. Chaos was dead. As was Evanescence. The people of the city had managed to push most of the invading army back into the Broken Lands. Most of the city had been evacuated, deserted as the people of Providence moved back to the south valley.

Nathan and Pearl both knew those tall, dark cages—the ones containing the monsters that Pearl loosed with her birthmark—were coming their way. And once the creatures arrived within the city walls and were unleashed, it would all be over.

Nathan glanced down the tunnel. Somewhere down there was the SilverTech laboratory that Jasper and Hush had found—and their ticket out of Providence, out of California, and away from Earth. For good.

Pearl sat on the edge of the cement platform overlooking the tracks, staring at her bare thigh, where her black key mark used to be. Nathan sat next to her, offering her his drink. "Want some?"

She shook her head. "I don't have need for food anymore, Nathan."

"That's a little weird."

"I've seen the face of God, Nathan. Do you realize…do you understand what that's like? Just…just looking at Him? I felt at once destroyed and renewed. It was unlike anything I've experienced before. I know I've only been in creation for a short while, but…I can't get over it." She scratched at her thigh. "And I can't get over that I don't have that stupid mark anymore."

Nathan gently stroked her thigh. Her skin felt soft, like a bed of cotton. "I love you," he blurted out.

She grinned, taking his hand in hers. "I love you, too." She kissed him on the lips.

He wanted to take Pearl into his heart and soul completely, become one with her, to wash away the grief that came with all the death that surrounded them.

"Don't think I haven't thought about you, Nathan." She fell silent, staring at the tracks. "You'll always be my one and only love, you know."

He thought he saw sadness in her eyes and realized she was referring to her immortality. Nathan would only live so long—and then Pearl would have to go on into the future, without him. Alone.

"There won't ever be another, you know?" she said. "I'll live out eternity alone, with the memory of you in my heart. That will be my fate."

"I'm sorry."

"You have nothing to be sorry about. I'll enjoy these years with you. Every second, every minute, every hour, every day. There will be a day, though, when I will join you with my

Father. We can be together again then. That's why I want to wait for you. Right now, let's just enjoy the time we have."

Hush, Jasper, and Ginger came down the ramp that led up to the street. Ginger handed the black Legion mask to Nathan.

"You found it?"

She nodded.

Nathan took the mask and stared at it for a while before he realized everyone was watching him.

Pearl took the mask from him, examining the sapphire inlay on its front. "There's a soul in here, isn't there?"

Nathan nodded.

"A soul?" Jasper asked.

"Legion traps human souls—and maybe other species—in these and then puts the souls on puppets to do Legion's bidding," Nathan explained. "There's a woman in this one—Margaret—who lives in a prison of her own home and is constantly tortured by ghosts of her life here on Earth."

"You've been inside the mask?" Pearl asked. "I didn't know that was possible."

"It is. And you don't want to go there. It's terrible. I don't know what to do. Margaret refuses to accept God—"

Pearl put a hand on his shoulder. "She's asked you to destroy the mask, hasn't she?"

Ginger took a soda from the machine. "Won't that destroy her?"

"Yes."

"If she's asked you to do it, don't you think you should?" Jasper wondered aloud. "Especially if it's a prison in there for her? I don't know much about this God of yours—although I've heard plenty since I've been here on Earth—but I think it should be up to everyone to worship or follow whatever deity they deem appropriate."

Nathan sighed, not really in the mood for a heavy discussion about Heaven and Hell. He conceded that Jasper did have a point, though. Margaret had been given freedom of choice by God, meaning she could accept or deny him. It was up to her. "You're right. It is her decision."

"Let her go," Pearl said. "You did what you could, right?"

He nodded. "I think I know what will destroy the mask, too." He stood, drawing *Shadowbanish* from its sheath. He set the mask on the platform and took a deep breath. Everyone stood, surrounding him, and watched as he stuck the blade into Legion's mask. As soon as the sword struck it, the mask burst into an explosion of colorful glitter and sapphires.

Nathan sheathed *Shadowbanish* and took a good look at the people before him. They were all he had left of anything resembling allies or family or friends. He wanted to mourn the loss of Heather, but she wouldn't want him to. She'd want him to celebrate her life, which is exactly what he planned on doing once he reached Anaisha.

Right now, they had to get to the shuttle. "Let's go."

Jasper nodded. "I'll lead the way. It's down the tunnel—"

Nathan Pierce of Earth, Nathan heard in his head.

"Legion?"

"What?" Ginger dropped her soda and readied her rifle.

You and I have much to talk about, human. Come outside and face me.

Nathan drew *Shadowbanish* from its sheath again. "Legion is outside."

Hush and Jasper started for the ramp. Ginger, with rifle in hand, followed. Nathan, surprised there was still fight left in everyone after defending the city, took Pearl's hand and led her up the ramp after them.

The dragon—Chaos—was gone. *I know I killed the man in the red suit*, Nathan thought, *but where did the body disappear to?*

Buildings burned within the city, and smoke and ash filled the street.

Nathan stopped behind his friends and observed the large orb hovering over the center of the street. It was roughly the size of a small house and looked to be made of black and purple clouds. Or black holes. He remembered seeing those same black hole symbols—black and purple swirls—on the walls of the insurance building back in Tucson.

"What the hell is that?" Ginger asked.

"Legion," Jasper answered. Nathan stepped forward, approaching the dark orb. Pearl held tightly to his hand, her beautiful blue wings expanding behind her.

I have no mouth, so I will speak to your spirits. All of you.

"What do you want?" Nathan asked.

Nathan knew the dark cages were approaching, somewhere far behind the hovering sphere. *The end of Providence is near*, he thought. *If we're going to get off this planet, we're going to have to do it soon.*

Legion is taking this planet, Legion said. *Earth is ours. Mine.*

"Haven't you already taken enough?" Jasper shouted. "You took—"

Yes, despicable Wedge! Legion won over your kind, and Rhodenine fell. Now, Earth will fall as well. But first, I will consume you and your friends. You have stood far longer than expected. It has caused discrepancies. Many discrepancies.

Nathan felt the orb staring at him with unseen eyes.

You irritate me, human, Legion said in his mind. *You wield that pathetic blade, not knowing that it cannot stop Legion. Legion is omniscient, omnipresent, and all-consuming. Soon, Legion is all there will be.*

Nathan lifted the sword. "No. This is where it all ends. We

were going to run, to flee from this planet. But seeing how you decided to come here and ask for an audience with me, I'm going to take *Shadowbanish* here and run you through."

Legion laughed. *Humans have so much humor. You are no different. You have seen the variety of forms Legion can take. Legion can merge with any species, infiltrate any society, and destroy anything in this universe. And soon, Legion will be the universe. This Sphere of Void—Legion's true form—will be the only thing in space, feeding off the stars.*

You have seen Legion in the guise of human females, and most of your males—with their uncontrollable chemistry—went after these females and were destroyed. You have seen Legion in the form of the Starry Visitors, wiping out your planet's electricity by feeding off your power supplies and your nuclear plants. You have seen Legion in a form unfamiliar to you, the great Broolers, who come through the portals and wreak havoc on your pitiful planet. They are coming this way, locked in cages so they do not release their rage until the appropriate time.

Legion is versatile.

You have seen Legion's weapons. We turn your human form into ash and blood. Legion destroyed much of your planet's cities with our vessels alone. And your weapons can no more harm Legion than your words can.

Legion is powerful.

Legion consumes the knowledge and wisdom of the planets we destroy, inhaling what you know to use it against you later on. That is how we knew to use the guise of your female. Legion watches, waits, and infiltrates your ranks to learn what is needed to turn yourselves on yourselves. How do you think your president and the other leaders of your world were so easily manipulated?

Legion is all-knowing.

Legion will destroy you. We will consume your tired flesh and strip it of everything familiar, leaving behind a rotting corpse forever trapped within Legion's depths. In the Hopeless Bastille, from where there is no escape.

Legion is unstoppable.

"You're forgetting one thing," Nathan said confidently. "My God. He will destroy you, even if I am not able to."

You speak of your deity, do you not? What is this God you strive to follow? Look around you, human, what has this God done for you lately?

"I'm still breathing. I have friends. Love. It's enough proof for me."

Inconsequential things. Items of no relevance. What is love, but a harsh emotion to destroy you from the inside out? What are friends, but those who will later betray you? And your breath has only brought you one step closer to destruction, not safety. You have tasted all these things, Nathan Pierce of Earth, and you still choose to lecture us. Lecture me. Have you not had enough death? First your parents, your caregivers. Then your sister—your beloved Daisy. Your friends died in the church camp slaughters. Your greatest friend, Heather, died in the battle with the Dark Army's very own Chaos.

And now you stand before the great Legion, spouting empty threats. You think you are so high and mighty, the one to stand as hero for the humans. But who are you really? Legion has observed that you are a mere human, full of inconsistencies and rebellion.

You grew up with religion, but not true admiration for this God you claim to believe in. You do everything your religious manual—the Bible— tells you not to do. And a dark road is what you went down when you slept with Cynthia Ruin, while your greatest friend listened through the wall in the room next door.

Shall I go on? Shall I call forth all of your heinous deeds, or have you had enough?

"There's a difference between what you say I am and what I truly am."

I am curious to hear what this difference is, human. So far, you have done little to impress me, except to stay alive when time after time Legion—and the rest of the Dark Army—has continuously sought to extinguish your pathetic life.

"I'm forgiven."

Forgiveness is an excuse for—

"I'm tired of trying to reason with you!" Nathan shouted. "You came here for a fight. I'll give you one." Nathan took a few steps back, realizing he would need to gain a little bit of altitude to reach the height of the hovering sphere. He glanced over his shoulder. Pearl nodded, indicating she would use her wings to give him the extra bounce he needed in his step. Hush and Jasper stood side by side, ready to attack as soon as Nathan found a way to get the sphere to the ground. And Ginger stood, rifle ready, to create a distraction if nothing else.

Nathan faced Legion's sphere. He ran, jumped, felt the lift under him, and let it carry his body straight up to the sphere. With a powerful swing, he dug *Shadowbanish* into the side of it. Although the orb looked to be made of clouds or black holes, the sword went in as if it struck Styrofoam. Nathan clung tightly to the sword's handle as the sphere began spinning.

He tightened his grip on *Shadowbanish*. "Hang on," he whispered to it, as he would if the sword were his only friend. The sphere spun around and around, so fast that Nathan felt his stomach churning in knots. Before he knew it, he was thrown off. His body slammed into something soft, and he realized Pearl had caught him.

The orb spun faster and faster, a swirling mass of black and purple chaos. Papers, bodies, building debris all got swept up in Legion's twisting rage. Pearl took Nathan back away from the orb while Jasper, Hush, and Ginger retreated toward the ramp leading into the Amtrak tunnel.

The swirling mass stopped instantly, completely. And then a bolt of lightning flashed from where *Shadowbanish* had pierced Legion's mass. The lightning burned throughout the entire sphere, filling it with bright blue and pink flashes of light.

Shadowbanish fell out of the orb and struck the ground, shattering into its many shards. Pearl took Nathan down, and he scrambled to gather each piece, shoving them into his backpack. Legion's Machine sat on the ground, intact, staring at Nathan. He picked it up and went to put it in his bag when Legion fell apart in a blizzard of shadows.

Darkness swept over the city in a violent gust, extinguishing every flame, every light. The air dropped to a temperature below freezing, and Pearl had to grab Nathan's huddled form, protecting Legion's Machine, and carry him down the ramp into the tunnel.

Nathan shoved Legion's Machine into his bag as he, Ginger, and Pearl used their wrist lights to illuminate their way across the platform. The five heroes headed straight for Mr. Silver's lab.

 *hadowbanish* had inflicted much more damage on Evanescence—powerful sorceress, Great Witch, lieutenant of the Dark Army—than she thought possible. The sword, as far as she knew, never had the ability to hurt Legion. *So then how did it shatter my gemstone? How did it get through my skin, puncturing my vitals? How did Nathan Pierce, a human, nearly destroy me?*

She lifted her face from the dirt. The Dark Army had passed her, leaving her alone in the middle of the Broken Lands, severely wounded, bleeding out across Earth's soil, only a lone torch stuck in the ground to light the area around her.

I have nowhere to go.

She gasped, trying to get more oxygen into her lungs. "Legion?" She saw no sign of the Sphere of Void.

The sword, Legion replied in her head.

"Yes. It...it did the same to me."

My vessel has been shattered. We are scattered.

She rolled onto her back. The pain felt unbearable. *Immortal does not mean invincible*, she reminded herself. She stared up at the dark sky. *I wonder where my brother is, and if he had any luck putting a stop to Nathan and his friends.*

He was slain, Legion answered. *By the human.*

"Nathan? He killed my brother?"

Yes. With the same sword he used on you. And us.

"How could one human...and he took my daughter, didn't he?"

They are gone. Away from this planet.

"Very well. I will have to—" She rolled onto her side and coughed up blue blood.

You are dying.

"I will…survive. The sword was not powerful enough to destroy all of me."

A piece was missing from the blade. I doubt the human knew that.

"But how did the blade…" She took a deep, painful breath and let it out slowly. She felt more blood traveling up her throat but forced it back down. "How did that blade defeat Legion? It never had the power to do so."

Shadowbanish is able to consume technology. When the sword shattered, I saw one of our Relicors fall out of the blade. The same Relicor that was used to destroy the part of us who called herself Viranda DelaCourte.

"How did Nathan get his hands on that?" *I underestimated Nathan Pierce on a number of occasions*, she admitted. *But this may have been the worst of it.*

A traitor within my ranks, Legion answered, venom etching the words in her spirit.

"Legion can betray…Legion?" She had never heard of that happening before in all the time the Dark Army had been aligned with Legion to destroy creation. *How can an entity go up against itself?*

We are one. And many. And at times, our many do not agree with the one. The traitor was willing to help the human destroy you and your brother. She pointed him in the direction of Shadowbanish.

"Wonderful."

I cannot wander without form for long before I—we—disappear. We need a vessel to take refuge in, so we can heal.

Evanescence took another deep breath, realizing that Legion was hinting at using her as that vessel. "I don't have much strength left myself."

If we combine our strengths—temporarily—we can assist each other. Once we are safe and strong enough, you can assist in finding a new, more permanent vessel for me to reside in.

What do I have to lose? she wondered. At the moment, I want nothing more than to get revenge on Nathan Pierce. It seems unlikely that I will be able to do so anytime soon. And my daughter took off with him. I will have to create another, more obedient child once I return to the Depths. As Evanescence struggled to sit up, her entire chest and stomach felt on fire. She glanced at her hands—wrinkled, bony, aged.

My time fades, Legion said to her mind. *Would you be willing to carry the great Legion for the time being?*

Evanescence wanted to return to the Depths to heal. But she didn't want Roshoru'm, the Dark One, her master, knowing she had failed. *If I can regain my strength, I might still stand a chance at destroying the human species…in time, after they've had a chance to settle on Anaisha and become engrossed in humanity's illusions of security.* "Yes."

Very well.

Shadows swarmed around Evanescence. She felt something enter her body, filling her empty parts with substance. Taking a breath, her lungs no longer hurt. She retained her decrepit condition, but she was able to move, to get to her feet.

"What now?" she asked, looking out on Providence. The city burned brightly against the dark sky.

Release the Broolers from their cages. Let them run rampant across this entire planet, and instruct the army to destroy everything and everyone in sight. It is time for the fall of Earth. But you and I—we—need to find shelter, to rest and heal for a time.

"I would like to stay a while and witness the destruction."

CHAPTER 33

A side from the tunnel being dark, Nathan's group didn't see any sign of Legion as they walked with Nathan's, Ginger's, and Pearl's wrist lights shining brightly along the path in front of them. Nathan still couldn't will the light to life. It seemed to have a mind of its own and activated when it needed to. The rest of the time, the mark just leaked light like the face of a cell phone. Nathan would have liked to think he destroyed Legion for good, but something in his gut told him he hadn't.

The underground track led straight into another station platform at what looked to be the end of the tracks, a wall abruptly stopping any further progress through the tunnel. They found a doorway protected by a password panel. Nathan had no idea what the password could be, but Hush stepped forward and typed one in, giving them access.

The door led to a cavernous room. Lamps expelling soft light hung from chains in the stone ceiling. Below the lights, on the tracks, sat a large black shuttle in the shape of a sideways milk carton with wings, the SilverTech logo painted in red on the tail wing. This shuttle looked significantly different than the ones SilverTech had advertised on television, in magazines, and on billboards for travel to Anaisha. This one was smaller, and the wings didn't appear to be able to retract into the body of the shuttle, as they did in SilverTech's advertisements. Dark tinted windows had been installed along the sides, possibly to protect from the sun's ultraviolet rays.

The room smelled of dust and grease. On both sides of the

shuttle sat clusters of desks covered in lab equipment like beakers and microscopes, and piles and piles of document folders. It was clear someone, or many, had at one point spent a lot of time here.

"So this is our way out of here," Ginger whispered, approaching the shuttle. She reached out and ran her hand along the wing. "It looks like it will hold all of us."

Nathan found the whole idea of leaving the planet bittersweet. *Earth has been my home. I had hoped to save it, especially when I was told by an angel—if that's what she was—that I would need to fight.* And he had done so. He had fought with everything he had.

Yet now it was time to leave. To retreat, so humanity could fight another day. It wasn't God's day to reach down and stop all evil. It was simply the day He reached down to rescue His creation.

Jasper examined document folders and notebooks, flipping through coffee-stained pages. He showed some of his findings to Hush, who simply shrugged or nodded or shook her head.

Nathan noticed a large chalkboard hanging in a corner of the room. Equations and formulas—all of which were foreign to him—covered its surface.

"I don't know what all this is," Jasper said, holding up handfuls of paper, each sheet scrawled with partially unreadable cursive and crude illustrations. "It looks like Mr. Silver's research on...well...everything. There are folders here talking about Hush and the Legion vessels and—"

A loud humming sound emanated from the other side of the room. Nathan made his way over the tracks, past the shuttle, toward the sound. He found a large circular pad with tiny particles of light floating in the center of it, creating a colorful pillar.

Ericka Shane stumbled out of it. Nathan caught her in his arms.

"Thank you," she said, holding her head. "Ah…" She knelt and retched.

Another female walked through the cloud—a woman with blue hair. The same woman who had publicly challenged the president's policies many times since Legion's vessels had fallen.

Before the light pillar vanished, a young man walked out, glasses sliding down his nose, long hair falling around his eyes.

"What are all of you doing here?" the woman with blue hair asked.

"Calm down," the spectacled man said. "I think we should introduce ourselves. My name is Samuel Grey. And this is Marigold," he said, pointing to the blue-haired woman. "And this is Ericka Shane."

Ericka wiped her mouth and waved at the group.

"Is that…a teleporter?" Nathan asked, staring at the circular pad.

Samuel moved in toward the shuttle. "Yes. And I see you all found Mr. Silver's private escape out of this hellhole. I believe there's room on board for all of us, so how about if we—"

The lights in the room went dark. The cement walls shook violently, raining dust and making the hanging light chains creak.

"What was that?" Ginger asked, shining her wrist light around the room. Nathan noticed that only he, Ginger, and Pearl had the glowing mark on their wrists. The newcomers said nothing about the wrist lights, although they did cast curious gazes.

I wonder if everyone has just seen so much weird that nothing is surprising anymore, Nathan thought.

Another tremor knocked some of the room's lights crashing down on the shuttle.

The circular pad hummed loudly again, and the light pillar

reappeared. Wrist lights aimed toward the emerging figure—a short woman in a dark lab coat. She seemed upset when she took a look around and saw, by the glow of the wrist lights, how many people were gathered around the shuttle.

A woman with long dark hair, wearing a Kevlar vest and a short skirt, came through the pillar, and then the beam disappeared behind her.

"I see everyone found my shuttle," the woman in the lab coat said.

Samuel chuckled. "Nice try. It's Mr. Silver's. And we're taking it for ourselves."

"As an employee of SilverTech Industries, this shuttle is my property—"

The woman with long black hair put a gun to the shorter woman's head. "You're going to fly us out of here, or you'll end up like Mr. Silver. Got it?"

"What happened to Mr. Silver?" Samuel asked, sliding the shuttle's door wide open.

"I killed the bastard."

"Who are you?" Jasper asked. "You look familiar."

"My name is Mira. I worked for Mr. Silver—undercover so I could assassinate him. It just took me a few tries." She shoved the shorter woman forward. "And this woman here designed the shuttle and knows how to fly it." Mira looked up for a second as Ginger's light shone on Hush. Mira's eyes lit up. Nathan thought she was going to speak, but she bit her lip and kept silent.

"Good," Samuel said. "I was hoping we'd run into a pilot."

"What?" Marigold shouted. "You don't know how to pilot the shuttle?"

"I would have done my best. Our priority is to get off this planet before—"

Another vibration, and more hanging lamps fell. Samuel ducked into the shuttle before more glass could rain down on him. Ericka, Marigold, Jasper, and Hush followed after him. Mira held the gun steady on the shorter woman's head, prompting her onto the shuttle and into the pilot's seat.

Once Nathan and Pearl slipped onboard, Jasper pulled the shuttle door closed. The ship's engines started. Another tremor, and dust and debris rained down on the shuttle. Nathan's heart raced as the massive hangar doors, which had been hiding the shuttle from the rest of the tunnel, slowly slid open.

He had never been in space before—like most of his fellow passengers. Fear quickly dwarfed his excitement. *Will the shuttle make it out of Earth's atmosphere without issue? What about those who couldn't escape Earth—the ones who escaped to the south valley? Or—*

Pearl squeezed his hand. "It's just us now."

He took a deep breath as the shuttle started forward along the tracks, headlamps illuminating the path ahead.

"This isn't a train," Mira grunted, shoving the gun into the back of the pilot's head.

"No shit!" the woman snapped. "The shuttle is programmed to run on autopilot until we clear the tunnel. Then it will dismount the tracks, and we'll be airborne. Just get your gun away from me so I can get us off this rock safely."

Mira silenced herself but kept her gun aimed on the woman.

The shuttle gained speed, racing through the tunnel. Nathan closed his eyes and gripped Pearl's hand tightly in his. He felt a soft kiss brush his cheek and imagined a life full of her presence. A place where the sun shone, where darkness hid from the light, a place safe for their children. For his future.

He opened his eyes just as the shuttle left the tunnel. The vehicle broke free from the tracks and jolted into the air. The pilot had to tilt the shuttle sideways last minute to pass through the middle of the two cages in the center of the city. Nathan felt his stomach turn as the ship evened out and soared higher into the sky.

Through the window, Nathan could see only darkness below. *Did I kill Legion?*

No, God replied.

Nathan sighed.

But you wounded Legion, God added. *It will take years for it to regain its power. There is much work to do until then.*

The shuttle crept into the dark ceiling. Minutes later, the vessel broke through the black sky, and sunlight spilled into the cabin. The shuttle's passengers shielded their eyes from what had eluded them for so long. The shuttle continued to climb until it broke through Earth's atmosphere and entered space.

"Now I'm putting it on autopilot to take us straight to the wormhole," the pilot explained.

"Wormhole?" Mira asked.

"Yes," Samuel answered. "That's the quickest way to get to Anaisha."

As Nathan stared out the window, he saw Earth, only it had no resemblance to the photos or videos he had seen in school or on news weather maps. The planet's surface looked charcoal black in most areas, with purple cracks forming along its once beautiful sphere.

Is that real? Nathan wondered. *Earth. Destroyed?* Within days, he knew the planet would be no more...just floating debris.

Ginger began sobbing. Samuel shook his head, mumbling something about one more chance. Mira fell speechless at the sight.

"That's horrible," Ericka whispered. "Our once beautiful planet."

Jasper held Hush's hand. "Rhodenine looked almost the same when we escaped its destruction. It's awful the power Legion has."

"Not just Legion," Nathan added. "No, Legion isn't our only enemy."

"The Dark Army is too," Ginger said.

"Yes. And ourselves."

The story of humanity's survival continues in
The Expired Reality Series